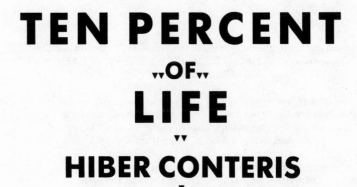

TEN PERCENT
ᵥᵥOFᵥᵥ
LIFE
ᵥᵥ
HIBER CONTERIS

A FIRESIDE BOOK

PUBLISHED BY SIMON & SCHUSTER, INC.

NEW YORK ▲ LONDON ▲ TORONTO ▲ SYDNEY ▲ TOKYO

Grateful acknowledgment is made to the Estate of Raymond Chandler
for permission to use the character Philip Marlowe and other
Chandleriana.

Simon and Schuster/Fireside Books
Published by Simon & Schuster, Inc.
Simon & Schuster Building
Rockefeller Center
1230 Avenue of the Americas
New York, NY 10020
Originally published in Spain by Editorial Laia, S.A. as
El Diez Por Ciento de Vida
SIMON AND SCHUSTER, FIRESIDE and colophons are registered trademarks
of Simon & Schuster, Inc.

Designed by **SNAP•HAUS GRAPHICS**
Manufactured in the United States of America

1   3   5   7   9   10   8   6   4   2
1   3   5   7   9   10   8   6   4   2 Pbk.

Library of Congress Cataloging-in-Publication Data

Conteris, Hiber.
Ten percent of life.

Translation of: El diez por ciento de vida.
"A Fireside book."
I. Title.
PQ8520.13.053D5413   1987   863   87-26521
ISBN 0-671-64589-7
ISBN 0-671-63419-4 Pbk.

Grateful acknowledgment is made to the Estate of Raymond Chandler for permitting publication of *Ten Percent of Life*. Without its support and encouragement the appearance of this work would not have been possible.

To my son, Marcos, killed at the age of twenty-four, while fighting for his ideals and the struggle for liberation in Latin America.

C O N T E N T S

Preface   13

PART ONE ▸ Los Angeles, September 1956   15

  Monday the 23rd   17

PART TWO ▸ Big Bear Lake, Summer 1950   45

PART THREE ▸ Los Angeles, September 1956   59

  Tuesday the 24th   61

  Wednesday the 25th   106

  Thursday the 26th   134

  Friday the 27th   176

THE CHANDLER TEST   216

The realist in murder writes of a world in which gangsters can rule nations and almost rule cities, in which hotels and apartment houses and celebrated restaurants are owned by men who made their money out of brothels, in which a screen star can be the finger man for a mob, and the nice man down the hall is a boss of the numbers racket; a world where a judge with a cellar full of bootleg liquor can send a man to jail for having a pint in his pocket, where the mayor of your town may have condoned murder as an instrument of money-making, where no man can walk down a dark street in safety because law and order are things we talk about but refrain from practicing; a world where you may witness a holdup in broad daylight and see who did it, but you will fade quickly back into the crowd rather than tell anyone, because the holdup men may have friends with long guns, or the police may not like your testimony, and in any case the shyster for the defense will be allowed to abuse and vilify you in open court, before a jury of selected morons, without any but the most perfunctory interference from a political judge.

It is not a fragrant world, but it is the world you live in, and certain writers with tough minds and a cool spirit of detachment can make very interesting and even amusing patterns out of it.

—Raymond Chandler, "The Simple Art of Murder"

The reader familiar with the life and work of Raymond Chandler could be disturbed by more than one anachronism that appears in the course of the novel. The most notorious is the one which occurs at the beginning of Part Two ("Big Bear Lake—Summer 1950"). According to the chronology established by MacShane, the season Chandler and his wife spent on Big Bear Lake—when he was working on a new novel *The High Window*—was the summer of 1940, that is ten years before the date I chose. I have chosen that date simply because it would have been difficult to mention at that time Heidegger, Sartre, Camus and other philosophers and writers who are quoted in the chapter. The same can be said about the quotation by Terry of Jack Kerouac's novel *The Dharma Bums*, which actually was published in 1958. The reader should understand these anachronisms as one of the many and arbitrary forms of freedom of fiction and literary re-creation of reality.

At some undetermined point during the leisurely, alcoholic winter of 1952, Raymond Chandler wrote an article that provided me with the title for this novel. The article was called "Ten Percent of Your Life," and it appeared in *The Atlantic Monthly* in 1952, when Chandler was sixty-four years old. He had spent but two of his six decades tending his budding literary vocation, and had five novels, twenty-three stories, and four articles to his credit. With the memorable exception of "The Simple Art of Murder," an essay that appeared in *The Saturday Review of Literature*, all of Chandler's essays had been published by *The Atlantic*. It's not implausible that "Ten Percent of Your Life" described many of Chandler's own experiences, including some of the more sordid details of his career as a novelist and screenwriter. The role played by the literary agent responsible for peddling Chandler's literary output in the troglodytic jungle that was Hollywood in the fifties was one of these sordid personal details. Swept away by his own sincere and rancorous rapture, Chandler consecrated the bile-filled paragraph that follows to the species that extracted nothing less than ten percent of his own life (it was the medullary portion of the article, and as Mac-Shane* recognizes, served as a sort of catharsis for Chandler, although it didn't solve any of his problems). "This brings me," Chandler wrote, "not too eagerly, to the orchid of the profession —the Hollywood agent—a sharper, shrewder, and a good deal less scrupulous practitioner. Here is a guy who really makes with the personality. He dresses well and drives a Cadillac—or someone drives it for him. He has an estate in Beverly Hills or Bel Air. He has been known to own a yacht, and by yacht I don't mean a cabin cruiser. On the surface he has a good deal of charm, because he needs it in his business. Underneath he has a heart as big as an olive pit... The law allowed him to incorporate, which, in my opinion, was a fatal mistake. It destroyed all semblance of the professional attitude and the professional responsibility to the individual client." The consequence, according to Chandler, was that the clients, whether writers, directors, or actors, "became the raw material of a speculative business. He [the agent] wasn't working for you. You were working for him."

—Hiber Conteris

---

*Frank MacShane, *The Life of Raymond Chandler*, edited by Jack Macrae (New York: E. P. Dutton, 1976). The quotations and episodes from Chandler's life used in this novel have as their sole source the inventory of facts and documents contained in this excellent biography. It was impossible to gain access to any other essay on Chandler during the period in which I wrote the tale.

PART ONE

LOS ANGELES
SEPTEMBER
1956

▶ **9:45 A.M.** **Brentwood Heights** In the middle of making breakfast Philip Marlowe abandons his half-cooked bacon and eggs and dashes out of his apartment and downstairs to pick up the mail in the box on the ground floor. It's the end of summer, 1956. These days Marlowe's living in a small penthouse in the Bristol Apartments in Brentwood Heights, right outside Pacific Palisades. His new building is four stories tall and structurally somewhat baroque. Its honeycombed, arched windows and Mediterranean-style stuccoed walls recall the architecture of Gaudi. There isn't anything unusual about this, since Brentwood Heights is just a short distance from the Pacific and the building was designed to withstand the brutal California summer sun. A stiff wind off the distant, quivering, mist-shrouded ocean leaks into every seam.

The apartment's living room is right off the foyer. Sliding glass doors at the far end of the room open onto a balcony. The living room contains a sofa, an oak desk, two armchairs, and a large breakfront that serves as both bar and bookcase. Next to the window, something resembling a Georgian credenza supplies a horizontal surface for the telephone, the record-player, and a disorganized record collection. An arch-shaped opening leads to the kitchen; the penthouse's bathroom and only bedroom are in back.

This seems to be a prosperous period in Marlowe's life. The four floors of the Bristol Apartments are serviced by a somewhat rickety elevator, in addition to the exterior staircase, but Marlowe doesn't get on the elevator until he arrives at the third floor, not because he's superstitious, but in order to sneak a hungry look at the group of barely post-adolescent dryads sunning themselves around the minuscule swimming pool on the rooftop terrace next door. Despite this understandable distraction, he gets back in time to keep the bacon and eggs from burning. He takes the Pyrex flask of boiling coffee off the flame and settles down at the kitchen table, one eye still squinting off toward the Cytherean pool. He throws away the bills and junk mail, and unfolds the wide pages of a thin, boring September Monday edition of the *Los Angeles Times*. A pigeon flutters off somewhere behind his back, casting its distracting fleeting shadow against the kitchen wall.

On the first page, Eisenhower has returned to the White House after a restful weekend at Camp David, the aborted Hungarian revolution has attempted to resign itself to the European geopolitical map, and Nasser is still maliciously exploiting the nationalization of the Canal. The only piece of news that attracts Marlowe's attention is on page twenty-six, in the section reserved for crime news. It barely fills two columns and briefly relates the discovery of the dead body of literary agent Yensid Andress; he is presumed to have committed suicide in the face of imminent bankruptcy and accusations of fraud brought by his prestigious clients. Andress had lived well, spent a lot, and apparently permitted himself luxuries whose costs he defrayed with the funds that circulated freely through his hands but which in point of fact belonged to his clients. A terse suicide note was found in his typewriter (the newspaper printed it in full), right next to where his body lay with a bullet in his brain and a Colt 7.65 in his right hand.

Marlowe reconstructed in his mind the scene of the crime: a glassed-in study on the top floor of the 250,000-dollar Bel Air mansion, with stucco walls, ashwood *boiserie,* vermilion carpeting, two Prendergasts or Everett Smiths (he couldn't remember which—in any case a safe investment in the rising prestige of the Group of Eight), violent noon light spilling in through windows overlooking the neatly manicured lawn and the chlorinated green surface of the enormous swimming pool. Definitely a form of the good life, but not an overly extravagant one. Marlowe thoughtfully chewed a piece of toast and told himself that the death of a man as notorious on the Hollywood scene as the agent Yensid Andress should have commanded a more important space in the newspaper—a banner headline on the front page at the very least. He was a high-wire juggler of writers, directors, rising stars, and even a stray producer or two, a lovable hustler who managed to extract a respectable percentage of his clients' assets for himself while also making himself the smiling creditor of the appreciation of the injured parties. Marlowe also figured that even at this relatively early hour of what was going on to be another lukewarm California fall day, assorted members of the versatile Hollywood population were raising glasses of bubbly in Andress's memory.

Marlowe refilled his coffee cup and lit a cigarette. He managed to come up with an alphabetical list of half a dozen names with no help but his own short memory. The list could be extended to ten names or even double that; never had the deceased Andress inspired as many toasts as he would on this mournful occasion. And that led him to ask himself if the agent's death could really have been a mere suicide, as the paper asked its readers to believe, or if some anonymous and vindictive hand had carried out, on its own behalf or someone else's, a premeditated, unusual, and beyond any doubt excessive plan for getting even.

▶ **12:48 P.M.** **Lonely Sands** The sun had passed the meridian and was casting a slanting cone of yellowish dust on the floor. Marlowe was trying to decide whether to look for a place for lunch or to finish a Steinitz-Blackburne match when the telephone rang. In the frame of the window, the sylphids were still spreading their legs in the sun like a group of Cézanne nudes. "Existence consisted of living always to test the limits of life, the last frontiers of one's own identity," he'd read somewhere.

He picked up the phone and announced, "Marlowe."

"Philip? Morton here. Could I come over and see you right now or are you too busy?"

"Depends where you are."

"The *Times* newsroom."

Marlowe glanced at his watch. "I can wait."

"Okay, I'll be there in twenty minutes. Is that all right?"

"Is this some kind of first fruits?"

"Wait and see. It's about the Yensid Andress suicide. Did you read the paper this morning?"

Marlowe said he had.

"Then this might be a case for you. That is, if you find a client."

"That's my job," Marlowe replied before he hung up.

He watched the show from his balcony until Charles Morton's Jaguar convertible pulled up in front of the building. Morton was a fan of English sports cars, and the man responsible for Marlowe's recent purchase of a Triumph. Beyond the rooftops and still palm trees Marlowe could just make out the misty blue gleam of the Pacific. Marlowe quickly called down to Morton to wait for him downstairs. He picked up his tweed jacket and ran down the staircase.

"I can't remember the last time I put something hot in my stomach," he said to Morton in jest. It was a little after one in the afternoon. "Why don't you tell me what's on your mind over lunch by the beach?"

"You took the words right out of my mouth."

Morton put the Jaguar back in gear and Marlowe stretched out next to him. The car coasted down Shetland Lane. They waited for the lights to change at Iliff Street, left Brentwood Heights behind, and with a powerful roar, sped down the Strip, abandoning Pacific Palisades. The wind whipped around their ears.

"Where do you want to go?" Morton yelled.

"You decide. As long as it isn't more than half a mile from the ocean." He leaned back in his seat; the sun hit him full in the face. "I forgot my bathing suit."

"Inexcusable." Morton mused for a moment. "Okay, I know of an okay place with a nice sea breeze, good chow, and a little privacy."

"Is this confidential?"

"Confidential?" Morton thought that over. "Anyone but you or me would call it top secret. What I'm going to share with you right now are some intriguing indiscretions. And a discovery I made. I want to supply you with confirmed facts and the outcome of that little personal investigation of mine. I'm not drawing any conclusions, understand? That's not my area, okay? That's why I came to you."

Marlowe observed him closely. It wasn't difficult to imagine why a newspaperman would want to adopt such precautions. He turned his head away and decided not to ask any more questions for the moment. Anyone who knew him well would have recognized this as Marlowe's elusive and long-established method of agreeing with something.

The place they stopped at was called Lonely Sands and it really was lonely. Not many tourists knew it existed. It was located in a corner of the Santa Monica beach half hidden in the bluffs at the end of a macadam road known only to connoisseurs of the temperate Californian equinox. Morton and Marlowe glanced inside. The not particularly attractive dining room stretched out like an oversized railroad car: globes of orangish light hung over the bar, window-side booths looked out over the sea, and quilted chintz upholstery and a discreet environment saturated with the aroma of seafood helped muffle the interior ruckus. The monotonous rhythm of crashing waves filtered in through the windows.

20

All the tables in the dining room were occupied by the predictable clandestine couples, so they decided to sit on the outdoor cement terrace raised a yard or so above the sand. Now and then a warm breeze kissed with saltpeter sprayed a gust of fine sand across the floor. That and the need for discretion had drawn most of the clients to the protection offered by the terrace's high-backed chairs. Four women at a nearby table cheerfully and provocatively observed the newcomers. Somewhat farther away an older married couple hung on the joyful antics of a sweet-eyed cocker spaniel, far and away the most sociable creature around. Morton ordered a whiskey and a lobster (twenty-five minutes). Marlowe decided on his usual rare steak, an unlimited quantity of french fries, and a bottle of beer.

"I assume you knew Andress," said Morton. "Do I need to fill you in?"

"Let's not bother with that." Marlowe had to cup his hand against a gust of wind to light a cigarette. "I've been to Andress's house a couple of times. I wasn't what you'd call a close associate, but he did require my services once."

"I thought as much." There was a hint of deviousness in Morton's voice. "A guy like that... It was natural for him to be stuck in some jam. You know what they say about his line of work here in Hollywood, don't you? An agent is the only individual who works for his enemies. I don't think it's as bad as that; I think that goes for anyone who consorts with the movie business. What did he hire you for, if you don't mind my asking?"

"Now that Andress is dead it doesn't matter in the least, but I'd rather not change the subject." Marlowe waited for the waiter to open the bottle of Carlsberg; he watched it foam and pressed his hand against the pearly glass surface until he could feel the cold liquid. "We'll get more accomplished if you just say your piece."

"Okay." Morton seemed annoyed. "Unless you find some connection... we'll see. Well, you know the basic facts. The body was discovered last night by the woman who cleaned and cooked for Andress. He shot himself in the right temple with his own gun. At least that's the official version. This woman lives with her husband, who did all sorts of odd jobs for Andress; he was the gardener, the mechanic, even the majordomo when Andress threw parties. Their place is about thirty yards from Andress's house. They say they didn't hear a shot, which is perfectly plausible. It was much simpler than that. When the study light

21

stayed on so late, the woman thought something strange was going on. Andress lived alone; he'd been separated from his wife for a couple of years and it wasn't unusual for him to have company once in a while. But he was a real creature of habit and his study was kind of off limits for certain things. What I'm saying is, it wasn't where he usually brought his twilight moths; it was for business only, and business was something he usually attended to during the day. And if you believe what they say around here, it seems his business dealings took up less time every day. Well, the fact is that the woman finished working around six in the evening, left something warming in the oven per the boss's orders, and turned in for the evening. She and her husband watched TV until midnight; that was when they noticed the light was still on in the study and decided it was odd, since the rest of the house was still dark. That wasn't normal—Andress usually kept at least the main floor of the house lit until late at night. Two hours later the woman woke up and looked out the window again. And all the lights were still on."

"And?" Marlowe had already attacked his steak but he was beginning to show interest in Morton's discourse.

"She decided she'd thought enough. She put on a robe and went to check things out."

"And risk making a *faux pas?* Andress had every right to discuss business or whatever the hell he felt like discussing until whatever point in the wee hours of the morning it took him."

"Could be. It seems the woman didn't see eye to eye with you. She knew Yensid Andress's habits better than you or I. So as I was saying, she went to the house, turned on the lights, called out, and when nobody answered she went up to the study. The rest happened more or less the way the *Times* says it did."

"Including the suicide note about his financial disaster?"

"The note, yes. As far as Andress's actual financial situation is concerned, it would take a lot more than that note to verify it. That's part of what you'll have to do."

"Why?" Marlowe sounded skeptical. "Up to this point your story has contained no sensational revelations."

"You'd accept the suicide theory at face value?"

"Until someone convinced me otherwise."

"Okay. I don't know if this will be enough to convince you, but I'll give you a newspaperman's perspective of how this business was handled. Get the sequence of events. First: by the time we heard about it the police had already been on the case for two

22

hours. That's not normal; we pay, that is the paper pays, for the news to filter through immediately. We have a man permanently assigned to the Homicide Division Press Office. Usually the police and the newspapermen get to the scene of the crime at about the same time. You know that."

"I suppose so. I always arrive a little earlier or way too late. I never run into you guys or the police."

"Second: I couldn't tell you who, but someone—evidently someone much higher up than the officer in charge—threw every possible obstacle in our way before we got into the study. And then once we finally got there, they didn't let us snap a single picture. Did you see one in any of the L.A. papers? Can you think of one good reason, even an off-the-wall one, not to allow a suicide to be photographed, especially when he's a well-known Hollywood personality, an infamous 'show-off,' a man who never missed an opportunity to be shown with anyone, the kind of guy who was always in the news?"

"Precisely for that reason." Marlowe pushed his plate to one side. "The man's picture had already been taken too many times in happier circumstances and more attractive settings. Anybody with a little common sense or sensitivity would think to himself: why ruin Andress's image now? Let's not tarnish his tinsel."

"Third: management didn't exactly push to give the story the attention it deserved. It didn't even defend its own interests. I've been working on the *Times* for years—I know perfectly well when a story ought to be on the front page in headlines and when it shouldn't, and this story should have, no doubt about it. I know how much mileage management can get out of throwing its weight around, how it monitors everything that happens, even the most routine story off the police blotter. What the devil happened this time? The *Times* doesn't like to let a story like that one get away without making sure to double its usual press run. And when somebody dug up a nice picture of the dead man to run with the story, somehow the negative got lost on the way to the print shop. And then the guy upstairs said there wasn't enough space. I can assure you that wasn't any standard editorial decision. Someone higher up, much higher up in management, is very interested in making sure Andress's suicide or murder gets as little play as possible."

"Fourth," Marlowe said.

"Fourth," Morton continued, "no one knows the autopsy results. We don't even know if there was an autopsy."

"Isn't it a little soon for that? What time did they find the body?"

"About two in the morning, like I told you. Usually, by ten in the morning they've already concluded the autopsy in a case like this one. When I called you we were still waiting in the newsroom; it was almost one in the afternoon. No news—just major confusion. No one could tell us anything; one police department referred us to the next. Who was the coroner? We don't even know if anyone bothered to call in the coroner."

"What else?"

"What else?" Morton, at the peak of his exasperation, practically jumped on Marlowe. "As far as I'm concerned that's plenty to whet a detective's appetite. Nobody on the entire Los Angeles police force will breathe a word about the case. They're anxious as hell to write the whole thing off and file it away. No one requested an investigation. There wasn't any official questioning; the woman and her husband merely told what they knew at the scene of the crime and no one has called on them again so far. And you can calmly ask me what else?"

"The ball's in the D.A.'s court," Marlowe said. "Can't you cool your heels for a while?"

"So much for you." Morton, thoroughly annoyed, pushed away his plate of half-eaten lobster. "Then I have to tell you that I did in fact decide to undertake a little investigation of my own. I don't intend to take it much further, of course—that's not my business and I value my job at the paper too highly to step out of line. Someone might get mad."

"Now we're getting to the bottom of this. That's when you decided to call me." Marlowe blew a mouthful of smoke in Morton's face. "Naturally, I wouldn't be risking anything with this, but I can't tell what I have to gain, either. And I have a feeling I'm not going to find out until we get to what you called the results of your private investigation."

"As far as what you might get out of it, we'll get to that," Morton said. "From a newspaperman's point of view the entire affair is quite fascinating. But I can't play detective, because I'm on the newspaper staff and I like it too much to put my job on the line. But you can. If you discover something on your own, I can assure you the *Times* will pay you very well for it."

"Are you capable of making a call on something like that?" Marlowe sounded skeptical.

"I'll swear on anything that strikes your fancy. That's where

I come into the picture, understand? Up until then, I'm more or less ignorant, but as soon as you have something pretty definite, I plant myself in front of my managing editor and say here's what I've got, how much is it worth?"

"How much will it be worth?"

"A thousand dollars. Is that okay with you?"

"Five hundred and five hundred?"

"A thousand dollars for you. Tax free."

"And your cut?"

"My cut is breaking the story. And that's no small thing."

"Suppose I accept. What was it you discovered in that private investigation of yours?"

"Something that kills the whole suicide business," Morton said abruptly. "I don't believe Andress had any real financial reason to eliminate himself, as they say. My conclusions aren't definitive yet, but according to the facts I've gathered so far, Andress was still very solvent. He maintained good business relationships, represented some of the best writers in Hollywood, and did well by them. His official percentage was the standard ten percent, but everyone knows he finagled some very juicy bonuses out of the studios who were interested in his scripts. He was the consummate operator; he knew what he had in his hands and how to make people bid for it. Lately he seemed to have had some problems with the movie studios, perhaps as a direct result of what I just told you, but he still managed to maintain his prestige. His tastes weren't very eccentric, and he didn't make risky investments. Guys shoot themselves for all kinds of reasons, but Andress had no financial motivations for doing so."

"Are you sure or is that just a hunch?"

"A hunch? After everything I've told you?" Morton tore off a hunk of lobster with his fingers and popped it in his mouth. "Let me make one thing very clear: I'm a newspaperman, and newspapermen tend to be bigger believers in what you call hunches than men such as yourself, believers in chess and mathematical equations. I repeat: Andress wasn't the kind of guy who'd peel the lid off his brains because of one, two, or ten financial problems. And he definitely wasn't the kind of guy who'd bother to close the safety catch of his automatic pistol after he shot himself in the head. Not Andress or anyone else I ever met could pull off such a feat."

Marlowe put his half-finished glass of beer down on the tablecloth and sat there looking at him.

▶ **3:45 P.M.** **Bristol Apartments** Around 3:35 the Jaguar stopped in front of the Bristol Apartments. Morton parked there for ten more minutes, brandishing his heated dialectic. By the time he left, he'd managed to extract a promise from Marlowe that he'd see what he could do, and that satisfied him. As far as Marlowe himself was concerned—tall and stooped, his ill-fitting tweed jacket falling off one shoulder—you can imagine his reaction. For the first time in his life he was probably having the uncomfortable suspicion he'd let himself be seduced into something that smelled much more of commercial enterprise, something completely foreign to his nature, than of private investigation. Obviously, Marlowe couldn't consider Charles Morton a run-of-the-mill client. The two of them had just finished forming a silent partnership to get something out of the *Times,* but the downside of the silent partnership was that only fifty percent was really silent. Marlowe knew he was the front man, and the one who'd have to take the consequences.

It's a good deal in spite of everything, Marlowe thought. *A thousand bucks—it's been a while since someone hired me for this much money.* Entering his apartment, he threw his jacket on the first armchair in his path, poured two fingers of Talisker into a glass, added a couple of ice cubes, and put a record on the turntable. As he savored his whiskey Thelonious Monk's piano beat the opening bars of "'Round Midnight" out into the damp, suffocating afternoon air. It was a ten-year-old, 1947 version—George Taitt, trumpet; Sahib Shibab, alto sax; Robert Paige, bass; Art Blakey, drums. The piece became a classic of the sort of jazz that was beginning to flow in those days, but that's another story. *No, no one could say money-wise it's a bad deal,* Marlowe tried to convince himself. *But on the other hand the whole business looks like a long shot, and Morton's hunch might turn out to be nothing but a hunch sniffed out by a newspaperman with an atrophied sense of smell.* (The species thinks it has an overdeveloped scenting apparatus, but not everyone shares that opinion.) The investment certainly had its risks: Marlowe didn't doubt Morton's word, but there was no advance payment and no possibility of reimbursement for his time and expenses if nothing turned up. And even worse, it wasn't even a sure thing there was anything behind Andress's suicide that needed to be cleared up. *Of course, there is the detail of the pistol's safety catch,* Marlowe told himself, at the moment the only real clue. Morton got that out of the man who worked for Andress, but the man could have made a big mistake. Did he know anything about guns? Morton hadn't even taken the time to find out. That was the difference between a newspaperman and a detective. *Nevertheless,* he admitted reluctantly, *a careless detective who refuses to do a simple preliminary investigation when a case is pushed under his nose doesn't deserve to be called a faithful member of the guild.* At this point Marlowe felt a mild depression invading him. How would he begin to untangle the skein? Obviously, with Andress's former majordomo. His first task, therefore, seemed to be a trip to the Bel Air villa.

Instead of leaving, he peered out the penthouse balcony and went on reflecting or doing whatever else it was he felt like doing for around fifteen minutes. The late-afternoon sun began to eclipse itself behind the Bristol's four stories; the Cézanne nymphs threw Marlowe hateful looks, as if he were personally responsible for the earth's elliptical path and swift twenty-four-hour orbit. They gathered up their towels and broke camp. A blonde who couldn't have been more than nineteen years old turned around and looked at him one more time; hers was a thin, lithe silhouette, tender and ardent as a ripe fig. Marlowe thought he could make out a smile or some other sign of complicity, at which point his earlier doubts about the business came back to assault him and the idea of pursuing the deceased Andress momentarily erased itself from his mind. Then the minuscule white bikini disappeared behind the rest down the staircase; Marlowe persuaded himself that she was just a high school student about to start college or something of the sort, but he had to admit a hip-swinging strut like hers wasn't something you learned in commerce school. A gust of wind curled the surface of the abandoned Estigia. It was much too hot, Marlowe had the feeling it was going to rain, it was time fall showed its face. He couldn't think of a reason to stay out on the terrace, either. He washed down the watery remains of the Talisker, decided to put on a vaguely sweaty shirt, and with no goal other than that of thrusting temptation aside, descended once again to the street to find his car.

▶ **5:08 P.M.** **Bel Air** The Triumph bore down toward Sunset and then west. It turned right on Lost Canyon Road. The afternoon was filled with radio music and the blue sputter of televisions behind window glass. I passed the University and turned right again. The high iron fences that led to Bel Air, the Hollywood suburb that reminded me of a zoo, began to parade by on either side—the only difference being that in this zoo the animals seemed to be outside of the bars instead of inside them, at least as far as the owners were concerned. In that neighborhood high-rise apartment buildings practically didn't exist; instead you saw gigantic mansions with plenty of space between them, and spacious green expanses with carefully kept gardens and little statues and birdbaths. There also seemed to be an ongoing covert competition for size and originality of swimming pools: the traditional rectangle had completely lost its prestige. A persistent soft breeze touched with sap and the penetrating odor of invisible eucalyptus trees was blowing in from the hills. It still felt like rain. The smoke from a couple of cigarettes floated stubbornly under my nose.

I found the Andress estate around five. A uniformed cop walked out in front of me as I pulled into the driveway.

"You can't go any farther, pal," the officer said. "The house is under police custody."

"What's going on?"

"Don't tell me you don't know what's going on." The gentleman sounded surly and aggressive, but evidently he was bored of being stuck there with nothing very important to do. At least I gave some meaning to his pointless routine. "By now I don't think there's anyone in all L.A. or even in the vicinity who doesn't know a guy killed himself here last night."

"And what's so exciting about suicide?" I put on a face that matched the occasion. "If the L.A. police had to keep an eye on every house where somebody'd killed himself they wouldn't be able to find enough officers in the whole country! Wouldn't it be more effective to regulate the sale of Nembutal and sleeping pills instead?"

I got out of the car. I took my Camels out of my pocket, put one in my mouth, and held the package out to him. He turned down my offer with a gesture.

"Then you don't know nothing," he said. "The guy who offed himself last night didn't die stretched out on silk sheets, full of beautiful dreams. In case you're interested, he put a gun here." He poked at a spot traditionally favored by suicide victims. "And then he pulled the trigger. It might seem like a neat way to make an exit, but let me tell you, no way is it pretty to look at. Sometimes their skull-bone splits open like a nutshell. And if the hole is big enough, after an hour or two you have enough blood to wax the whole floor. No, it's not a picture I'd recommend to anyone, no siree."

"You saw it?" I asked without too much interest.

"I saw him when they carted him away. I've been here since nine this morning, pal. And I've seen a dozen cases like this one in my time."

"Well, who was it? Don't tell me it was Yensid Andress?" I let out abruptly.

"You got it."

"I can't believe it. Andress isn't the kind of guy who'd have a reason to kill himself."

"So you knew him? Well, yeah, he was the type. A pretty important so-and-so, so they tell me. If not, why would I have to stand here all day like a jerk just to keep people from getting into the house?" He turned around to glance at the villa, perhaps with the purpose of obtaining a view of the scene. "I guess they want to keep out ransackers," he added. "The guy lived alone, if I understand correctly."

"Well, no. There's a married couple on staff who live in the cottage in back." The moment was right to ease myself back there. "And now that I mention it, it's them I came to see. I've got news about their daughter, terrific news: she's finally going to be in a movie. And it's no second-banana part: those old folks are the progenitors of a future star, let me tell you. Would it be okay if I walk back to the house? You can watch me from here."

The policeman turned around and appeared to calculate the distance between the hedge at the entrance to the estate and the white stucco walls shining on the far side of the pool. He turned to give me a professional once-over.

"Do you work for Hollywood or one of them movie studios?" he asked.

"Something like that. I'm an agent."

"Well, I guess there's no reason you shouldn't go see those old guys," he said finally. "I don't have any orders about that. As long as you don't try to get near the house."

"I'll leave you my car as collateral," I said. I threw the keys in my pocket, waved to him, and moved off, staying far away from the driveway to avoid any misunderstandings. The officer answered my gesture by slightly tipping back the visor on his cap.

I knocked on the door a couple of times. The door itself was somewhat rustic—pine planks varnished white to match the walls of the dwelling, which was modest but not without a certain charm; the window shutters were painted green. A woman of about fifty-five opened the door to me. Her face looked tense and haggard, her eyes sunken in their sockets. Evidently she hadn't had a good night.

"My name is Marlowe," I said. I opened my wallet and showed her my private investigator's license, hoping she couldn't tell the difference between it and an official police document. "I know you and your husband aren't in the best of moods, but I need to talk to you both. I promise it won't take long."

She stood there without knowing what to say. She seemed to hesitate, looking for an excuse, but finally opened the door and stood aside to let me in.

"We already told the Lieutenant what happened, and then we told the Inspector and the gentleman who came along with him," she hesitated. "My husband and I are heartbroken. We were very fond of Mr. Andress, and we have no idea what we're going to do now. The estate will probably be put up for sale and we'll have to leave."

"I understand," I said. "But it's a little soon for you to be worrying about that. The process could take months, and whoever the new owner is, he'll probably want to be able to count on your services. A trustworthy staff is hard to come by."

I looked around for somewhere to sit. It was a narrow little room, but arranged with a certain degree of taste, and it had a window that faced the western side of the mansion. The afternoon sun burst against the glass panes of Andress's studio. It would be impossible not to notice a lamp that stayed lit there through the early morning hours.

"Make yourself comfortable," the woman said, interpreting my hesitation. "I'll get my husband."

I was careful not to reveal my true identity. Nor did it seem like a good idea to make them repeat yet again the whole story. The man's name was Fuentes; he'd been born in Mexico, but he was a legal U.S. citizen, as was his wife. He looked as tired and apprehensive as she did. There is a moment just after an intense

30

interrogation when all you have to do is push the right button, and everything a man has inside him will gush out, even his confession, if necessary. I wasn't expecting that much. I decided to go right for what interested me.

"I understand you were the one who found Andress's body, Mr. Fuentes," I said by way of testing the waters.

"Actually, it was my wife," the man corrected me in muted tones. "She saw him first; she came to get me immediately, and I checked to make sure he was dead. My wife was too overcome to do anything else."

"Did you call the police right away?" I inquired.

"Yes, she did it while I stayed with him. It wasn't in the least pleasant to stay in that room, with Mr. Andress's body slumped over the desk and blood pouring down his face, but I felt I had to stay. I couldn't leave him alone."

"Do you think much time had passed since he'd fired the shot? Blood usually stops flowing after a while and clots around the wound."

"Yes, I think that must be so. I don't know when it could have happened, really. The police must have established that. I think the blood on his head was dry, and there was a thread that came down past his cheek, and a puddle on the desk. It wasn't very big, but it was fresh."

"You said you made sure Yensid Andress was dead. How did you do that, Mr. Fuentes? Did you take his pulse? Did you check for a heartbeat?"

"I took his pulse," Fuentes answered. "It was the first thing that occurred to me. But you didn't have to know much to see Mr. Andress was already dead. It was just a natural impulse. I felt I had to do something."

"Was that why your wife called the police before she called a doctor or the hospital?" I proposed.

"What?" Fuentes stammered, suddenly alarmed. "I don't know what you mean. In such a case, one always calls the police. It was the first thing that came to mind."

"Of course. But if you had believed Andress had a chance of survival perhaps you would have called a doctor. In such cases, a fraction of a minute can make all the difference."

"Yes, of course," Fuentes accepted. "But Mr. Andress was quite dead. A person couldn't shoot himself in the head and lie there still like he did if there was any life left in him. There was no doubt in my mind from the moment I walked into the room: Mr. Andress was no longer in any condition to receive any sort of assistance."

"Still you took his pulse."

"As I said, it was an instinctive reaction, just because I felt I had to do something. A person doesn't think very clearly under such circumstances."

"The pulse of the right hand or the left?"

"The right. It was closer."

"That was the hand holding the gun."

"Yes," Fuentes said.

He seemed to be avoiding my eyes.

"But you didn't take the pistol out of his hand, did you?"

"I could only have done so with great difficulty. His hand was stiff. I could barely turn his wrist to take his pulse. Then I realized that had been a mistake. The police prefer that the scene of the crime remain untouched." Fuentes brushed one hand across his forehead. "As I explained before, in that kind of situation it's hard to know what you should or should not do. I was desperate. I knew nothing about treating a serious injury. Even if Mr. Andress still had had a little life left in him, I wouldn't have been able to do anything for him."

"I understand," I said. I held out the Camel package. Fuentes accepted and thanked me in a barely audible voice. His hand trembled as he put the cigarette in his mouth. The flame went out when I held my lighter up to his cigarette; his lips trembled. I lit a cigarette of my own and waited until he was calm again. "Let me make it clear I haven't the slightest doubt about the truth of your story," I said so he would relax completely. "Nor do I believe Yensid Andress had the slightest chance of being saved. I'm only interested in a minor detail, but it's one that could be crucial to solving the case. A detail you can provide me with."

He raised his gaze and observed me with new signs of terror in his eyes.

"Were you familiar with the pistol Andress used to kill himself?" I spat out.

"Yes," he answered doubtfully. "I'd seen it on his dresser many times."

"Can you assure me it was his pistol?"

"If it wasn't his it was one just like it. I didn't look at it very carefully. Everything led me to believe it was his automatic."

"A Colt 7.65 caliber, isn't that right?"

"Yes, I believe that was the gun's caliber."

"Do you know much about pistols, Mr. Fuentes?"

Once again suspicion or fear surfaced in his eyes.

"Why?" he replied. "I'm no gun expert, but I can recognize gun calibers. I have one of my own. Actually, it belonged to Mr. Andress too. He insisted I hold on to it. He thought since I was in charge of the house I should have a gun within reach."

"Also a Colt 7.65?"

"A revolver," he clarified. "A Colt .38 Special. The boss bought it for just that purpose."

"What purpose?"

"To protect the house. At first he was considering a pistol, but I advised him to buy a revolver. It's almost a military weapon, much more potent and reliable."

"So you know something about guns?"

"Even a child could tell you that," he replied.

"And exactly when did you realize the safety catch on the pistol Andress had used had been shut again?" I sprang.

He put his cigarette to his lips. His eyes searched out his wife's. I didn't turn around to watch her. She was there, next to me, not entirely beyond my range of vision, but I had no special interest in verifying what they might be able to silently communicate to each other. Fuentes wasn't the murderer.

"I don't think I mentioned the safety catch," he said finally.

"Maybe you didn't mention it to the police, but you mentioned it to someone, Fuentes. You and I both know that. That's the detail that interests me."

"I told the police too," admitted Fuentes. "It was the first thing I told them when they took my statement."

"Nevertheless, the newspapers didn't mention this fact at all."

"I had nothing to do with that," he answered. "I don't write the crime news."

"You drew to the attention of precisely which policeman the fact that the safety catch had been closed after the gun was fired?" I asked.

"Lieutenant Nulty. I believe that's the name. He didn't say anything," Fuentes said. "I don't think he thought it had the smallest significance. It wasn't in the statement they made me sign."

"But he must have asked you something," I insisted. "Didn't

33

you make him think twice about it? Didn't he make you realize that you were probably too upset to have been able to notice a small detail like that?"

"As a matter of fact he did mention it," Fuentes acknowledged. "But as I said, he attached no importance to it. He made me see it would be an unnecessary complication for me if we reported that fact. It didn't make sense to give written evidence that I'd touched the body before the police arrived. My wife and I would avoid a lot of trouble that way. Being questioned by the D.A., testifying before a judge, all of that."

"And so the Lieutenant thought the catch could have closed all by itself, after Andress fired the gun?"

"To put it bluntly, the Lieutenant thought I might have done it myself when I tried to take his pulse. He reprimanded me. But like I just told you, I was too stunned. Now I know that you should never touch a corpse before the police examine the scene of the crime."

"That's probably good advice," I admitted. Fuentes seemed more relaxed now and he'd stopped sweating. He assiduously flattened the cigarette in the hollow of a ceramic ashtray with Mexican markings. "And what do you think, Fuentes?" I pressed. "Do you really think you could have closed the safety catch when you tried to see if Mr. Andress was really dead?"

"It's possible," he said, in a thread of a voice. "It's very possible that I myself shut the catch."

"But your fingerprints weren't on the gun, were they?" I insinuated.

"Not as far as I know," he replied. "No one took my fingerprints during the questioning. The police don't have the slightest doubt Andress killed himself, although my wife and I don't understand their reasoning. They also told me they weren't going to bother us again, and they even left a guard at the entrance to the estate. But now you're here, and it's starting up all over again. Which department are you from, Mr. Marlowe? I suppose the Lieutenant found it necessary to question us again, didn't he? I already warned my wife things weren't going to be wrapped up so quickly. A death, after all, is a death. And Mr. Andress was an important man. If you want my honest opinion, I think they should pursue the investigation. But I have nothing else to say, Mr. Marlowe. I can swear myself in and repeat everything to a court if it becomes necessary. Although I don't know what good that would do. If Mr. Andress really decided to kill himself, we'd prefer they not stir up his life too much. Not because we're afraid of what might come out. He was a good man—a good, honest man. I don't know much about the way he conducted his business dealings, but I know when I'm working for an honest man. And my wife and I worked for Mr. Andress for twelve years."

I cauterized the ceramic ashtray patterned with Aztec faces with my own cigarette and stood.

"Don't worry," I said with the most conviction I could muster. "I don't think they'll bother you or your wife anymore. Not for a while, at least. As far as Andress goes, well, I don't know. We'll try to make sure his body doesn't turn over too often in its grave."

▶ **6:05 P.M.   Bel Air**   "It looks like you made a killing on the stock market, Marlowe. Congratulations." Lieutenant Nulty was examining the car parked in the driveway. He was dressed in street clothes, as usual, and as he spoke he shook the end of his Dutch cigar so the ash scattered over the immaculate scarlet sheen of the Triumph's hood.

"When did you get a new car?" he continued. "Last time I saw you, you were driving a little number that was a lot less spiffy than this buggy."

He took a small notebook out of his pocket and rapidly glanced through it, following the column of numbers with his index finger. "Here it is. 1952 Mercury, dark blue, California plates, number 12-216." He examined the car admiringly from end to end. "What the hell is this? One of them English numbers, huh? This car doesn't do you justice, Marlowe. You deserve a more reliable form of transportation."

He stood there and looked at it. He was a fairly tall, hefty man with a certain something about his sparse golden hair and sky-blue eyes that proclaimed his Germanic or Scandinavian ancestry; he almost always wore brown. More than once it had occurred to Marlowe that substituting the simple mnemonic epithet "nutty" for "Nulty" would have given the Lieutenant the most appropriate patronymic. It wasn't that Marlowe was a word-game fan, but the word "nutty," meaning crazy, loony, was especially popular in the police-speak of the day, and even in the lingo used on the other side.

Nulty drew a line through his old notes on the Mercury and began to pen in new information, repeating out loud what he was writing down:

"Marlowe, P., Car: Triumph cabriolet, two-door, model 56, red with black roof, California plates, 13-572. How much did you pay for it? Twenty-five hundred, something like that?"

"Much less. I bought it secondhand."

"I gave you a citation for illegal parking. The officer here will write out your ticket."

"Illegal parking?" Marlowe repeated, looking for the nonexistent No Parking sign. He lit a new cigarette.

"Your car is obstructing the entrance to the house."

"I should have noticed," Marlowe acknowledged. "There is so much going on around here. I suppose the funeral cortege will have to pass the house by because my car is still in the way. Isn't that right, Lieutenant? Why didn't you have it towed?"

Nulty's thorax grew to enormous proportions as he executed a long, contemplative puff on his cigar.

"No funny business, Marlowe. Didn't the officer advise you that this house is under police custody? What are you doing here?"

"Is that what's going on?" Marlowe threw an erratic glance through the autumn dusk: the day was leaving evanescent traces of light along the horizon and the damp breeze smelled of algae and fog. "Don't you think the wind's changed, Lieutenant? I think we're going to get some rain."

"Is that so. Well, you don't have to tell me," Nulty said, changing the subject. "The Fuentes' daughter is going to be a starlet, isn't she? And you're the happy bearer of the glad tidings. How lovely. How nice. I'm bleeding internally. And just now, when the old folks were so desperate. What would have become of them without that girl ascending the misty stairway to Hollywood paradise on her way, way way up high, to stardom?"

The Lieutenant held out one fist and smashed it on Marlowe's shoulder with the force of a piston engine. "Huh?" he shouted. "What would have become of them?"

"That's what I asked myself, Lieutenant," the policeman began to stammer. "I didn't see anything wrong with..."

"You," Nulty interrupted sharply, his basaltic stare boring into the uniformed man while his claw continued to pulverize Marlowe's shoulder, "you belong there." He pointed his outstretched arm and its damp-cigar appendage. "Stay at the gate until this individual and his vehicle vanish from your sight. And then come back here, understand? And no one, absolutely no one, is allowed to enter the estate—not the mansion *or* the old folks' house. Not even if blonde Marilyn herself arrives to give her parents a good-bye kiss or put on her bikini and take a dip in the pool. No one. This property—you hear me? The entire property is under police custody."

"Roger, Lieutenant," the policeman mumbled, stiffening. He began to move backward.

"But first make out a parking ticket for a twenty-five-dollar fine. Fifteen for illegal parking and ten for refusing to mobilize the vehicle."

"I took down the information, boss, but I don't have any forms here. I'm not from the Traffic Department."

"So send it to him," Nulty growled.

The officer touched his cap with his right hand, turned around, and moved off toward the villa. With great effort, Marlowe removed the hand that was still squeezing him. He carefully shook off the ashes that had grazed the shoulder of his tweed sport jacket.

"Well then, now you and I are going to have a little chat," the Lieutenant said.

"There's nothing I'd like more," Marlowe improvised. "But I've got a date. Believe me, Nulty, I'm sorry down to the bottom of my soul. You are one of the few people on the force with whom a conversation is always meaningful."

"A date, eh? Blonde or brunette?"

"Redhead," Marlowe said. "But it's just business."

He reached out toward the Triumph's door handle.

"Hold it right there," Nulty barked, grabbing the nickel-plated handle and, along with it, Marlowe's hand. "Redheads usually wait, and I'm in a very bad mood. What were you doing here, Marlowe? You don't belong in this cast of characters. Why did you go see the old folks? Don't tell me they called you up and contracted your services."

"There you go again, never giving me the benefit of the doubt, Lieutenant," Marlowe replied. "You know very well I'd never take money from servants."

"That's exactly what I told myself. So who hired you?"

"Well, I have my professional standards to uphold, you know. I'm not required to reveal my client's identity."

"And why exactly is your client concerned about this matter? Andress killed himself. Doesn't your client read the papers?"

"My client wants to know when the funeral will take place. And if there will be an open-casket wake. And what state the body was in after the autopsy was performed. And at exactly what time last night the unfortunate Andress passed away. And if he pulled the trigger on account of his poor digestion or as a result of some other harmful substance that might have been in his stomach. And whether he had a will, or if some other sort of document exists, an insurance policy for example, whatever, that may be of some interest to the immediate family. And who is going to answer to his creditors, seeing that Andress was bankrupt. And where he can send a wreath, or at least a telegram of condolence to the immediate family, if he had one. That sort of thing."

"And what else?"

"What else?" Marlowe lifted the cigarette to his mouth. He'd heard it said tobacco could cause lung or throat cancer, but so far all he'd been able to determine was that it stimulated his imagination. "He also wants to run a front-page obituary with a photograph of the deceased in all the West Coast papers. You know, one of those oodles of photographs of Andress with a smile on his face as wide and shiny as Long Beach, and surrounded by a slew of important people. A sort of post mortem homage. He thinks the press didn't do the guy justice when the story broke."

"Oh yeah? I'm fighting back the tears. Nothing moves me more than discovering someone who is generous and grateful to dead people. Usually someone dies, and zap! People cross the guy's name out of their address book—one less person to keep track of. Do me a favor, Marlowe. Give your client my regards."

"With great pleasure, Lieutenant. He'll appreciate it, take my word for it. Coming from a man like you, so familiar with all of this, a man long accustomed to crossing names out of his phone book...really, this means a great deal. I'll tell him. It's a promise."

As Marlowe began to open his car door, he felt Nulty's restless right hand close over his own.

"What's the hurry?" the officer said. "Tell me something else, Marlowe. How far does your client's curiosity extend beyond mere generosity? What else does he want to know?"

"I already told you: almost everything." Marlowe reasoned with him. "The remaining details are insignificant and almost in bad taste. How did he manage to shut the safety catch on the pistol after he poked a hole in his own cranium, for example? And what kind of wound did the bullet leave in his skull? Did it leave a sharp-edged opening, a bruised wound, a raised surface, all that complicated lingo coroners throw around. Between you and me, he's lost sleep over this. He can't imagine the sight of a guy as devilishly clever and meticulous about his appearance as Yensid Andress spreading his valuable gray matter all over that elegant desk and pretty red carpeting. And I can understand his point. It's a real shame, don't you think?"

Nulty looked at him thoughtfully. The interminable cigar had stopped shaking between his teeth, but as he calmly took it out of his mouth he loosed such a heavy curtain of smoke Marlowe had to fight it off with his fists.

"So he's familiar with Andress's study. Has he been upstairs recently?"

"I wouldn't say he'd been upstairs very recently," Marlowe said. "But the rug was very bright, and Andress was more the conservative type. I don't imagine he'd have changed it since then."

"Your client is well informed," Nulty acknowledged. "And you came to confirm the facts with old Fuentes, is that it?"

Marlowe didn't answer.

"The autopsy results say Andress died around midnight." The Lieutenant paused. "There was nothing lethal in his system but his usual dose of whiskey. That didn't kill him, and it didn't put him out of action, either. Apparently Andress moved a few inches right as he was being shot. I still don't understand how the devil a doctor can tell things like that from somebody's destroyed cranium. So the shot had to have been fired from a few inches away—two or three at most—meaning the guy who did the job wasn't a conscientious professional. Those mathematical calculations are also a mystery to me." Nulty took another abominable drag on his cigar. "Well, I guess that's why they have coroners."

Marlowe opened the door of the Triumph.

"Now you're going to go and tell the first imbecile who crosses your path what I just told you," Nulty harrumphed.

"You know I won't," Marlowe promised. "It so happens you can count on my unconditional loyalty, and from this moment onward, my client's eternal gratitude."

"In case you didn't know," the Lieutenant added, "Andress's

secretary isn't a redhead. I seem to remember she's more on the blonde side, although I wouldn't swear to it. She's one classy dame. The office is in the Avenant Building, near the Hollywood Brown Derby. Don't use the Boulevard entrance, use the one on Vine. But you won't find her there until around nine tomorrow morning."

"I said my date was urgent," Marlowe protested as he sat behind the wheel.

"And tell your client the burial is tomorrow at Hollywood Cemetery. If he's interested in the religious service, he should check the papers."

"There's nothing I find more depressing than a funeral service," Marlowe replied.

He put the car in first, turned around at the top of the driveway, and sped off toward the multicolored swarm of light and neon that was the distant city.

▶ **7:13 P.M. Wilshire Boulevard** The night began slowly wrapping itself around Los Angeles as I drove down Lost Canyon Road toward Sunset. I was hungry and not much in the mood to finish up the day's work, but I really didn't know what else to do. The information Nulty had given me threatened to turn the Andress affair into an enormous quagmire, but now, beyond any doubt, I knew I had a case on my hands. A call to Morton appeared to be in order. I let the Triumph coast down Canyon Drive and stopped in front of the first telephone booth I found on Wilshire Boulevard. I was lucky. I found Morton at the *Times* newsroom.

"Where are you?" he immediately wanted to know.

"In a pay phone. Right outside L.A."

"On your way out or coming back?"

"On my way home to soak in a hot tub and three fingers of whiskey."

"Would you mind if I stopped by?"

"I wouldn't mind if you brought some barbecued chicken and some french fries with you—I'll provide the liquid refreshment. I have a burgundy around here somewhere I keep on hand for special occasions. It reminds me of Paris."

"I didn't know you'd been to France. When?"

"When I went to see Gene Kelly in *An American in Paris*."

"I should have known," Morton groaned. "It's settled. Expect me around nine."

I hung up the phone and went back to the car. Once again I sniffed a change in the wind and decided rain was imminent. As I pulled away from the curb, I noticed in the rearview mirror that another car had lit its headlights and had pulled up behind me. It had been parked about thirty yards down the Boulevard. I drove at medium speed, one eye in the mirror, more out of professional habit than any real suspicion I was being followed. I left Wilshire for Sunset, maintaining the same speed for about a mile: the other car insisted on keeping a constant distance behind me. I braked for a light, and the other car hurled itself to a halt against the curb about twenty yards away. At this point I began to seriously consider the possibility that its driver's number-one priority was persecuting me. There was a second silhouette next to the first. I turned right unexpectedly and entered the old section of Bunker Hill. I went around the block; the automobile appeared again. I crossed the Boulevard toward South Lafayette Place, turned into Idaho Street, continued toward Ventura Avenue, and without signaling, reconnoitered Altair Street and Brayton on the way to Sunset. It was an absurd, repetitive route and the car was still behind me. There couldn't be two crazy guys with the same obsessive maze in their brains. It occurred to me Nulty might have decided to find out my client's identity and had put a pair of bloodhounds onto my trail. It fell within the rules of the game and I didn't worry about it anymore. It was just a nuisance to drive with two yellow headlights nailed in my rearview mirror. I thought Nulty's people must be imbeciles; they should approach things more skillfully and subtly if they really wanted to find something out. Then it occurred to me they might not—maybe what they really wanted to do was make it clear they were following me. Why? To slow down my movements? I couldn't think of any other good reason. I got to the Strip and decided to test my pursuers' skill by slipping into the traffic. The headlights began to fall behind and finally blurred together with dozens of other dots of light moving down the Boulevard in the evening mist. I went through an intersection just as the yellow light turned red, and after that the headlights were completely lost. I slowed down; when I got to Pacific Palisades I turned toward Brentwood Heights and got on Shetland Lane with the needle at forty.

Morton was due to show up an hour later. In the meantime I tried to float away the tension of being followed and the day's string of interrogations by spending forty minutes just slightly above the waterline of a full bathtub, savoring half a glass of Talisker on the rocks. Then I wrapped myself in a big warm robe, lit a cigarette, and put on a record. Goodman was sobbing his own memories to himself, melancholically blowing "Benny Rises Again," when Morton showed up. We listened to music a while longer, devouring the chicken along with my last bottle of burgundy. It wasn't the dinner we would have enjoyed in a place like La Tour d'Argent, but Los Angeles wasn't Paris, either. Nothing resembling the Seine wended its way through Pacific Palisades, and I couldn't look out the balcony and see the trunklike towers of Notre Dame emerging from the thick glow of the spotlit fog. As far as I can tell all the two cities have in common are boulevards, and even so I was still in for a big surprise when I saw the Gene Kelly picture. Maybe it was a perversion of the technicolor, but apparently the curving, cobblestoned Parisian boulevards had nothing at all in common with their very long, straight, desertlike Californian brethren.

Morton couldn't contain his astonishment when I recounted Nulty's revelations.

"Its incredible," he said, after listening to me for a while without so much as opening his mouth. "None of that was officially passed on to newspapers. The only official story so far is the suicide story. The only version. The managing editor wasn't in the least bit interested in poking around some more. There's something a little strange about Starret, but I can't believe he could be in on a conspiracy like this one. He said he doesn't want any trouble and we shouldn't do anything until the police turn something up and bring us in on it."

"And what will he do if we give him a cake we baked in our very own oven?"

"If we got that far he'd have to back down, that much I'm sure of."

Considering the official reticence on the subject, it was hard to tell what had been on Nulty's mind when he slipped me the autopsy results and the rest of it; if I took his words at face value, we were looking at a criminal act, now that the suicide theory and its possible explanation had been disproved. We considered the possibility that Nulty wanted to send us off on a wild-goose chase. After all, the Lieutenant wasn't naturally the helpful type; he worked out of 77th Street and was one of the tough guys, the men in charge of softening up any suspicious characters and those sorts favorably inclined to pleading guilty to anything once they'd been worked over two or three times. Nulty certainly owed me a few favors and had for me, shall we say, a certain professional respect. But he was also one of those cops who were acutely aware of the line separating private investigator from public might; he shared his comrades' conviction that they were the ones who had the handle on every case, and that anyone else who came sniffing around was nothing but a nuisance—an opinion based on envy or privilege, depending on the observer's point of view. The role he'd indirectly given me in the Andress case had an implication neither Morton nor I could divine. Remember, we'd ingested a bottle of burgundy and at least a couple of scotches each.

Despite that, after two cognacs and a binge of forties jazz we finally came to an agreement. We had enough to go on to continue the investigation. Obviously the next step (in our condition everything seemed very obvious) was to take a trip to Andress's offices in the Avenant Building to see what we could find out. We'd try to verify the agency's true financial status, get hold of a client list, and sound out whoever we found there about who could have had a motive to kill Andress. I'd handle that end, and in the meantime Morton would see if anything came out in the whispering at the funeral. Neither of us was very optimistic, but we did feel carefree, and it was the most rational way to proceed.

Morton left way past eleven. Out of pure inertia, I went out onto the balcony and watched him get into the Jaguar. The evening damp had intensified—a creeping, teary, coastal fog had begun to invade the city. We could have been in London. As Morton started up his car I saw a pair of yellow headlights blink on about a hundred yards down Shetland Lane. Instantly, I knew those two lugubrious owl eyes were the same ones that had followed me down Wilshire Boulevard and into the labyrinthine pirouettes in Bunker Hill. The car slowed down to shift gears, and I made it out to be a gray Plymouth sedan, although I wouldn't have sworn to it in court. The streetlights' diffuse yellowish gleam was reflected back up by the thick, ornate arcade of fog. Morton turned right down the next alley and the Plymouth's red parking lights turned surely behind him. My first impulse was to run for my car and join the convoy, but instantly I realized that the time it would take me to get dressed

43

was in itself enough to give them a significant head start. Presumably Morton was on his way home, but considering he was a newspaperman, and a single one, it wasn't a sure thing. I'd see what I could find out in the morning. I switched off the record player, straightened up the living room a little, and took Chandler's latest novel, which I'd promised myself I'd read, off the shelf. I think I got to page forty, double thanks to another gulp of Talisker and half a dozen Camels. The things Chandler thought up were impossible—his detective would never have been able to solve a mystery in real life.

PART TWO

BIG BEAR LAKE

SUMMER

1950

After some five months in Arcadia, a residential suburb northeast of Los Angeles, Chandler and his wife, Cissy, went to spend the summer of 1950 in the mountains overshadowing San Bernardino. First they tried out Fawnskin and then they rented a cabin on Big Bear Lake. The seven-thousand-foot altitude provided a refreshing change from the city's stifling captivity. In those days Big Bear was still an inviting wilderness with a spectacular view: granite boulders came all the way down to the eastern shore of the lake, there were endless forests of vivid green pine trees, and the mountain peaks were snowy all year round. According to Frank MacShane, the landscape and vegetation are reminiscent of those of the low Alps: wildflowers and evergreens dot the mountainside and the air is cool and clear. During summer the sun is warm. Arrowhead Lake lies some fifteen miles away, and the tiny resort village of San Bernardino slightly beyond it.

John Butler, one of the *Black Mask* writers, lived nearby. At one point during the summer, W.T. Ballard and Cleve Adams, two other writers in the group, journeyed to Big Bear with their respective wives. Chandler had just begun work on a new novel, which would eventually be published as *The High Window*. The reunion of the four writers and their neglected spouses developed into a lively get-together at the Chandlers' cabin.

"The main trouble with most detective stories, as I see it, is that the people who write them are bad writers," Chandler succinctly affirmed in the middle of a round of bourbon and ginger ale. They were sitting in the cabin's ample, comfortable main room, its large lakeside windows swathed in mosquito netting.

"They don't make for satisfying literature," he continued, "because in general the mind which can produce a coolly thought-out puzzle can't, as a rule, develop the fire and dash it takes to write vividly."

"What about Poe?" Butler replied with liveliness. "He certainly had the sort of mind you're describing; he was a man capable of diagramming the plot of a story exactly as he'd diagram a crossword puzzle or chess problem. But not for lack of fire, impetuousness, or what you call dash. He was a great writer, one of the best in English, and the creator of the detective story genre to boot. That refutes your argument."

"I admit he was the first to write a certain kind of crime story," Chandler said. "But not every crime novel is by nature deductive. Poe isn't under discussion here—he hadn't yet been deformed by his profession. He was a true writer, a poet, and he couldn't have done anything with his life but what he actually did. I often think he must have written his first mystery stories as a sort of joke or pastime. He possessed such an exuberant intelligence he had to use his analytic faculties somehow. 'Murder on the Rue Morgue,' 'The Purloined Letter'... There is something satirical, insulting, about those stories. Poe was sending up the traditional police investigation techniques of the time. He wanted to show that a superior mind could, with complete precision, solve a mysterious crime like the one in the Rue Morgue without getting out of his parlor armchair and with no facts except the ones that were printed in the paper. He detested the pointless police mobilizations, the mass arrests, the interrogations, and decided to make fun of them."

"He certainly discovered a completely original form of entertainment. And to call it a form of entertainment is an understatement." Ballard leaned back in his armchair next to the window and watched the fluctuating afternoon sunshine. "His stories may be too cerebral to be entirely convincing; in this sense I agree with Raymond that Poe's stories have neither fire nor passion, and hence neither life nor action. But Poe intended to provide a strictly intellectual form of pleasure, just the sort you gentlemen were describing."

"But he was an honest guy," said Chandler. "He was a genius. He didn't have to play games or keep an ace in the hole. Not like the deductive novel that followed him, the classic crime novel, which didn't always play by the rules of the game, and in that it was dishonest. Of course, the people who wrote them didn't have Poe's intelligence, so instead they resorted to filling themselves with esoteric knowledge that they kept to themselves, just giving the reader enough information to disorient him. The truly honest detective story or novel of detection is one that gives the reader all the material for solving the mystery, where nothing significant is underemphasized and nothing insignificant overemphasized, and where the facts themselves carry their own interpretation and don't have to be analyzed under microscopes to disclose their meaning."

"And what about Conan Doyle?" Adams asked. "Was he an honest writer?"

"Honest—probably. Intelligent too. But Doyle's greatest strength was knowing when to resort to eccentricity. Sherlock Holmes is a completely atypical character, an eccentric. That fas-
48

cinates the British. He has the mind of a scientist or a mathematician and the sensibility of an artist; he plays the violin, he is completely devoted to his pipe, he is a morphine addict and definitely a misogynist, if not homosexual. An unusual combination of characteristics, but one that awakens incredible nostalgia in his readers for all those repressed qualities. And so the interest in Holmes derives more from what the character itself symbolizes than it does from any intrinsic interest in Doyle's plots and hypotheses. Anyone who is familiar with Scotland Yard and the way it operates, for example, will find his policemen completely absurd. Their scientific theories are very unreliable, and there is hardly any mystery in a Doyle novel. A very sophisticated mind won't be satisfied with one."

"And what about Agatha Christie?" Butler wanted to know.

"Agatha Christie?" Chandler puffed on his pipe unconsciously. "Look, John, I just finished reading one of those little novelettes of hers, *And Then There Were None,* and I'm convinced Lady Christie decided to write detective novels the same way she probably decided to crochet, to make a cake for a get-together of her girlfriends for five o'clock tea, or to accompany her second husband on his archaeological adventures. This book of hers isn't an honest crime story: it doesn't give the reader the slightest chance of figuring things out for himself, and the motives and plot devices are pure bunk. The story is based on a man who acts in one particular way, and then suddenly, without any convincing explanation, begins to behave in another, completely unexpected, way. And then Lady Christie is abysmally ignorant of lethal drugs and their action. I found the book good for one thing only: for me it finally and for all time settled a question in my mind that had at least some lingering doubt attached to it—whether it is possible to write a strictly honest mystery of the classic type. It isn't. To get the complication, you fake the clues, the timing, the play of coincidence, and pretend fifty percent probabilities are one hundred percent certainties. To get the surprise murderer you fake character, which hits me hardest of all, because I have a sense of character. If people want to play along, it's all right by me. But for Christ's sake, let's not talk about honest mysteries. They don't exist."

"But you can't tell me her hero, that Belgian policeman Hercule Poirot, isn't a guy with a clearly defined, charismatic personality," Adams observed. "I admit Sherlock Holmes is too much of an archetype—too cold and intellectual to be real. But

Monsieur Poirot is a fully realized character—his manners, his courtesy... Consider *Murder on the Orient Express*. Don't you agree?"

"Not in the least," Chandler replied categorically. He picked up the ice bucket containing some water and a few pebble-sized cubes, walked to the kitchen, and opened the refrigerator. "Look, Cleve," he continued from in there. "I don't deny the mystery writer the privilege of making his detective any sort of person he wants to make him: poet, philosopher, student of ceramics or Egyptology, or master of all the sciences, like Doctor Thorndike. Mrs. Christie dreamed up her very own Hercules and she was within her rights. What I cannot bear is this affectation of gentility, which does not belong to the job and which is in effect a subconscious expression of snobbery. The kind of thing that reached its high-water mark in Dorothy Sayers. Perhaps the trouble is that I'm an English public school man and know these birds inside out. And the only kind of public school man who could make a real detective would be the public school man in revolt, like George Orwell."

"I don't see how you can dictate in advance how a real detective must behave," Ballard said. "Does he always have to be a guy like Sam Spade? That Spade is no aristocrat, that's for sure. Neither is Dashiell Hammett. But even though Hammett was an agent with Pinkerton and knows the job backwards and forwards, there is something about the way Sam Spade talks and acts that doesn't ring true to me. Of course, a policeman doesn't usually spend time in elegant places or with highly educated people. But Spade is always such a tough guy and he's often needlessly vulgar. In a way that's snobbery, too. Hammett wanted to break away from the classic ideal of the educated, aristocratic, well-mannered detective who applied himself to solving a crime or any other mystery with the gusto of a dilettante, as if it were a clever form of diversion. But Spade is rude, insolent, and provocative even when he doesn't need to be. If we're talking realism, I personally prefer James Cain's. Maybe he hasn't had Hammett's real-life experience, but he's just as crude and violent, and his characters rise far enough beyond the superficial to achieve a certain literary value. Their feet may be buried in mud, but they don't spend all their time grumbling or feeling obliged to act tough. Spade is a kind of machete."

"Look, Ballard," Chandler said. "A real-life private detective is a sleazy little drudge from the Burns Agency—a strong-arm guy with only slightly more personality than a blackjack and the moral stature of a stop and go sign. If Hammett had stuck to reality, no one would have been interested. Hammett re-created this detective as literature, with legitimate precedent. I'm not entirely sure Cain has done the same: what he writes is even more sordid than real life. If we're going to be completely honest with each other, we just have to admit the fictional private detective doesn't and couldn't really exist. He's the personification of an attitude, the exaggeration of a possibility. The detective exists complete and entire and unchanged by anything that happens; he is, as detective, outside the story and above it, and always will be. That is why he never gets the girl, never marries, never really has any private life, except insofar as he must eat and sleep and have a place to keep his clothes. His moral and intellectual force is that he gets nothing but his fee, for which he will, if he can, protect the innocent, guard the helpless, and destroy the wicked, and the fact that he must do this while earning a meager living in a corrupt world is what makes him stand out."

"Philip Marlowe," Ballard commented ironically. "The modern knight in shining armor."

"I don't disagree," Chandler admitted. "Marlowe has something of that. Look," Chandler confessed in a slightly inebriated state, addressing an audience that constantly multiplied and dissolved among the alcohol fumes, "when I started out to write fiction I had the great disadvantage of having absolutely no talent for it. I couldn't get my characters in and out of rooms. They lost their hats and so did I. If more than two people were in a scene I couldn't keep one of them alive. The most difficult thing of all was creating plots. With me a plot, if you could call it that, is an organic thing. It grows and often it overgrows. I am continually finding myself with scenes that I won't discard and that don't want to fit in, so that my eventual plot problem invariably ends up as a desperate attempt to justify a lot of material that, for me at least, has come alive and insists on staying alive. I have no compunctions about helping out my novels with slices of narrative I've already used elsewhere; I 'cannibalize' my own work. Well, then...I was making another point. Ah, yes: using a first-person narrator makes for great inconveniences—especially in a mystery novel, where a lot has to go on while the detective isn't onstage. But a character who sees things from his own point of view also has advantages: he enriches the texture of the prose and gives it a character the omniscient narrator doesn't have. I learned that from Joseph Conrad. He named his character Marlow and I adopted the name for myself, as a form of acknowledgment. I tried to make my Philip Marlowe less solemn than Conrad's, to make him somehow lighter, sharper, perhaps a bit more ingenious and intelligent—and definitely more cynical and romantic. For me, Marlowe had to be the spokesman for that 'controlled half-poetical emotion' that must be an essential part of every novel I write."

"What was it Chesterton had to say about that?" Cleve Adams interjected. "'The essential worth of the mystery novel lies in the fact that it is the first and only form of popular literature in which some sense of the poetry of modern life is expressed.' It was a brave defense of mystery novels, when you realize it was made in 1902. Of course, it was a way of justifying the adventures of his own Father Brown and his entire body of work."

"It's still absolutely true," Chandler chimed in. "A form of the poetry of violence. The mystery novel has the elements of tragedy without being tragic, and the elements of heroism without being heroic. It is a dreamworld which may be entered and left at will, and it leaves no scars. That's the nature of poetry; and to be a poetic expression of modern life, the mystery novel has to necessarily transform the violence of the world we live in into poetry."

"And there's a lot more," decided Butler, who had been silent and contemplative for a while. "A good mystery novel immediately submerges the reader into a tumult of events. Just as Horace recommended in his *Ars poetica:* tragedy must begin 'in medias res,' in the middle of the thing—with a crime that has already been committed or a war that has already been unleashed. You begin to read Homer's *Iliad* and rapidly you find yourself in the midst of a dispute, witness to Achilles' terrible wrath and Agamemnon's stentorian fury. Something similar happens in the crime novel; the situations that develop are always limit situations, the sort of occurrences that approach the edges of existence and permit its meaning to suddenly be discovered. More than once I've begun to think existentialism has given tragic literature a new dimension, and the mystery novel as well. Jaspers discusses limit situations; Heidegger defines existence as being-for-death; for Sartre it's a precarious balance between being and nothingness, where the only factor that can push the faithful to one side of the scales or the other is individual freedom, choice. Camus' affirmation that suicide represents the fundamental philosophical problem seems a logical one: existence has an ontologically contingent or accidental nature; death, on the other hand, is a necessary and inevitable event. For mankind, suicide represents the most extreme option of exercising its freedom."

"Very complex," Chandler said. "I agree the aim of the police novel isn't essentially different from the aim of Greek tragedy. But we're dealing with a public that is only semiliterate, and therefore we have to make an art of a language they can understand. I think it's paramount to squeeze the last drop out of your chosen medium. All my activity is based on the idea that the formula isn't important; what counts is what you do with it. In other words, it's a question of style."

"Eh, one minute," Butler jumped in. "A question of style, but fundamentally a question of substance, of content. I insist: the mystery novel's uniqueness lies in how it confronts the reader with one of those limit situations of existence: a death, a murder, a suicide, a kidnapping, an act of revenge, a missing person. Even, in a minor way, a robbery or swindle. In any event, it's the content that determines the tragic nature of events. Generally, this content has to be a decisive, unexpected, sudden event, one that overtakes the reader when he least expects it. The mystery novel always hovers on that sharp line separating law from crime; justice from injustice; the respectable, conventional world, bourgeois decency, from the criminal underworld. It's a line like the one between good and evil, security and peril, imprisonment and freedom—and, more than anything, the ultimate, conclusive boundary between life and death. You don't just achieve that by polishing your style, boy; to get that far you have to tell meaningful stories, full of tragic content, and tell them well."

"And isn't that exactly what style means?" Chandler replied. "How, otherwise, can you tell a story with that certain power of persuasion? For example, I'm among those who believe in what is called inspiration, to a certain extent, although the word has been so perverted I prefer not to use it. I believe that any writing with any life in it is done with the solar plexus. It is hard work in the sense that it may leave you tired, even exhausted. In the sense of conscious effort it is not work at all. The important thing is that there should be a space of time, say four

hours a day at least, when a professional writer doesn't do anything else but write. He doesn't have to write, and if he doesn't
feel like it he shouldn't try. He can look out of a window or stand
on his head or write on the floor, but he is not to do any other
positive thing, not read, write letters, glance at magazines, or
write checks. He writes, or nothing. Two very simple rules: A)
You don't have to write; B) You can't do anything else. The rest
comes of itself."

"Yes, that's a good, disciplined way to work. If you want to do
it professionally, I suppose there is no other way." Cleve Adams
had approached the window. He threw a melancholy glance at
the lake's smooth surface and found himself looking at the
mountainside plunging into the water's eastern edge like a knife
into a body. He turned back to the group. "But to be able to work
you have to already have amounted to something. You can't turn
yourself into a professional writer overnight, and this preliminary step, this stretch of the road you have to cover entirely on
your own steam, depends entirely on your personal talent and
your determination to write. Writers are born, or they aren't.
Perhaps many more are born with enough talent and stop halfway—we have no way of knowing—but I doubt anyone has become a brilliant writer just because he decided to be one, the way
at one moment in your life you can decide to be a bank employee,
or business executive, or throw yourself into a perilous job as a
civil servant."

"Well," Chandler said, "I published my first story when I
was forty-five years old. Until then I hadn't amounted to much
except a good accountant and a business manager in the oil business. My inclination toward letters certainly comes from way
back. I was educated at Dulwich College in England, and quite
honestly I was an excellent classics student. If I hadn't studied
Greek and Latin I doubt I'd know today how to draw the distinction between what I call vernacular style and what I would call
faux naïf. In my opinion there is an enormous difference. So don't
be upset, Cleve, if I still think to this very day that the hardest
part of writing is style, and that perfecting his style is also the
best investment a writer can make with his time. The payout is
slow; your agent will make fun of you, and your editor won't
understand you. But there will also be people you never heard of
who will slowly convince you that the writer who gives his writing his individual stamp will always make money. Of course I
mean the sort of style that's something like a projection of the

personality; so to be able to project it, you have to have a personality first. I agree with you, Cleve; you can't make yourself a writer just by applying yourself to your style. Style isn't a product of the quality of your emotions and perceptions; it's the ability to transfer them to paper that makes a man a writer, as opposed to the large number of people whose emotions are just as keen and whose perceptions are just as sharp but who can't put them down on paper for anything in the world."

"At heart I suspect that's a rather romantic and expressionistic theory of the creative process," Ballard rejoined. "You can't be saying that writing is a completely subjective process. Of course that counts, but you have to concentrate on form and technique. If you don't you end up with a sentimental and tearjerking sort of product. The difference between the good writer and the bad writer isn't the quality of his emotions, or the sharpness of his perceptions, it's in what he does with his material. A good novel is the result of many hours of hard, intensive work, like any form of craftsmanship. Except instead of polishing wood, soldering metal or chiseling rock, you work with a language, language is your raw material."

"You could say the same of a good magazine article," Chandler rejoined. "And I have no doubt today a great many skillful articles disguised as novels are being written—and probably will continue to be written. But those novelistic articles will always lack a certain emotional resonance. Even when the subject is death, and it often is, they aren't tragic. It's not unexpected: an age that is incapable of poetry is also incapable of any other sort of literature, except for the literature of decadence. These boys know how to say anything they want—their scenes are quite tediously rounded out, they have all the facts and know all the answers—but they're little men who've forgotten how to pray. As the world shrinks, men's minds shrink with it. Someday a novel written by a robot or computer will go on the market. And I'm sure it will be a best-seller."

"Have you read that Somerset Maugham essay, 'The Decline and Fall of the Crime Story'?" Butler asked. "You and Hammett come out very well, especially you," he emphasized, addressing Chandler. "But in spite of everything, Maugham says that the detective story is all washed up, except for the two of you, because no other original talent emerged. Nothing but imitators, more brutal, more vulgar, more interested in sex. I suppose James Cain and perhaps one or two of us must be among them.

But in any case, you rescue the honor of the group, Raymond. 'I do not see who can succeed Raymond Chandler,' Maugham says at the end. Comforting, isn't it?"

"I suspect that's Maugham's elegant way of returning my admiration for him," Chandler said, tamping down into the bottom of his pipe. "I never knew him personally, but I once suggested to my British publisher, Hamish Hamilton, that I'd like an autographed copy of *Ashenden,* and he got me one right away. *Ashenden* is heads above any other spy novel ever written. The rest of his novels, as good as they are, don't really outclass the field."

"And do you agree with him when he says he doesn't see who could follow you as a detective-novel writer?" Ballard asked, his tone somewhere between taunting and admiring.

Chandler inhaled deeply on his pipe. He sat back thoughtfully, his eyes wandering through the disorder of glasses and empty bottles, as if the labyrinth of his own life would be reflected somewhere in this chaos of glasses, cigarette butts, and empty fifths of bourbon. He raised his eyes and watched the afternoon shadows begin to thicken in the window frame; behind the net curtains the yellowish air above the lake was being beaten by the wings of myriad insects. Taki the cat approached the group and jumped suddenly on Chandler's knees, sprawling out until she found the most comfortable position. Chandler caressed her haunch complacently.

"Who knows," he finally said after breathing out a small, diffuse cloud of aromatic Dutch Amphora smoke. "I thought quite a bit about what you said, John, in the middle of your philosophical detour. Something about suicide being the only way to resolve on your own an event that must occur sooner or later. After all, anything you can possibly do is destined to slowly burn out in that expendable flame called life. The things by which we live are like the distant flashes of insect wings in clouded sunlight. If I were convinced no one who came after me could ever take my place, suicide would be a beautiful way of passing on into immortality. But I sincerely don't believe it's true. The detective novel will go on renewing itself, and all of us will pass on without much pain or glory into the pantheon of anonymous heroes as unknown soldiers who did something to maintain the vitality of the genre, incorporating into it the very language and crime and violence of the style of our own lives. If with all this we achieve something resembling poetry, that's al-
56

ready plenty. If I were sure I'd accomplished that, I personally would be satisfied. And so if someday I don't have any good reasons to live, like whiskey, tobacco, Taki the cat, or my wife, I'll probably fall back on that old philosophical recourse: I'll look for my old .38 in the back of some bureau drawer and shoot myself in one of those no-fail spots at the most convenient moment."*

*In fact, according to Frank MacShane, Chandler carried out a failed suicide attempt on February 22, 1955, two weeks after the anniversary of the death of his wife, Cissy. Chandler fired two shots from a .38 revolver while standing in the bathtub behind a closed plastic shower curtain and wearing a bathrobe. Here is Chandler's own account of this vaudeville situation: "I couldn't for the life of me tell you whether I really intended to go through with it or whether my subconscious was putting on a cheap dramatic performance. The first shot went off without my intending it to. I had never fired the gun and the trigger pull was so light that I barely touched it to get my hand in position when off she went and the bullet ricocheted around the tile walls of the shower and went up through the ceiling. It could just as easily have ricocheted into my stomach. The charge seemed to me to be very weak. This was borne out when the second shot (the business) didn't fire at all. The cartridges were about five years old and in this climate I guess the charge had decomposed. At that point I blacked out. The police officer who came in then told me later that I was sitting on the floor of the shower trying to get the gun into my mouth, and then when he asked me to give him the gun I just laughed and handed it to him. I haven't the slightest recollection of this. And I don't know whether or not it is an emotional defect that I have absolutely no sense of guilt or embarrassment at meeting people in La Jolla who all knew what had happened. It was on the radio here, on the wire services, in papers all over the country, and I had letters from all over the place, some kind and sympathetic, some scolding, some silly beyond belief." (From a letter Chandler wrote to Machell, dated March 5, 1955.)

PART THREE

LOS ANGELES
SEPTEMBER
1956

▶ **9:03 A.M.** **The Avenant Building** Fall had just begun; it
was strange to have so much rain already. I woke up a little after
nine with the nagging thought there was something I had to do.
Call Morton? I decided it wasn't so urgent after all. I glanced out
the bedroom window. The morning was dissolving under a violent burst of rain and a shroud of pale and misty light. Vines of
ivy streaming with water disguised the buildings on the other
side of the street. The roof terrace next door was empty; water
splashed thickly into the pool and threatened to overflow onto
the tiles. That meant farewell to the Swan's Lake until next
summer. I ate breakfast quickly and got my raincoat. I dove into
the Triumph; while the motor warmed up I glanced quickly
through the *Times*. Nothing about Andress except a brief death
notice: place and time of service. Hollywood Cemetery, four in
the afternoon. The mere thought of the choreography of open
umbrellas around the open pit made me shiver. What's more, it
was cold. I folded up the paper, put it next to the seat, put the car
in first, and let the cabriolet slip over the pockmarked pavement
toward Hollywood.

There were a few parking spaces on the Strip. I chose the
best one but I still had to walk almost fifty yards to Vine. In case
you've never been there, I'll remind you that Vine is where they
have the coral stars with the holy names on them, so walking
over those slabs was practically desecration. I crossed the street
toward the side entrance on Avenant. A slanting lash of rain hit
me and I swore at Nulty between my teeth—my suspicions that
Morton and I were victims of one of the Lieutenant's tricks were
deepening. But no, the name Andress was on the lobby directory.
I got on the elevator and got off on the twelfth floor.

The agency's offices occupied at least two suites at the far,
eastern side of the hallway. A plaque on the main door suggested
I enter without ringing the bell. I obeyed. There was a small
reception area and then came a main room where somewhere
between six and eight people probably worked. The desks were
unoccupied. A woman was replacing the flowers in a vase that
balanced precariously on one of the work tables. She raised her
head and looked at me. She wasn't blonde or young, and apparently she wasn't expecting any clients that morning, either. She

61

left her task and came to meet me, sending a light spray of water in my direction as she shook off her hands.

"What can I do for you?" she said. "We're not working today, we're in mourning."

"I'm looking for Mr. Andress's secretary," I said. "Is that you?"

"You want Miss Valento—Mr. Andress's partner," the woman corrected me. "I mean his ex-partner. Mr. Andress died yesterday. Why do you want to see her?"

"It has to do with the unfortunate event."

"I'll see if I can help you."

She finished drying her hands and deposited the vase in a niche in the wall behind her desk. The little placard said *Mrs. Prendergast*. She pushed the intercom button.

"Who am I announcing?"

"Marlowe. Philip Marlowe."

"A Mr. Marlowe is asking for you," the woman told the gadget.

A metallic squawk answered: "We're not receiving anyone. The office is closed until further notice." In spite of everything I liked the sound of the voice.

"You heard yourself," the woman observed.

"Please tell Miss Valento it's important."

"Important? Why?"

"It would take too long to explain it twice."

"Tell him to come in," the intercom crackled.

Mrs. Prendergast pointed to a walnut door on the other side of the office. I went by the empty desks, opened it, and found myself in what could have passed for a smaller replica of Andress's sumptuous Bel Air study. The windows looked south and took in a wide view of the long serpentine appendage that was Los Angeles. The violet mountains emerged out of the background of rain and the wooded areas were a discolored green; I thought of the landscapes of Pissarro or Marquet. The attractive and elegant woman Nulty had described had her back to the door, except she wasn't blonde; her hair was almost the color of almond wood and gave off a pale rosy sheen in the dim rainy light. She contemplated the mountains, the far-off mass of central Los Angeles, or the end of the road, with what seemed to be a mournful and cheated expression. She took her time before turning to me.

"Speak, Mr. Marlowe," she suggested as she sat behind the

immense desk. "I assume what you have to tell me is truly important. I'm in no mood to discuss business today. Actually, all business relating to Mr. Andress's affairs has been suspended."

"I didn't come here to talk business," I said.

I stood there waiting for an invitation to sit down. The three comfortable red leather armchairs appeared to be unoccupied.

"Then?"

"Do you mind if I sit down?" I asked.

"I'd mind if that meant what you have to say will take long. Believe me, Mr. Marlowe, I'm in no mood to discuss anything. I would be infinitely appreciative if you were as concise as possible."

I sat down. I had an impulse to take out my pack of Camels, but I repressed it. Miss Valento's icy eyes observed me with an impenetrable mixture of impatience and uneasiness. She was a beautiful woman, sure of herself and without doubt efficient. She was probably around thirty-five. One of those executive women shaped by Hollywood and the entertainment business—it wasn't difficult to imagine her as Andress's right hand. She also could have been an actress or a television announcer. A woman like her was essential for insuring the best possible public relations. I asked myself what there might have been between the two of them aside from a professional relationship. Despite her forced firmness and stubborn coldness she appeared fragile, troubled, and on the verge of a breakdown.

"What I have to say isn't very pleasant," I said. "But I prefer to get it over with out of consideration for your request and your state of mind. Did you know Yensid Andress was murdered?"

She looked at me for what seemed like an embarrassingly long time. She studied my face, or more likely the bottom of my soul, to decide what kind of person I was, what motives or hidden purposes might be behind my words and how much credit she could give them. She stretched her arm out toward a wooden box ornamented with inlaid work, executed a delicate maneuver, and extracted a cigarette. Her hand was long and slender, the fingers agile and sensitive. She tried to appear unperturbed, but she couldn't help trembling slightly. I came to and lit her cigarette.

"Thank you," she mused.

She sighed a long sigh and momentarily her gaze was lost. Once again I sank down into the blanketlike folds of the armchair and lit a Camel. Again I felt myself subjected to a relentless examination, but now there was a gleam of vulnerability hidden deep in her eyes. I asked myself if she'd ever let the gleam out, even if it was a tear.

"Who are you?" she finally asked. "The police?"

"Private investigator," I said.

"I suppose you have a good basis for making that statement."

"I do. I know there is nothing official about it—or better said, that the official theory is still suicide. But the facts at my disposal come from impeccable sources."

"What facts are these?"

"The shot that killed Andress came from a short distance away. Maybe two or three inches. At that kind of distance a black or gray stain, sort of a cloudy aureole, forms around the wound, an effect of the gunpowder's combustion. On top of this stain is what is called the tattoo, gunpowder grains that have been embedded in the skin. The mark looks very different when the weapon is firmly held against the cranium. You don't find this tattoo in a suicide. I never heard of anyone bent on killing himself who relied on the steadiness of his own hand. If the weapon moves just a few fractions of an inch as it goes off there's a good chance it won't hit its target, but that the target could become a vegetable for life. A man like Andress had to know that."

"Is that all the evidence?"

"They were holding a gun on Andress, but the evidence shows he still tried to move when they shot him. The murderer was only inches away; he wasn't shaking and he couldn't have missed. Still, he didn't take the precaution of resting the gun barrel on his arm. There's no doubt it was Andress's pistol; after the murderer fired it he put it in Andress's hand to simulate suicide. It was during the course of this maneuver that he committed the conclusive careless act. The pistol's safety catch snapped shut. I don't know if you know enough about guns to know what that means."

"I know very little or nothing about guns," she said in a quavering voice.

"The safety catch is the mechanism that holds down the trigger. To shoot a Colt, you have to slip it off. If you shoot yourself in the head and die instantly, it would be very unlikely for the safety to return to its normal position. The mere thought is absurd."

"Not even accidentally?"

"A one-in-ten-thousand chance."

She became thoughtful, slowly inhaling the mentholated smoke of her cigarette. She rose from her seat and turned, revealing three-quarters of her profile, toward the enormous windows and stood there watching the lead-colored darkness of the rainy morning. I suddenly realized I could easily fall in love with this woman. There was no doubt in my mind that Andress had been in love with her.

"Why would someone want to have Yensid killed? It's impossible to imagine," she said.

"That's why I'm here." It was the right moment to say it. "I thought you'd be the person who could give me some help."

"Help?"

"A clue."

"I don't feel the least affinity for your profession," she said. "What's more, I'd like to forget about all of this as soon as possible. Sometimes I think I'm in the middle of a nightmare, that I'm going to wake up any second and everything will go back to being the way it was. I don't plan to go on with this line of work and I may not even stay in Hollywood. In sum, I'll stay as long as I have to to put everything in order at the agency, just as Yensid would have done. Then I'll leave all this behind."

"And what will happen to Andress's studio and his assets? Can you tell me who his heirs are?"

"Yensid and his wife were divorced. They have a son who is traveling somewhere in Europe at the moment. We haven't been able to find him yet and we don't know if he knows what happened. He inherits the personal effects. I'm Andress's partner and fifty percent of the agency's proceeds and of this office belongs to me. Also, things were arranged legally so that in the event that something happened to Yensid I would take over as head of the agency."

"And you still want to retire?"

"In my present state of mind, yes. I don't know—I have to let all this play out and then reconsider the situation. At the moment I would like to go far away from here as soon as possible."

"I suppose you're familiar with Andress's alleged suicide note. What is the business's financial situation, Miss Valento?"

She thought for a few seconds before she answered me.

"This is a representational agency. Actually, we're intermediaries between the movie studios and those who write for the film industry. We negotiate our clients' properties for the best possible returns and we retain the established percentage for such transactions. We represent many of the best writers in Hollywood; our financial situation fluctuates, but we have a solid base and the company is never in the red. The writers' payments are made within a period previously agreed upon by the parties concerned. In the interim, the agency works with the money forwarded by the producer. Some amounts are significant; one hundred or two hundred thousand dollars. If Yensid used a portion of such an amount for a personal matter and was unable to replace it when the payment came due, it was without my knowledge. In any event, the firm has enough capital to cover that kind of emergency. At the moment our bank account contains something over half a million dollars. Of course, this capital belonged to the business, and I can imagine Yensid didn't want to mix his personal affairs up with the concerns of the agency. That was the kind of person he was. Nevertheless, his scruples were excessive; he knew very well I wouldn't oppose him in the eventuality of any circumstance that forced him to withdraw the required sum."

"It couldn't have been a sum much larger than the half a million in the bank?"

"I sincerely don't believe so."

"What kind of connection existed between you two, Miss Valento? I mean, aside from the one you told me about. You don't have to answer if you don't think the question is opportune."

"It isn't opportune, but I'll answer it anyway. Yensid asked me to marry him several times. He was convinced I would eventually say yes. We loved and respected each other. Not just in the professional sense. That was all."

"And would you have ended up marrying him?"

She contemplated me for a few seconds with detached indolence. Then she turned the armchair away again, as if she needed to sustain her reflections on the gray turbulence of the day. Something about it must have corresponded with her internal state, perhaps with her feelings toward Andress.

"Does this have anything to do with your investigation?" she finally said.

"I don't know yet. I shouldn't tell you," I said. "This is still a very confusing case. The police haven't officially opened it yet. Even you wouldn't have doubted the suicide hypothesis. I don't want to compromise my client."

"Is your client Andress's ex-wife?"

"I don't know who she is, or where she lives, or even what her relationship with her ex-husband was like. All I know is that they were divorced. Might she have some reason for being interested in the case?"

"I couldn't say. I rarely saw her, and our meetings were not pleasant. She'll doubtless be at the funeral this afternoon. Yensid had to make her a significant payment every month, and I suppose she thinks she has some right to this."

"You mean to the agency?"

"Exactly."

"She could demand it legally?"

"Impossible. Yensid's son is twenty-two years old. He isn't dependent on her. His father's share of the agency belongs to him."

"I understand. And you probably don't feel terribly drawn by the possibility of working with him, perhaps in his mother's protective shadow."

"You are a persistent man, Mr. Marlowe. I suppose a private detective has to be. How much can you hope to earn if you prove Andress's death was a crime and find his murderer?"

"A thousand dollars. At the moment it's a remote possibility."

"A thousand dollars." She seemed to weigh what that sum might mean to me. It might have been an unconscious or conscious method of establishing the different circles of democratic society in which she and I moved. "Yensid had an insurance policy," she added then, as if making an involuntary association between the two facts. "To the best of my knowledge companies don't pay premiums in cases of suicide. Is that true? You don't work for the Doreme Insurance Company, by any chance?"

"No. But I appreciate the information. Evidently, if there is someone who clearly benefits by Andress's death officially being considered a suicide, it's the insurance company."

"And if there is someone truly interested in demonstrating the contrary, it is none other than Andress's son, who would receive the insurance premium. But Terry isn't here, nor is he the kind of person who would be that interested in the money. His mother, on the other hand, is."

She inhaled nervously on her cigarette, and her eyes had a different shine to them when once again she lifted them to meet mine. "Why don't you come clean with me, Mr. Marlowe? I understand perfectly well that this is how you earn your living, and I'm willing to admit it's possible that the methods you are using are quite standard for your line of work. But I don't want Yensid's death to get turned into some sordid little affair just because someone doesn't want to lose out on an insurance premium. Please don't invent a crime where none exists. I'll pay you the thousand dollars myself if I have to. After the funeral this afternoon I'd like to try and forget all this as soon as possible; I'd erase it from my memory if I could. You seem bent on making sure I don't. Well then, it's worth a thousand dollars to me to spare the feelings of the living and the memory of an honest man who decided to kill himself for some unknown reason. Do you accept my offer?"

I stood up. In my line of work you don't usually get worked up enough to feel indignant, offended, or insulted. You get used to dealing with all kinds of people—murderers, hoodlums, psychopaths, plenipotentiary millionaires, and policemen who think they have carte blanche to push you around like some intruder they found *flagrante delicto* on the inner patio of their private garden. But this was one of the few times I felt utterly humiliated. Maybe it was because the aforementioned Valento was a real knockout, or because she'd innocently stumbled on just the right way to show up the subtle yet unbreachable distance between her and me. Or maybe it was because she seemed so sincere about defending what she perceived as Yensid Andress's spotless memory. Maybe it was just that not everyone could afford to be quite so blasé about a thousand dollars. But was she really as blasé as she seemed? It must have been that shadow of a doubt that made me stop in the tracks I was making and turn back toward her.

"Were you in love with Andress?" I asked suddenly.

She answered me without the slightest hesitation, which made me even more uncomfortable. "No. I already told you. We loved and respected each other. But Yensid was emotionally unstable. I've just escaped from a disastrous marriage. I'm not even sure I'm home free yet. It's an experience that leaves deep wounds and one I don't plan on repeating." Once again she held out her delicious hand and put out her cigarette in an onyx ashtray. "I don't know why I'm telling you all this. I think you're getting more out of me than most detectives would get. Or maybe you just happened to catch me with my guard down."

68

"I promise you one thing," I said with every ounce of persuasiveness I could muster. "I'm not working for Andress's ex-wife."

"Suppose I believed you. What else would you want to know?"

"Who might have a good motive for wanting to see Andress dead?"

"I can't think of anyone. He was great at public relations. He gave equal time to every player in a deal, and conscientiously defended the interests of the writers, who made up the weakest group. His life was a relatively open book—he avoided complications and fulfilled his financial obligations religiously."

"I've heard it said that Hollywood agents always skim off slightly more than ten percent of their clients' proceeds. That they get secret bonuses out of studio auctions for the rights to a particularly prized project. Did Andress go for that?"

"I won't deny he resorted to such tactics on occasion. It was part of his flair for playing the Hollywood game. It saved him a lot of haggling and it won his clients some of the highest fees in Hollywood for their work. It was only fair for him to get something out of it too, and it didn't violate any contractual clauses on either side."

"But doesn't that feed a certain kind of resentment? A screenwriter can't help but think someone is making more than he is from his own work."

"I know there are people who see it that way. I think they're wrong. Why don't you look over Yensid's client list? It includes the most desirable names in Hollywood. They were all quite anxious to be represented by him, and the fact that they were gave them a certain prestige, a sort of halo. I doubt a single one thought of Yensid as his enemy."

"Not even during the occasional tiff over the date or amount of a payment?"

"I can't answer that."

"One more thing. Could I really have a copy of that client list you mentioned?"

She pushed the intercom button and asked Mrs. Prendergast to give me a copy of the list.

"It will tell you everything you want to know." She was thoughtful for a few seconds. "Let me see...today is the twenty-fourth, the last Tuesday of the month. Most of the writers with

69

the agency usually get together for a monthly dinner at Steven's café, the Nikobob. It's on the corner of Novena and Wilshire. They started a club called the Fictioneers; they meet in a small private dining room and you can catch them there around nine. If you'd find it useful, you could probably question a good number of them right there."

"It would be extremely useful. Can I use your name?"

"You can if you want; it won't make any difference."

"Legally, you represent them now."

She sat back in her armchair. Her face went serious and worried, as if she'd just become aware of this new responsibility, but on her it looked good.

"I know. I hope not for very long."

"What do your friends call you, Miss Valento?"

"Velma. Do you find that useful too?"

"I go by Philip. Next time we get together I'll call you V.V."

"What makes you think there will be a next time?"

"Just a hunch. We have something in common, don't we? We both want to get to the bottom of Andress's death."

"I'm still not sure I do. But you know where you can find me for the next few days."

When I let go of the front door of the Avenant Building, the rain was pouring down and Vine Street had become the swiftly flowing tributary of Hollywood Boulevard.

▶ **3:13 P.M.** *Los Angeles Times* Charles Morton glanced nervously at his watch. It was a sporty Rolex that kept perfect time and perfectly matched his car, his wardrobe, and his philosophy of life—he was extremely proud of all three. It was later than he'd thought; by now it would take a good fifty minutes to get to Hollywood. He locked his desk drawer and, without finishing the page that was still in his typewriter, left the *Times* newsroom behind.

The *Times* parking lot was behind the building, and it was raining cats and dogs. Morton lowered his head, put his back to the wall, and inched his way toward West 54th Place. There was no reason he should have noticed the silhouette that rose from one of the tables at Shamey's, the coffee shop right across the street, hastily left the amount of his check at the cash register, and started after him. This individual was tall, over six feet, and hefty-looking, although it wasn't easy to tell how he was built, on account of the gray, bulky raincoat that covered most of him up. His face as well was half hidden under a rain hat turned down over his eyes. He crossed the avenue, skirting the cars splashing water on each side of the street and provoking curses from a driver forced to stop short. He reached the corner in time to see Morton disappear into the lot. West 54th Place was a one-way street going east. The man stopped in the middle of the intersection and shook the water off his hat brim a few times. A few minutes later Morton's Jaguar emerged from the parking lot, turned left, waited for the light to change, and merged with the northbound traffic on Sixth Avenue. About fifty yards down the street a gray Plymouth sedan started up. It hurtled to the intersection, paused just long enough for the giant in gray to jump in on the driver's side, and sped down the street until it was a safe distance behind the Jaguar. Morton couldn't take full advantage of the Jaguar's horsepower in the middle of the rain and the heavy afternoon traffic. The two vehicles kept up their forty- to forty-five-mile-an-hour speed through Greengrove Avenue, Spring Street, Canyon Drive, and Sunset Boulevard until they arrived in Hollywood.

The burial of Yensid Andress certainly wouldn't go down in history for large attendance. The rain was incessant. The Presbyterian minister gave a perfunctory reading of the ceremony while an acolyte sheltered his spectacles and the prayer book with an enormous black umbrella. Rain fell mercilessly over Yensid Andress's coffin, awaiting its final resting place under the green meadows of Hollywood. It was probably the place Andress himself would have chosen if he'd had the chance. The hill rose like some immense natural stage above the capital of celluloid, and most of its sacred monsters had been laid to rest there. Alienated by the minister's drone filtered to an unintelligible murmur by the rain, Morton repeated a different set of words, his own profane apodosis to the Holy Scripture: *"What did it matter where you lay once you were dead? In a dirty sump or in a marble tower on top of a high hill? You were dead, you were sleeping the big sleep, you were not bothered by things like that. Oil and water were the same as wind and air to you. You just slept the big sleep, not caring about the nastiness of how you died or where you fell."*

Completely untouched by the ceremony, Morton stayed a

few yards beyond the small huddle of Andress's debtors, friends, colleagues, and collaborators stoically bearing up under the torrent. He had no protection against the weather but his wide-lapeled white trench coat, so he was grateful when a black umbrella (that classic instrument of British elegance, yet so decidedly opposed to British elegance's pragmatic view of existence) suddenly moved above his soaking-wet hair. He was even more astonished to discover that the hand holding up the cloth toadstool rippling in the blustery wind belonged to his old acquaintance Lieutenant Nulty.

"What a surprise to find you here," Nulty said. "Are you going to write an obituary?"

"The surprise is mutual," Morton replied evasively, but without rejecting the shelter of his umbrella.

"My conscience told me I ought to liven this shindig up a little," the Lieutenant answered. "Don't you think it's odd that so few people showed up to say their final good-byes to such a prominent man? Look," he added. "That woman is his ex-widow; the other two over there are his private secretary, Miss Valento, and his receptionist. I can identify a couple of Hollywood writers and a half-dozen colleagues, his closest sidekicks. When Andress was still with us they flayed each other alive. And who's representing the movie business? After all, almost every studio owed Andress more than one favor. I hear he supplied them with more tons of first-class material than any other agent. That translates into millions of dollars. Hollywood is a godless world. It's a heartless industry, yessiree. The space reserved for that respectable organ is occupied by a safe."

"Don't try and tell me you just figured that out, Lieutenant," Morton said.

"No, but it pains me to notice how often the point gets rubbed in." Nulty moved the umbrella to his other hand, and Morton began to get the slanting lash of rain on his left side. "You know more than I do about these things. Wasn't Andress the founder of the Hollywood Association of Literary Agents?"

"He was one of the people who worked the hardest to start it, at the very least."

"And where are his fellow Association members? I can't believe it isn't any larger than this little handful of agents. It was a rather powerful and united organization, wasn't it?"

"Almost every agent in Hollywood belongs. Andress's great

achievement was to force the big studios to deal with the agents in a bloc, and to submit to most of their demands."

"And to those of the writers as well, I suppose," Nulty deduced. "Which probably didn't make the studios jump for joy. The agents got used to sucking a little blood here, a little blood there. A sort of organized vampirism. Wasn't that more or less it?"

"Let's just say the Association required writers to take advantage of a powerful intermediary. There's a law protecting them. From where I sit, the writer comes out ahead. Before, he had to make heads or tails of everything by himself and was at odds with a group of very powerful companies that paid what the market would bear for scripts. By protecting the agents the Association also protects the writers. If that organization bugs anyone, it's the studios."

"And Andress was the brain behind the union, right?"

"He was the toughest and the most skillful of the bunch, that much I'm sure of. And he also took away the lion's share. He represented the best-paid writers in Hollywood."

"That's just what I was saying," the Lieutenant reflected taciturnly. "There should have been an impressive cortege here. And how many of us are there? Twenty, maybe twenty-five. Without counting those two bodyguards, who're keeping, who knows why, such a distance it's almost a sacrilege. On your left there. Why do you think I moved the umbrella? Tell me, Morton, did you bring them along for protection, or are they tailing you?"

Morton just barely turned his face in the direction Nulty's glance was imperceptibly pointing. He made out the dark silhouettes, one the height of a basketball player, behind the curtain of rain. They were so far away it must have been real tough to follow the liturgy.

"I've never seen them before. They look like they might belong to your force's *gardes du corps,*" he ventured.

"They aren't from my department," Nulty protested. "Either they're protecting someone important, or they represent the legion of Andress's anonymous followers."

"You think so?" Morton replied skeptically. "There aren't any of those captains of industry who always travel with a driver and a bodyguard at this funeral?"

"What else could they be doing here?" The Lieutenant managed to take out a cigar, lift it to his mouth, and light it in the gusting rain using nothing but his one free hand. "To change the subject, Morton, what else is your newspaper going to publish about this unfortunate occurrence? I imagine you didn't come all the way here just to throw a handful of mud on the coffin?"

"And what else would we have to say?" Morton complained. "You guys put a lid on the whole thing. Why so much mystery this time, Lieutenant? Are we going to get the official autopsy results, or aren't we?"

"Listen carefully," the Lieutenant said. "But please don't write anything down. Remember as much as you can and make do with that. A bullet fired point-blank leaves powder burns and an irregular, gaping orifice; a bullet fired point-blank against a sealed cavity like the cranium can have rather explosive results. Got it? Well, Andress's head didn't show evidence of any sort of explosion; there was a black powder stain around the point of entry, and on top of the stain there was an oval-shaped tattoo. That means the shot was fired from two or three inches away, and not point-blank nor much farther or closer than those two or three inches. Understand? The bullet's path slanted from top to bottom—at a pretty steep angle. The character who fired the shot was on his feet and Andress was sitting down. Decorate all that with a few of those formulas you use so expertly: according to what is known, unofficial sources maintain, etcetera, etcetera. If I find myself quoted in the newspaper I'll have you thrown in jail for slander. For the moment, the investigation is strictly confidential. Officially, Andress still committed suicide. Don't forget it. The fact that in my opinion a small leak could give us a little push doesn't mean my superiors agree with me."

Once more, with an apparently careless and expert gesture, the Lieutenant turned his head toward the men stationed some twenty yards away. "We've got to find out whose trail those two bloodhounds are on," he added. "And now I'll be on my way. Look, they already threw the last shovelful on Andress's body. That miserable minister of God must have been numb with cold, to fulfill his obligations that way."

Nulty turned and began to walk away in the direction of the cemetery entrance. Morton waited for the group to break up. He considered approaching Andress's ex-wife, then decided it wasn't the right moment. He turned up the collar of his trench coat and walked back to his car. As he closed his hand over his keys he remembered the two characters Nulty had pointed out. He turned around and tried to pick them out through the rain, but he was already too far away. They must have left with the rest of the cortege or melted away into the early evening darkness. He didn't give it any further thought. He waited for the motor to warm up, lit a cigarette, and began a leisurely drive back to Hollywood.

▶ **8:17 P.M.** **Bristol Apartments** Once you're on Sunset, providing the traffic is light, it's only twenty or twenty-five minutes from Brentwood Heights to Steven's café. I woke up from my mild evening torpor to the metallic murmur of a plane overhead and the phonograph needle slipping across the last notes of a Bud Powell record: "Dear Old Stockholm," a drugged dream of Hesperides and Valkyries, except Bud Powell's rough fingers were pounding out the dream with a strange melancholy, as if the tune were a premonition of his own lot—sex, booze, and that sad hangover either exhaustion or life can leave behind. These seem to be essential elements of jazz; so are drugs sometimes, but drugs aren't as necessary as they used to be, because on the cotton plantations and even in the brothels of New Orleans blacks didn't need anything but white religion and Puritan licentiousness to get off. Marijuana, heroin—all that came later and claimed its victims, Bud Powell among them. But a scalding hot shower and about fifty cc's of bourbon or Talisker were all I craved to put me right. Along with a pretty strong dose of resolution.

The more I thought about it, the fewer possibilities I saw for my raid on the Nikobob. The prospect of jumping into the middle of a writers' get-together without an invitation seemed in and of itself discouraging. I could assume my chance of finding the group immersed in some scholarly or even merely literary debate was remote; there was a chance the topic of discussion would be the club itself, but that also seemed unlikely. As fate would have it, Yensid Andress had been buried that very afternoon, and therefore it would probably resemble a macabre celebration more closely than it would a run-of-the-mill club meeting. How could they get rid of all the Hollywood literary agents once and for all? This, possibly, would be the only important item on the evening's agenda.

Miss Valento's opinion aside, I was still convinced writers

had well-defined criteria concerning the proper role of their representatives—a role that was the least of all evils, but an evil nonetheless. But I'd already resolved to go to the meeting, and after glancing at my watch I realized I'd better hurry. If I arrived much past nine it was quite possible I'd discover the club members in the middle of some Bacchic rite. As far as I could tell, the Fictioneers were not known for their moderation. W.T. Ballard had once said that the meetings were always casual; their principal purpose was for club members to placidly inebriate themselves and then attend one of the neighborhood burlesque theaters en masse. Alcohol's tendency to induce confessionalism might or might not work in my favor. A drunken writer will talk and talk—the hard part is trying to figure out how much fiction and how much reality there is in the stories he tells you. The list the Andress Agency had supplied me with included most of the writers I might find at the café: Ballard, Cleve Adams, Dwight Babcock, Erle Stanley Gardner, Norbert Davis, George Harmon Coxe, and my old acquaintance Raymond Chandler.

As I finished dressing I couldn't stop myself from going over all the angles. Chandler and I had met at least half a dozen times, almost always as he was beginning to write a new novel. He was a difficult and unpredictable man; you could never tell what mood you'd find him in. He might be quiet, sullen, on the defensive, and sealed up tight as an oyster, or he might well be feeling garrulous and sentimental—ready to cry on the nearest shoulder, list his marital misfortunes one by one, and even mercilessly dissect his own inconclusive autobiography. If Chandler were immersed in a brand-new story, it was likely we would talk more about me than about him. On such occasions he tried to squeeze the best juice he could from me; he became more interested in my affairs and wanted to know what the life of a private detective was like from "the inside." I was never really sure what he meant by "the inside"—whether he was referring to my monklike privacy, my domestic disorder, or just my methods and forms of working. He was especially interested in knowing how I could stand living alone, in an empty and silent bachelor's apartment. I suspect that at heart he was terrified by all these things —solitude, isolation, and silence. The first time he questioned me I did everything I could to convince him I experienced great tranquility each time I came back to my cave. It's not a place you could call home, but there is a homey smell, a smell of dust and tobacco smoke, the smell of a world where men live, and keep on living. At heart, I suppose my reply let him breathe easier. There are people who feel solitude so acutely they can't even bear to hear about the solitude of others.

In short, whatever mood I might find him in, Chandler was, by far, the man I was most interested in talking to. He was the best writer in the group and without doubt the most notorious. A wise observer who didn't cross over the line into cynicism, he was objective and truthful without being skeptical. For a writer who invariably found his inspiration in the flora and fauna of our angelic California society, that was already saying enough. Chandler had been, in addition, the writer who had sounded off with the most frankness and depth on the subject of the proper role of the Hollywood literary agent, a subject that was now acquiring particular relevance. The opinions he expressed were shared by the whole group, but the difference was that Chandler had had the courage to make his public in the prestigious *Atlantic Monthly* magazine. Since then he had probably earned the enmity of a few agents, including Andress himself, along with that of a few producers, directors, and other local varieties, but his stock was still high. No one in the movie business (and especially in the sect of agents) who valued his own hide could permit himself to dispense with Chandler's services entirely. Billy Wilder came to admit after a hazardous collaboration *(Double Indemnity)* that Chandler was one of the most creative men he had ever met. Now, as a result of a curious chain of events, Chandler's article on the "orchid of the profession," the Hollywood agent, had come to command unexpected power and placed him in a privileged position with respect to Andress's death.

I considered this possibility: was Chandler the kind of guy who could pump another guy's head full of lead (even if it was only the head of a literary agent) over a few thousand dollars? Or even for the sake of some less concrete but more romantic dilemma of principles? I couldn't believe it. Nevertheless, one never knows to what point a writer is capable of making reality out of his own fictional world in some isolated moment of mental disturbance, imbalance, confusion, or spite. And on top of that, mystery writers are perpetually walking the narrow line between fantasy and reality—it is impossible to write about crime and death without imagining over and over again what's going on inside a guy who's deciding to squeeze the trigger of a gun pointed at someone else's chest. In a case like that financial motives, personal motives, any other motives or vulnerabilities at all become secondary. A mystery and crime writer might decide to kill merely because his unconscious and his reflexes have become so intimate with violence and death that such alternatives are just part of his everyday psychological repertoire, part of the storehouse of possible options. For him, a real murder can come to mean something as simultaneously simple and complex as the cathartic urge to knock off the decisive paragraph of a good story with a violent burst of words typed out at top speed. All the better if the act's sweetened with that indispensible dose of excitement, intrigue, fury, passion, or what have you. In short, I considered the possibility very carefully, but it still seemed completely irrational to conclude Chandler had killed Yensid Andress; I was convinced he hadn't, and it was a hunch as solid as a proven fact. All I could expect of Chandler, provided I found him sober and receptive, was that he would tell me something I didn't already know about the professional relationship between Andress and whoever might have been interested in permanently retiring him from the Hollywood scene. To pull off this minor achievement, I had to arrive at the Café Nikobob before the Fictioneers had gotten much beyond the third or fourth toast of their monthly dinner and before they set off in a jovial group over the damp pavement of Novena Street or Western Avenue toward the most alluring burlesque show in that merry district.

I left Pacific Palisades around eight-twenty. I decided to take the Coastal Highway. There was a paragraph in one of the Chandler stories, *The Little Sister,* that described a trip to Oxnard by the same route: "On the right the great solid Pacific, trudging into shore like a scrub-woman going home. No moon, no fuss, hardly a sound of the surf. No smell. None of the harsh wild of the sea. A Californian ocean." The description was close enough to reality, I thought, a slightly sordid reality, the kind Chandler'd had a taste for about ten years back. There had been changes. At the moment I was pedaling the accelerator of a vehicle that in just a few seconds could go from zero to eighty-five or ninety miles an hour and it had become necessary to build two-way highways with three lanes on each side and overpasses that did away with intersections. The new technology of the automobile industry and the quickened pace of production were largely responsible for the transformation of the urban landscape that had taken place over the last decade. The old Coastal Highway, for instance, had turned into one of those double bands of asphalt shimmering with the soft, diluted reflection of a necklace of mercury lamps. The truck going in the other direction hurled endless streams of light against a night drilled through with fine darts of drizzle. The windshield wipers danced crazily to the beat of who knew what music, and the parking lights of the cars in front of me pointed back into the darkness like the antennae of invisible insects about to be devoured by the black throat of the highway. I suppose that the automobile had given individuals a new and very contemporary illusion of isolation and power, one that made a person feel not unlike the lauded Homeric gods: closed in and protected, like livestock. So much for the transformation of the Coastal Highway. As far as the ocean was concerned, it was still there just as it had been in Chandler's story—that much was inevitable. But I didn't know why it had occurred to him to compare it with a humble maid on her way home. It could be immense and solid (a point in its favor), but impetuous and voracious as well—it broke against the coast with a rhythmic and choleric din that came to my ears wrapped in the wind and the rain, above the snore of the motor. And it wasn't at all pacific—it was as sinister and threatening as the deaf murmur of California.

Then I recalled another passage from the same trip in Chandler's novel: "I smelled Los Angeles before I got to it. It smelled stale and old like a living room that had been closed too long. But the colored lights fooled you. The lights were wonderful. There ought to be a monument to the man who invented neon lights. Fifteen stories high, solid marble. There's a boy who really made something out of nothing." He had created the poetry of the modern city, and Chandler had drunk it down without the least flinch of continence, he had gotten high on it, before he vomited it into his writing. I looked up and met the sensual, blinking mask of Los Angeles. Neon and marble—skyscrapers that dissolved into rain. The city, up around those steel towers, had also changed somewhat over the last decade. The pinnacles were perpetually pulling themselves up by their bootstraps to more dazzling, streamlined heights. Neon signs announced a world of pleasure and consumption, an artificial society of luxury, a dazzle as fascinating, prestigious, and fragile as money, success, and, at times, life itself. But it was worth the trouble to take a closer look from street level, from the basements and alleys, the nightclubs, the hidden shacks, the brothels. It was worth taking a prudent walk through the worst bars and suburbs of that central cluster. There the urban labyrinth was as sordid, dirty, dark, and duplicitous as it had been ten years back. Even more dangerous than you thought it was, Chandler, old pal: "Twenty-four hours a day somebody is running, somebody else is trying to catch him. Out there in the night of a thousand crimes people were dying, being maimed, cut by flying glass, crushed against steering wheels or under heavy tires. People were hungry, sick, bored, desperate with loneliness or remorse or fear, angry, cruel, feverish, shaken by sobs. A city no worse than others, a city rich and vigorous and full of pride, a city lost and beaten and full of emptiness."

Suddenly I found myself obliged to maneuver to leave the Coastal Highway behind. I crossed the overpass and penetrated the reeling nocturnal periphery of the tentacular city. Wide deserted avenues, darkened buildings. Life, that insomniac, flowing inside it and underneath it. Ten minutes to go to the Café Nikobob. More than enough to be convinced that in Los Angeles anything that doesn't grow, anything that slithers back into the basements and hovels, will surely die.

▶ **9:12 P.M. Café Nikobob** I walked through the carpeted vestibule and entered the tenuous and purply half-light of the Café Nikobob. Glasses tinkled weakly. There was the dim sound of voices, and the notes of a piano tucked away in some invisible corner were syncopating "My Little Buckeroo." The place had tall dark walnut panelling and booths separated by solid brown leather backrests. A discreet candle burned on each table, and the farther back one ventured the more discreet and enveloping the half-light became. The place wasn't considered very elegant. It was practical for certain types of meetings and it was located on a hotly contested corner of the business district. Once in a while one of the more notorious Hollywood characters could be found there, but due to an unwritten code to which everyone secretly seemed to subscribe, no one indicated they were aware of or recognized the presence of anyone else except their exclusive companion. Newspapermen were practically banned from the place, and private detectives probably fell into the same category, but that night I managed to infiltrate without any resistance. The pianist ran one thumb down the keyboard, hitting a few notes, and then began to improvise on "We Can Still Dream, Can't We?" I approached the bar. The barman was stirring a
80

cocktail to the piano's beat. I recognized Steven's blond, smooth, shining mane of hair behind the cash register; he seemed to be chatting happily with a man emptying a whiskey bottle with no company but his own loneliness, but in reality Steven was paying very little attention to the man. Steven was a man who gave off smiles and affability; he had the face of a falcon, a curved nose, fine lips dripping with irony, and green eyes that flashed into alert suspicion when they saw me approach.

"If it isn't Marlowe!" he exclaimed. "I'd like to know why I pay a six-foot bouncer if a guy with an aura as prestigious as yours can get as far as the coatroom without any kind of interference."

"Calm down, Steven," I replied. "This has nothing to do with business."

"Oh yeah? And so to what do I owe the privilege of this visit?"

"My love of literature. Isn't tonight the meeting of the writers' club?"

"What club?"

"The Fictioneers. Isn't that what it's called?"

"Could be. Were you invited?"

"I'm tonight's speaker."

He shot me an incredulous glance, but it was followed by a look of perplexity that made me suspect my statement was just crazy enough to seem true.

"Are you going to announce me or shall I go on my own steam?" I suggested.

"Do you know where they meet?" he asked.

"No idea."

"The staircase after the restrooms. Mezzanine, first door to the right."

I raised one hand in an ambiguous gesture somewhere between thanks and so long. The drunk wanted to snare me, in hopes of starting a conversation. I left without giving Steven time to think. I felt the spark of his jaundiced eyes following my steps as if I were leaving a trail of dust behind me.

I passed a waiter on the staircase. He was on his way back to the bar, balancing a tray with three empty bottles in his right hand.

"Excuse me," I intercepted him. "By any chance are you coming from the writers' meeting?"

"I sure am," he replied. "Should I set another place?"

"That won't be necessary." I extracted a dollar bill from my pocket. "I want to talk to someone there, but I hate interrupting. I know how sensitive intellectuals are." I made the bill glide to the center of the tray. "Raymond Chandler's the man."

"I'll see what I can do for you. What's the name?"

"Marlowe. Philip Marlowe."

"Yes, sir. Follow me and wait in that booth near the wall. You're going to have to wait a bit."

Chandler appeared five minutes later. He seemed sober, but I never trusted appearances. He looked thinner than he'd been the last time we'd gotten together. I knew he wasn't bearing up well under the strain of his wife's death, and there were all kinds of rumors about the way he was conducting his private life. I'd always been of the opinion that a man's private life enjoys a unique privilege: it's private—it's a matter that concerns him primarily if not exclusively. Chandler took his symbiotic pipe out of his mouth and adjusted the bridge of his glasses with one index finger. He didn't offer his hand nor did I attempt to hold mine out to him. He said he had a skin problem and scorned that chummy American custom.

"Now I believe it—Philip Marlowe in person." He spread his 176 pounds on the empty seat across from mine. "My God, I thought I'd finally gotten rid of you."

"When and why?" I asked.

"When? Any number of times. Let me see...once I wrote Hamilton that you were beginning to bore me. Hamilton is my British publisher. That was after I finished off *The Little Sister*. I suppose you haven't read it."

"I rarely read mystery novels."

"You do well. I don't read any but the ones I write. And then only because somebody has to proofread the galleys. Frankly, I thought we'd seen the last of each other with *The Little Sister*."

"That was five years ago?"

"Seven, to be exact. It was my fifth novel. You were becoming more artificial to me every day—your attitude, I mean. A man of your parts is beginning to look pretty ridiculous as a small-time private detective. However, something told me you were still too valuable. Then came *The Long Goodbye*. That was in 1953. You didn't read that either?"

"I glanced through it a couple of nights ago to kill time."

"To kill time?"

"I was curious about how far you'd taken your study of me."

"Too far. So far, they accused me of making you slack and sentimental. I almost married you off. Look, Marlowe. The years don't go by in vain. I've grown old; you're much older than you once were. Why don't you get another job? This sort of touch-and-go life isn't for us."

"I could be convinced," I admitted. "But after a while this turns into a habit as noxious as heroin or morphine. You know it's bad for you, but you can't give it up."

"I don't deny it." Chandler patiently began to fill his pipe. He didn't seem to be in any hurry—no doubt he'd been waiting for the smallest excuse to leave the meeting. I'd given him one. "Why don't you get away from here?" he insisted, looking at me over the rim of his glasses. "It's probably just a question of scenery. This is no place for you. I'm about to leave for England. Permanently."

"I like California," I answered. It was one of those rare occasions when Chandler was half sober, half sad, half jovial, and unusually communicative.

"California..." he repeated. "I've lived half my life in this, what they call the greenest state in the Union. It has the best climate, the most beautiful coastline, some of the fairest cities in the country. I'm in love with San Francisco... You know what someone once said about Switzerland? 'Un beau pays mal habité.' That describes this place to a T. I'm sick of California and the kind of people it breeds. I like people with manners, grace, some social intuition, and education slightly above the *Reader's Digest* fan, people whose pride can sit still for half an hour without a drink in its hands, although apart from that I always prefer an amiable drunk to Henry Ford. I like a conservative atmosphere, a sense of the past; I like everything that Americans of past generations used to go and look for in Europe, but at the same time I don't want to be bound in by the rules."

"Come on, Chandler. You must have had some reason for spending the best years of your life in this city or the vicinity. After all, you've always written about California."

"To get it out of my system," he replied. "But now I know that I squeezed too much out of this city, this landscape, and these people. Now they're squeezing me. Take my advice: get out of here before it's too late."

"And Hollywood?" I answered. "Don't tell me you don't owe

83

Hollywood a favor or two? Half your fame, and I presume, most of your fortune."

"Hollywood?" Chandler seemed to perk up quickly at the mere mention of the magic name—but who could guess at everything burning in the transparent ardor of his gaze? "Could be; I don't want to seem ungrateful," he continued. "Look, Marlowe, the first time I went to bed with the whore that is Hollywood was back around 1943. Billy Wilder called to ask me if I'd write the screenplay for *Double Indemnity*. Until then, I'd seen Hollywood as a sort of luxury call girl, understand? Something way beyond my means. Then Paramount granted me an interview; I get there like an almost virgin teenager and agree to write the screenplay for a few hundred dollars. Someone had to appear to teach me how you negotiate with the studios. I went to an agent and ended up with a three-month contract, seven hundred and fifty dollars a week. That seemed like an incredible sum to me. Two years later, in 1945, I was paying fifty thousand in income tax. Did you hear me? Fifty thousand dollars in taxes. Something inconceivable for a guy whose soles had been wearing through just a few years before."

"And then?"

"Incredible, huh? I had a salary and a contract. One night a very important producer called to ask me to do the screenplay for one of the most advertised projects of the year. It was a great opportunity, but the fact is that I had to do it on the quiet, with full knowledge that it would be a violation of my contract with another producer. Well, that's a small example of Hollywood ethics. It never even occurred to the guy that he was insulting me. Perhaps in spite of all my faults, I still had a certain sense of honor. When I quarrel, I put the point at issue down on the table, and I'm perfectly willing to let them examine my sleeves for hidden cards. But you know something, Marlowe? They don't; it would horrify them to find out my sleeves were empty. They don't like to deal with honest men." He dawdled a few seconds lighting his pipe, which went out in the middle of each paragraph; he sucked on it and went on. "I remember one of the first times I ran into a group of executives on their way back from lunch in one of the studio hallways. I was transfixed with sinister delight. They looked so exactly like a bunch of topflight Chicago gangsters moving in to read the death sentence on a beaten competitor. In a flash they made me see the strange psychological and spiritual kinship between the operations of big money business and blackmail. Same faces, same expressions, same manners. Same way of dressing and same exaggerated leisure of movement. That's more or less the image of Hollywood I've kept to this day: the pretentiousness, the bogus enthusiasm, the constant drinking and drabbing, the incessant squabbling over money, the all-pervasive agent, the strutting of the big shots and their usually utter incompetence to achieve anything they start out to do, the constant fear of losing all this fairy gold and being the nothing they have never really ceased to be, the snide tricks, the whole damned mess is out of this world. It is like one of these South American palace revolutions conducted by officers in comic-opera uniforms: only when the thing is over and the dead men are lined up in rows against the wall you suddenly know that this isn't funny, this is a Roman circus and damn near to the end of civilization."

"Agreed. But Hollywood didn't just give you the chance to make money. It also gave you the chance to write, and write about what you knew and liked."

"You're crazy, Marlowe," Chandler said patiently. "You haven't the slightest idea of what it means to be a Hollywood screenwriter. Screenwriters are treated like cows; someone rounds them up and puts them out to pasture. At one time I truly hoped I would find a way of working in the film industry without being cynical about it. But I couldn't, because there isn't. Look, the movies are like a picture of a woman in a bikini. If she were wearing more clothes, you might feel intrigued. If she weren't wearing anything at all, you might be scandalized. But as it is, all you can do is notice her knees are bony or her toes are too big. The illusion of reality in a contemporary film is so perfect that it doesn't require anything of its audience but that they eat popcorn. Something similar happens to writers."

The waiter who had arranged the interview unexpectedly opened the door and looked us over. He didn't seem entirely pleased.

"What about a drink?" I proposed to Chandler.

"That's the best idea you've ever had in your whole life," he replied.

I signaled the waiter and ordered a couple of double scotches.

"Will you be staying much longer?" he asked.

"Is there a problem?" I asked in turn.

"This booth," he said. "It was requested in advance. It has to be available in half an hour."

"Time to spare," I assured him. "Make it Talisker, will you? I just discovered the label..."

"Right away, boss. But don't forget your promise, eh?"

Chandler waited until he heard the door close.

"Let me make things clear to you, Marlowe; it's not that I think the movies are pointless. Completely the opposite. The cinema isn't merely an art form, but rather the only completely new art form that has appeared on this planet in hundreds of years. If Shakespeare had been born in this generation he would have prospered; he would have refused to die in a corner. He would have taken the false gods and made them over; he would have taken the current formulae and forced them into something lesser men thought them incapable of. Alive today, he would have written and directed motion pictures, plays, and God knows what. Instead of saying 'This medium is no good,' he would have used it and made it good."

"And then?" I interrupted him, intercepting his somewhat fantastical digression.

"Well, that simply proves one thing: it's not the movies that are sick. It's that the movie business has perverted them. And when I say movie business, here in the United States I mean Hollywood. That you know very well."

"I have a vague idea," I said. "You sign a contract, decide what to write about, argue with the producers, the director, and probably a few more executives in the bargain, draw a salary of... how much? Two thousand, three thousand dollars a week?"

"Up to four thousand," Chandler said.

"Fine. What's the problem?"

"Everything you mentioned, except the money, is only a half truth, which is to say it's not true at all. For starters, it is extremely difficult for the screenwriter to choose his own theme, and even if he likes the story given him, someone will make it his business not to let him do things his own way. In Hollywood you can't make a movie unless it is essentially a love story, a story where sex predominates. When I persuaded Paramount to buy Elizabeth Sanxay Holding's novel *The Innocent Mrs. Duff* and began to work on the script, immediately there were difficulties. The producer got Paramount to change the parts of the plot he didn't like. If Paramount had had the sense to let me

86

write my own idea of a rough screenplay about Mrs. Duff, I would have come up with something in a relatively short period of time that would have shown them at a glance where the picture was. But no—they simply didn't realize that what they want from me is what I write in my own way. You know what the clincher is? In Hollywood they destroy the link between the writer and his subconscious. After that what he does is merely a performance. His heart is somewhere else."

"I don't deny the strength of your argument, but maybe your take on the movies is too literary."

"And is it possible for a writer not to have a literary perspective on something? Literature is art, and the movies should be an art. Thinking in conceptual terms destroys the ability to think in terms of emotions and feelings. Producers, and sometimes directors, are full of ideas; they explain them very well, but in an intellectual way. That's when I feel the futile impulse to tell anyone who'll listen why the needs of the whole apparatus cannot be served by intellectualism. Literature is action; cinema is action—the rest is useless chicanery."

"I ask myself if the studio heads at places like Paramount or MGM don't notice this," I observed. "Why would they sign you up if what you come up with isn't of any use to them? Isn't it possible they have their own ideas about what is useful and what is not? After all, for those people the movies are just another high-profit business. Naturally they would run the industry just for what they understand it to be: a business."

"That's exactly what I'm trying to say," grumbled Chandler, looking at me rancorously from behind a cloud of smoke. "Even after all this time you haven't lost your perspicacity, Marlowe. For the Goldwyns, the Warners, and the Bracketts, the movies are an industry—a machine for making money and easy women. Everyone who plays a role is nothing but a bureaucrat, no matter how well he's paid. And he has to behave like a bureaucrat, understand? Have you ever known an employee of any industry, not just the movies, who's allowed his own ideas or initiative? No, sir—ideas are the boss's prerogative. I once saw Samuel Goldwyn beat a table and scream, *I'm sick and tired of writers chiseling on producers in Hollywood. So here is the deal. You can either take it or like it.*'"

His evocation of the choleric Goldwyn was so persuasive I almost broke out laughing.

"It's just as I say," he continued, suddenly serene, as if his cathartic pantomime had relieved him of all the rancor he'd been holding inside. "In an atmosphere like Hollywood's a writer can be briefly enthusiastic, but his enthusiasm is destroyed before it can bloom. He knows intelligent and interesting people, and he may even go so far as to form lasting friendships, but none of that has anything to do with writing. The wise screenwriter is the one who wears the suit of the day, artistically speaking, and doesn't take things too seriously."

The waiter came in without knocking and set down two glasses brimming over with amber liquid.

"That's five dollars," he said. "And the table has to be available in fifteen minutes. Steven's orders."

I reached for my wallet, but Chandler put his hand on my arm.

"Put it on the Fictioneers' tab," he told the waiter.

He held up his glass as if it were a trophy.

"Cheers!" I said.

Chandler took his pipe out of his mouth and made most of his Talisker disappear in one gulp.

"Good whiskey," he approved, watching the candlelight filter through the amber liquor. "This will probably be our last drink together for some time. But you didn't come all the way here to wish me bon voyage, Marlowe. Now out with it."

"Yensid Andress," I said.

"Ah, yes," he muttered. "I read that business about the suicide. Are you on the case?"

"He was your agent, wasn't he?"

"He used to be," Chandler said. "It's been a while since I worked with him."

"Your name is still on his client list."

"Remind his people to update it. Andress wasn't a bad guy. He was no better or worse than the rest of his kind—more diplomatic in his dealings with writers and less scrupulous in his relationships with producers. Anyway, the average length of my agreements with literary agents is about two years. Andress lasted a little longer, but not because he inspired me with more confidence than the others. Who'd have thought he'd end up killing himself? It's upped my respect for him. I've always secretly admired anyone who actually manages to commit suicide. I tried it once; it's not the kind of thing you should try, it's the kind of thing you should just do. Failed suicides always end up with the most abject old age."

88

"It seems to me that you don't hold Hollywood agents in great esteem."

"It seems?" Chandler swirled his whiskey, stirring up who knew what sort of memories in the bottom of the glass. "That doesn't take much insight on your part, Marlowe. My opinion of the sect of agents is public record. Like so many other things in Hollywood, they are an inevitable evil, and therefore a necessary one. Without agents to protect them, writers get eaten up by big business. But so far writers haven't found a way to avoid being eaten up by agents. That's the gist of it. I began here with Swanson, who was one of the most important in his day. Then I switched over to Ray Stark; he was a man with incredible energies, but when he sold a radio play series of mine to Century Artists, a company he owned a share of, things began to smell bad. So I left Stark and went back to Swanson. Stark was like a flickering light reflected on the wall; you could never get a fix on him. Swanson was solid; you could reach out and touch him with your hand."

"And Andress?"

"Andress was a slippery kind of guy. Look, Marlowe: when an agent tries to influence your work he becomes a nuisance. I have no patience for a representative who doesn't know where his usefulness ends. The best agent is not necessarily the best judge of literary material, understand? Nor is he necessarily the best organized or largest. I do not expect from him a detailed organization of my affairs; agents pretend to give it, but they do not do a very good job. What I expect from an agent is tough but scrupulous trading; a wide market knowledge; a respect for the fact that it might in the long run be better business for me to do an occasional article for the *Atlantic* for a few hundred or whatever, instead of putting the same time and energy into a short story for the *Post* at a couple of thousand. All this goes for literary agents and so for movie agents."

"And did Andress fit the bill?"

"Andress had a weak spot for politics. The way I see it, that got him into trouble he didn't need or deserve. I lived through McCarthyism and the House Un-American Activities Committee. Obviously I was deeply repulsed by that idiotic witch-hunt. But neither did I really understand why North American intellectuals decided it would be classy to call themselves leftists or communists; here the screenwriters got lumped into that group, the Hollywood Ten. Those people drove me crazy. They tried to protect themselves with the Fifth Amendment. But the bottom line was that they had very bad lawyers. They were afraid to say they were communists, and at the same time they were afraid to say they weren't. So they drifted around in a sea of lies. If they'd told the truth, the courts would have looked more kindly on them and they wouldn't have been quite so violently cut off by the Hollywood types who put their bread on the table. I don't think the Alger Hiss or Dashiell Hammett cases or the perjury accusation against the Ten were just government manipulation. The government had a lot to do with it, but the Ten were pretty damn clumsy themselves."

"And what does all this have to do with Yensid Andress?"

"I just told you: Andress had his political sympathies; as far as he was concerned the blacklist that still rules Hollywood didn't count. If he could place a script written pseudonymously by Dalton Trumbo or Albert Maltz, and get an Oscar out of it, that was fine by him. It was a brave and very commendable attitude, but in the long run he must have gotten a lot of grief from the studios for it."

"What kind of grief?"

"Oh..." Chandler drew a vague and impatient gesture in the air and washed down the rest of his Talisker. "I don't have to spell it out for you. In general, businesses don't want to get mixed up with the authorities or the FBI, and they can't allow someone to pull the wool over their eyes so boldly. Andress, with his innocent smile and that mellifluous courtesy of a Persian or Burmese ambassador, thought he could really pull the wool over their eyes. Well, he couldn't. There are things businesses don't excuse. Period."

"Agreed. Exactly where would you place that period, Chandler?"

He looked at me for a few seconds.

"I must have gone past my thousand-cubic-millimeters-per-twenty-four-hour bourbon capacity with the glass I just polished off. Of course this label you've just introduced me to is pure scotch." He peered at the bottom of the empty glass as if he could read its name in its etheric vapors. "Talisker, right? I'm going to remember that," he added nostalgically. "Well, the purpose of this digression is to suggest I didn't understand your last question very well. Would you mind rephrasing it, Marlowe?"

"Yensid Andress was murdered," I replied. "It was planned

well enough to make it look like suicide, but a small careless mistake indicates whoever carried out the plan wasn't very skillful. At this point, no doubt remains that a crime has been committed. Chandler, who would have had the most to gain by Andress's death? I came to see if you could give me any useful ideas."

"Me?" Chandler sat back in his chair and tried to light his uncooperative pipe for the nth time. "But Marlowe, up until this very moment you've always been the one to give me my best clues to solving mysteries. I'm fully retired. And if you want a last piece of advice, you're getting a little too big for your britches. You're beginning to try to live up to your name among the quasi-intellectuals. You used to be able to spit once in a while and talk out of the corner of your mouth. Know something? Last year the *Daily Express* ran a public opinion poll to find out who were the favorite authors, film actors, artists, and comedians of the highbrows, the middlebrows, and the lowbrows. Marilyn Monroe and I were the only ones that made all three brows. That's the only thing I'm proud of right now."

"Congratulations. But that doesn't do anything to help me solve the Andress murder."

"What that survey indicates," Chandler said imperturbably, "is that political power still dominates culture. The Americans are a shallow-minded people with awkwardly unstable emotions and no deep sense of style. Their language in the hands of the man in the street is probably a waste product, as empty of deep meanings as Nazi propaganda. Andress was a guy with political ideas. And the Hollywood machine is especially good at grinding up anybody who tries to gum up its gearbox with political dissidents or innovators. What else do you want me to tell you? As resentful as a writer can be of his agent, he wouldn't try to get rid of him by blowing his brains out. There are more effective and less compromising ways of doing the job. You change agents, and the problem is solved. I'd look for his murderer among the ranks a guy like him could permanently annoy, with the sort of nuisances that can't be gotten rid of merely with more or less money. In that sense, what you're telling me has earned Andress my respect. I suppose it's too late to send flowers, isn't it?"

"The funeral was supposed to be today at four," I said.

"Well, sorrow and repentance always come late," Chandler pronounced.

At that moment the waiter cautiously opened the door.

"I'm sorry, gentlemen," he said. "You have to vacate the table."

We got to our feet.

"I'm going to join my colleagues in the meeting," Chandler announced. "I'd much prefer to take advantage of this opportunity to escape, but I have to cover my share of the bill."

"When are you leaving for London?" I asked.

"I have to decide when I'm sober. No making decisions I'll regret later. I'm still in my apartment in La Jolla. Do you have my phone number somewhere?"

I nodded and we didn't say anything more. I went down the staircase quickly. As I arrived at the cash register, Steven glanced meaningfully toward one of the tables near the entrance.

"There are beautiful women who can waste time and patience on people like you," he said enigmatically. "Someone has been waiting for you for half an hour."

I turned toward where his hawklike profile was pointing and discovered Velma Valento. She was alone, the glass she'd had herself served was still full, and she still had her coat on. There was no doubt she was waiting for me.

▶ **9:07 P.M.** *Los Angeles Times* With a precise, well-practiced maneuver, Charles Morton slipped his streamlined Jaguar convertible between the painted lines labeled with his license-plate number. The fine, cold drizzle that was falling didn't belong to these September nights; it was more like the harbinger of a cruel, oppressive winter. There weren't many cars in the *Times* lot. In weather like this the editors preferred to finish off their sections during the afternoon rush and disappear around seven. Morton had left Hollywood Cemetery with numbed muscles and an unsettling feeling of emptiness inside, an unpleasant aftertaste or residue of nothingness, which left him with the pale and evanescent spectre of death dissolving in the turbulent afternoon light, and he had begun to experience a trembling he judged to be of pain or pity for Yensid Andress, who in life had never moved a single one of his more sensitive fibers. Death was a lonely and all-encompassing event; one day you had everything, and the next moment you were completely and irreversibly cut off. With this funereal torpor loitering in his spirit, he had ca-

92

ressed the steering wheel of his car, one of those objects he'd prefer never to have to give up, and had decided his fallen spirits required immediate rejuvenation from feminine companionship, and at least two snifters of cognac. Only once he'd completed those preliminaries had he driven in the direction of the newsroom.

Like most of the newspapermen on big morning papers, Morton was a night owl. He usually worked until after midnight, and it wasn't at all unusual for him to take a stroll by the print shop at around two in the morning, when the paper was put to bed, to catch a late-breaking story. It was from this diligence and the way he foraged for news in all the right places long after his colleagues on other papers were in bed—and not alone—that much of his professional prestige and rather privileged status emanated. When from his own glassed-in cubicle Vincent Starret, the managing editor, saw Morton burst into the room and hurl himself on his typewriter, he had no doubt Morton was on to something interesting. He watched Morton roll a piece of paper into the machine, adjust the Remington's cartridge, and begin to rattle away. Starret lit a cigarette and went back to the proofs on his desk. He calculated Morton would be pushing his office door open unannounced within half an hour.

The text Morton typed out without stopping, designed to fill a maximum of two columns, said the following:

WAS THE DEATH OF AGENT YENSID ANDRESS REALLY SUICIDE?

Yesterday afternoon at 4 P.M. in the Hollywood Cemetery the funeral for the well-known literary representative Yensid Andress took place. Among those in attendance were Andress's ex-wife, Miss Jessie Florian; his associate, Miss Velma Valento; and other close friends, relatives, collaborators, and colleagues of the dynamic Hollywood executive. It has been discovered that Andress's only son, the heir to his considerable assets, is still unaware of his father's death because he is currently traveling through Europe at an undetermined location. Perhaps it was the gloomy weather ruling Los Angeles for the last several days that reduced the world's farewell to a man with so many ties to the movie business into a small gathering.

As readers will recall, a report published in this very col-

umn last Monday, September 23, revealed Yensid Andress had been discovered dead the night before in the study of his Bel Air home, with his own gun in his hand and an unsigned suicide note in his typewriter. So far, there are no new developments in the police investigation, which includes an autopsy and other procedures routinely performed in cases of violent and suspicious deaths or suicides. However, based on information supplied by reliable sources, the Los Angeles Times is in a position to report that the initial suicide theory is being questioned by the officers in charge of the investigation. Our sources state the shot that killed the former literary agent was not executed point-blank (the barrel of the gun against the cranium) but rather from a few inches away, which eliminates the possibility that the victim himself pulled the trigger. Furthermore, the bullet is reported to have followed an oblique path from top to bottom as it entered the victim's cranium, permitting assumption that the perpetrator was standing and pointing the gun at the victim from somewhere a few inches above the point of entry. Viewed together, these two facts could be enough to prove that Yensid Andress's death was no suicide, but, in fact, a cold-blooded, premeditated murder.

The note found in his typewriter would in this case demonstrate this crime's perpetrator's (or perpetrators') intent to make Andress's death appear to have been orchestrated by the victim himself, with the obvious purpose of concealing the true murder motive. The Times has also requested and obtained sufficient information from the deceased's friends and associates to affirm that the financial motives for the alleged suicide contained in the alleged suicide note have no factual basis whatsoever. The deceased's economic, social, and emotional state was normal, and his behavior in the hours preceding his death—corroborated by the testimony of various witnesses—did not at any point reveal the emotional extremes or imbalances typical of a person contemplating committing suicide in the next few hours.

Since the authorities have not officially communicated this information to the press, we assume that the investigation is still in progress, and that police officials have decided not to make these preliminary findings public so that the search for the individual (or individuals) responsible for the crime will not be obstructed. However, and with no desire to interfere

with the serving of justice, the Los Angeles Times feels it has
an unavoidable responsibility to make these facts available to
its readers. Was Yensid Andress's death really suicide—as it
appeared to be at first—or do we find ourselves confronted with
an as-of-yet-unsolved case of brutal and treacherous murder?
This column will continue to report any new developments,
until the truth comes to light, and every detail can be pre-
sented to the public.

Morton tore the second page of the column out of his typewriter in a single movement, rapidly glanced over the entire
piece, penned in a few corrections, and walked in the direction of
the managing editor's office.

Vincent Starret threw his weight back against his reclining
armchair, put out his cigarette in the porcelain ashtray with the
brand name VICEROY printed on it in thick blue letters, and carefully read the two pages Morton held out to him. He deliberated
over each line, got to the end, and went back to the top of the
first page again.

"So, Charlie," he said without taking his eyes off the pages,
"who are your sources?"

"This is between you and me. Okay, Vincent?"

"Word of honor," Starret affirmed.

"Above suspicion," Morton replied. "Lieutenant Nulty."

"Nulty told you all this about the distance of the pistol and
the bullet's trajectory?" This time Starret raised his eyes and
examined Morton's face skeptically.

"Nulty, in person. He was my lady-in-waiting at Andress's
funeral."

"And he insinuated this information could be published?"

"He didn't insinuate. He went out of his way to tell me."

Starret scratched the back of his ear dubiously.

"Hell if I know what that Nulty's up to," he said. "He officially denies any new developments as if the case were already
closed, and then with the best intentions in the world hands you
a bomb that could blow this entire building into little pieces and
compel us to go on working in the ruins."

"It's not as bad as all that," Morton said. "It's not the first
time they've acted this way, is it? The Chief of Police considers
the case is closed, but then they leak something hoping someone'll make a false move. Notice my story doesn't compromise

anyone. 'Reliable sources,' etcetera, etcetera—all those worth-
less, deliberately vague formulas that don't implicate anyone,
not even the brass upstairs."

"That's okay up to a point," Starret answered hesitantly.
"I'm going to have to run this by Management, understand? If
the brass doesn't put a good face on it I'm not going to be in the
mood to publish it. I have specific orders to be unusually discreet
with the Andress case, even more so than usual."

"Straight from the top?"

"They called to warn me about it." Starret put Morton's
pages on his desk and lit another Viceroy. "Look, Charlie, I know
perfectly well when we're on to something that's worth the trouble. If it were up to me, I'd take you off page twenty-six and move
you straight to page one. I promise you I'm going to fight to do
that. I also promise not to mention Nulty, but I'm going to have
to risk my neck vouching for your sources." Once again he nailed
his penetrating eyes to Morton's very soul. "You haven't been
playing private detective, have you? All this evidence of yours
isn't the fruit of your little criminology hobby, right?"

"Vincent, I swear by all I hold most sacred—for instance, by
my Jaguar."

"And it doesn't come from your friend Marlowe, either,
right? I didn't think of that until right now."

"Nulty, Nulty," Morton swore. "You know I'd understand if
you absolutely had to mention it. But the Skipper better not get
any brilliant ideas about calling Seventy-seventh Street to confirm."

"Okay, Charlie—I'm going to give you a vote of confidence.
I'm going upstairs to talk to the old man, and I'm probably going
to have to leave one of my kidneys up there with him in order to
go ahead with this tomorrow. On the front page, if possible."

"Count on both my kidneys as a token of my appreciation,"
Morton said.

He said good-bye and excused himself. There was nothing
left for him to do at the newsroom. He'd done his day's work in
spades. He'd have to see what Marlowe'd been able to dig up in
the meantime. He remembered the half bottle of cognac and the
soothing female companionship he'd left in a warm apartment on
Drexell Avenue, the middle-class Hollywood neighborhood in-
habited by the sort of starlet who had yet to reach her zenith. No
matter, he told himself. Very soon she'd fly off toward a presti-

gious, futile, luxurious, artificial, and asexual world. Never again would she be a creature made from flesh and blood. Just a voice on a sound wave, a face on a screen.

The words really didn't belong to him; he had read them sometime, somewhere, but they could be adjusted to fit the case.

▶ **10:12 P.M. Café Nikobob** "You see? You said we'd meet again," Velma Valento said.

"But I never dreamed it would be so soon," I replied.

I started to sit down, but she stopped me with a quick gesture.

"Let's get out of here," she suggested. "I need to talk to you about a few things, but I feel too exposed here."

I took a look at her check and left two dollars without waiting for change. We walked past the coat check, and the giant seneschal stepped forth to push the revolving door. A gust of cold night wind whipped around us.

"Did you bring your car?" I asked.

"No. I left it in Hollywood. I hate driving in the rain."

"Magnificent. Mine is parked right here."

I took her arm and we crossed the street toward the opposite corner of Western Avenue. That brief physical contact created a new level of intimacy between us. I opened the door of the cabriolet; Velma slipped onto the seat and pulled her antelope coat tight around her shoulders. I walked around to the other side and sat down behind the wheel. I took out a cigarette, but I didn't offer her one. She wasn't the type who'd smoke Camels.

"Where are we going?" I said in a tone of voice that insinuated more than I'd intended it to.

"The best place I can think of is my house," she replied. "It's in La Jolla. Would you mind driving that far?"

I said that unlike her, I liked to drive in the rain. I took the Coastal Highway and maintained a low speed without actually making a conscious decision to do so. We glided through the silent, empty night; the road was almost deserted. The trip took fifty minutes. We didn't talk much, and I had the impression Velma was making an effort to suppress whatever it was she wanted to discuss with me. I didn't want to jump the gun. I just mentioned the burial and the desolate feeling that final ceremony always gave a person; I suspected her lassitude and subdued resignation were the result of the aftershock of Andress's death, the effect of his burial that afternoon and of the depressing, eroding backdrop the nasty weather had spread out behind the day's events. As I took a turn in the road Velma listlessly pointed out a slight elevation to my right and murmured, "It's over there." I veered and turned into a driveway between two rock promontories. The number 6005 stood out in dark relief against an illuminated plaque hung down low near the grass. The house was surrounded by a flagstone patio; the headlights' haze lit up a rock garden climbing up the hill in back. We walked into a large, airy living room about eighteen by thirty-six feet. It looked out on the ocean, and far away you could see the lights of Point Loma. There were a grand piano, a fireplace, comfortable armchairs, and a solid mahogany breakfront; here and there, strategically placed lamps cast intimate zones of light into the inviting half-light. I said it was a place that made you feel like living, and then Velma showed me the rest of the house. A hallway with windows that looked out onto the patio led to the dining room, the kitchen, the service area, the master bedroom, a guest room, and a study that contained many more books, an armchair, and a Chippendale desk. A window in the study offered me another view of Point Loma—scattered diamonds floating on the crest of the waves. We went back to the living room and Velma suggested I make myself comfortable wherever I pleased, mix myself a drink, and be so patient as to allow her another twenty minutes to bathe, change her clothes, and lift her spirits.

"I left here at nine this morning, and I've been taking punches ever since," she said, trying to inject a little humor into her metaphor. "I feel like a boxer about to be pulled out of the match. But a bath and a drink will perk me up. We'll have something to eat, if you like."

I told her it was an offer I couldn't refuse. She half-opened the door that separated the living room from the hallway, so I went into the study and looked through her books for a while. Art books and an eclectic collection of North American and European literature predominated. I discovered Scott Fitzgerald's *Tender Is the Night* and looked up a passage that had once meant something to me: "Nicole shook her head right and left, disclaiming responsibility for the matter: 'So many smart men go to pieces nowadays.' 'And when haven't they?' Dick asked. 'Smart men play close to the line because they have to—some of them can't stand it, so they quit.'" It seemed to echo Chandler's reproaches of a few hours back. I held onto the book and looked through the records. I put on an LP that had "I Ain't Got Nobody," a Williams tune that had to do with all that—Count Basie on piano, Walter Page on bass, and Jo Jones on drums. On the next cut Basie himself had played "Don't Be That Way," and they'd added Lester Young on tenor sax and Buck Clayton on trumpet, a combination capable of generating as much heat as the double martini I'd made myself to while away the time until Velma returned.

We devoured a cold supper she wheeled in herself on a little round table. She'd changed into a turquoise robe that set off the almond highlights in her hair. The wine was excellent, a Château Talbot far beyond my enological know-how; I was primed for any form of seduction. I still had no idea what Velma Valento wanted to talk to me about. But a little voice inside warned me that something had happened between our first encounter this morning and her surprising appearance at Steven's café, something to do with Andress's murder. So I hadn't been invited to fill up a presumed emotional void.

"After you left," Velma began while I held a match flame to one of her mentholated cigarettes, "I began to go through Yensid's papers. Believe me when I tell you I didn't expect to uncover any revelations. Yensid operated with a wide margin of freedom; it gave him a certain flexibility and the latitude to move dynamically and aggressively in a very tough market where results depend more than anything on initiative. He needed a certain elasticity that's indispensable for pinning down deals that are often closed during a casual lunch and sometimes revoked an hour later over the phone. Maybe this sounds a little shady to you. I'm trying to make you understand that although Yensid and I were business partners, he was the one who brought in the business, and I wasn't always entirely up to date on the contracts he was handling. There was often a brief period—when the relationship between a writer and the agency was still in its preliminary stages—when things weren't handled in the usual manner. So we had transitional formulas, temporary agreements for single scripts, that weren't necessarily recorded in our books. Am I making myself more or less clear?"

I nodded and Velma continued.

"Well, then, although these arrangements were often quite casual, Yensid was a very meticulous businessman, and as I said, I didn't expect to find anything unusual. I gave you a list of the Hollywood writers we worked with on a more or less ongoing basis; they're all under contract with the agency and we assume we represent them exclusively. I'm sure you found a good number of those writers tonight at the Café Nikobob."

"The list wasn't entirely up to date. Chandler, for example, was on the roster, but I spoke with him and he told me he wasn't represented by the agency anymore."

"That's only partially true," she replied. "As everyone knows, Chandler is a very unpredictable and temperamental man; sometimes he came to us and sometimes he didn't. It depended mostly on his mood and level of pent-up resentment. Since he's a big name Yensid decided to give him special treatment. He never officially broke off with us, and the agency never claimed to represent him exclusively. But we keep his name on our list."

"I understand," I said.

"The real surprise of the afternoon was discovering that Yensid kept a parallel list. And I don't mean contracts for a single screenplay or temporary agreements which had no reason for being logged in our books until the permanent arrangements were formalized. No, it was a secondary roster where, according to everything I saw, an ongoing relationship existed with the client, and each completed transaction was duly noted. In general, they were major transactions—Yensid charged some of the most impressive sums this agency has ever received for these writers' work."

"But the agency as such received no portion of those benefits?"

"I didn't say that. Accountability is one thing; specifying the property that produces the income is another. I think the agency received and worked with that money. What caught my attention is the fact that Yensid decided to keep a parallel list I never knew about, when he was dealing with such large amounts of money and such big deals."

I had my reservations about the bookkeeping aspect of Velma's affirmation, but I didn't see any point in arguing about it.

"What were the names on the list?" I asked. "That could clear up a lot of things."

100

"That's what I was getting to," Velma said. "It was in code. Apparently, Yensid had given the list the name *X:* the authors appeared as *X*-1, *X*-2, etc. I found two lowercase initials following the listings for two of those *X* authors."

"How many *X* authors appeared on the list?"

"Seven. It's a rather substantial number."

"And the total sum of the operations?"

"Close to a million dollars."

"Do you have the signing dates for the contracts?"

"Everything is in order. Yensid wasn't trying to hide anything except the names and the list itself. But if he'd wanted to swindle the agency, as you obviously seem to think he did, he wouldn't have had to keep up that list. On the contrary. And it would have been even less likely that he'd have kept it in the office, where I might find it at any time."

"Could it have something to do with taxes?"

"I considered the possibility. But if I accepted that, I would also have to admit that our percentages of those sums weren't being funneled through the agency's regular financial systems."

"And that apparently is what would hurt you the most to acknowledge."

"I have no evidence such a thing took place. As I said, our client list is one thing, our financial systems another. Yensid could have processed the funds through the usual channels. For example, let's say this list just duplicated some of the names that appear on the official register. Yensid could have included the corresponding sums in the total volume of that particular writer's fees recorded in our files."

"What purpose would that have?"

"That's what I don't understand."

"Unless it was the writer who wanted it that way. Could there have been something illegal going on?"

"I don't know. Yensid was too concerned about his reputation to get involved in something like that."

I stood up nervously and walked over to the window overlooking the ocean. The bracelet of light that was Point Loma traced an absurd dotted trail through the depth of the night.

"Something tells me you didn't bring that secret list with you."

"No. I thought it would be more prudent to leave it at the office."

"Could I take a look at it—tomorrow, for instance?"

101

"I wouldn't have told you about it if I hadn't thought you'd be interested in seeing it. But frankly, I don't think you'll find anything I didn't."

"Maybe not. Still, you think there's a relationship between that list and Andress's murder."

"I don't know that either. For the moment, I'm merely surprised by the coincidence of the two occurrences. Yensid dies—according to you he's murdered—and at the same time, after two years of working together, I stumble onto something going on behind my back at the agency."

"You wouldn't have gone through Andress's papers if he hadn't died. Nevertheless, the connection seems obvious to me. There is something you glossed over: the initials that appear after a few of those authors X. You couldn't figure out what they meant? Did they correspond with any initials of authors on the official list?"

"I already thought of that. No, they didn't. They could have referred to the author's name, but then what would be the point of coding them with X's? Yensid wasn't an imbecile; if he'd decided to leave the names in code he wouldn't be naive enough to put the initials after them."

"That makes sense." I lit a new cigarette. "You told me that the contract dates were on the list. Can you recall them? Tell me the years, if you remember them."

"They were quite recent. From last year and this year. Maybe it had something to do with a new financial system, a line of expansion for the agency, some experiment he'd decided not to tell me about for the time being."

"If the contract dates are accurate, we could use them to figure out which contracts had been signed on those days."

"That's an impossible task. The agency does business with almost every studio in town. We cut film contracts, radio contracts, television contracts. We'd have to dig around in every single conceivable medium. It would take months, providing no one gave me a hard time about getting access to his files."

"Suppose, Velma," I said, "that the X isn't really the letter x, a secret list. Suppose the X really represents the number ten in Roman numerals. Would that mean anything to you?"

Velma looked at me questioningly.

"And if it did? What progress would we have made?"

"It could mean that that X designates the Group of Ten, ten writers included on Hollywood's black list, X-1, X-2, X-7 representing the different members of the group. This would perfectly explain why Andress wanted to keep the list secret. It was too compromising a document to keep in the agency's official archives."

"You're suggesting that Yensid was working with a few of the authors in the Group of Ten?"

"I'm suggesting it to you, but you're the one who has to respond to the suggestion. You really knew Andress. You're the one who would know best whether Andress was the type who would be willing to risk himself for reasons that weren't exclusively economic, but that were also a matter of principle—whether he believed in those writers' innocence, and whether he could have been open to helping them out of sympathy, solidarity, or whatever you want to call it."

Velma took more time to think it over than I had expected.

"Some of the authors in the Group of Ten were among the best screenwriters in Hollywood. If for no other reason, Yensid might have taken the risk."

"Independent of any political consideration?"

"You don't work for the witch-hunt, too, do you, Mr. Marlowe?"

"We agreed that when we met again my name would be Philip," I said.

"And mine would be V.V., but I'm grateful that you haven't used it. We have a B.B. in the movies, and that's already quite enough."

"Velma sounds very nice," I agreed. "I like the sound of it. It's one of those names that's pronounced more or less the same way all over the world, isn't it? It could be Greek, Italian, Spanish, or French, and it would always sound like Velma, with very little variation."

"My father was Italian," she said. "A large part of the family is still in Italy. He wanted things to be just the way you said—to give his children names that wouldn't suffer phonetic alterations as they traveled along the family circuit. His secret wish may have been to return to Italy. Him, my mother, the children. He said this country was a good place to make money, and he made quite a bit. But it wasn't the place where he would have chosen to live or die."

"And what happened to your mother and your brothers and sisters?"

Velma studied my face for a few seconds. Then she carefully put out her half-finished cigarette.

"That's enough revelation for today, Mr. Marlowe. Now I'd like you to tell me something. I think you owe it to me, after the vote of confidence I've given you tonight." She looked at me from under her long dark eyelashes. I still hadn't been able to determine the exact color of her eyes. They gleamed in the living room's studied half-light; that morning they had burned with the mineral gray basalt that probed deep inside me even as it shielded and defended her. They were the sort of almond-shaped eyes that might take you by surprise in a gallery of portraits by Modigliani or Bonnard, shining with irony and self-sufficiency. "Tell me," she continued. "Who are you really working for? Who could be so interested in getting to the bottom of the mystery surrounding Yensid's death they'd pay you a thousand dollars to do it?"

I decided the moment for answering that question had arrived.

"I'm not really working for anyone in particular," I admitted. "I've got this newspaperman friend. He did the routine workup on Andress's death and came across the information that led us to believe a crime had been committed. It turns out that for some reason which we have yet to glimpse, there are some very powerful people who are insisting it look like a suicide at any cost. The two of us are working on the case together. If the truth about what happened and who was behind Andress's death comes to light, my friend's newspaper will probably buy the information for the price you mentioned. But although I don't expect you to believe me, seeing as a private detective makes a little of his living off dead carrion, I assure you my interest in this business is not merely financial."

"Then what is it?" Velma didn't take her eyes off me.

"It has something to do with what I'm beginning to find out about the character of your former collaborator," I said. "I'm beginning to feel a certain degree of sympathy for Andress. And mostly it's because of you. You can interpret that as positively as you'd like to."

"I believe you, Mr. Marlowe," Velma offered after a pause. "In my line of work I have to deal with all sorts of people; I have to look somewhat deeper than the surface. If I didn't believe you, I wouldn't have gone to find you at the Café Nikobob, you can be sure of that."

"Then let's continue the search together," I said. "And now I think I should go home."

"It just so happens that my car is in Los Angeles," Velma answered, reaching out toward the cigarette package. "If there isn't anywhere you're obliged to spend what's left of the evening, you'd do me a great favor by driving me in to town in the morning." She lit the cigarette and raised her face toward mine again. "I promise I'll call you Philip from now on."

▶ **10:07 A.M.** **Hollywood** Marlowe pulled up on Vine Street in front of the entrance to the Avenant Building. Velma Valento turned and smiled from the doorway. She had recovered her cool Hollywood-executive exterior. Marlowe fleetingly evoked the image of the tousled mane of hair on her naked back—lips parting in a silent gasp of pleasure. The scarlet car turned toward Sunset Boulevard and bore down on Los Angeles. It wasn't raining in the city proper, but foggy drifts of water admonished from a distance. The sky was a turbulent, threatening dark-stained mass, and the mountains in the East looked blurry, as if they'd been softened by the palette of Turner's late period or that watery sky into which Monet's cathedrals had once dissolved.

He continued down Shetland Lane and parked the car across the street from the Bristol Apartments. High above, the white walls of his modest penthouse rose. It was almost eleven in the morning; the mailman had already delivered his newspaper into the box next to the door, and the edge of a folded copy of the *Los Angeles Times* ostentatiously stuck out through the opening. He unfolded the large pages and was surprised to read on the first page: WAS THE DEATH OF AGENT YENSID ANDRESS REALLY SUICIDE? This was followed by the column Charles Morton had written in professional haste the night before. Marlowe began to read as the elevator ascended to his lair, asking himself what unexpected turn of events had occurred in Morton's neck of the woods, and why the *Times* administration had so meekly cast aside its reservations about this thorny case, whose solution was already threatening to unleash dark and presumably violent reactions, and even to make Hollywood shudder down to its very foundations. He climbed the two flights of stairs to his penthouse and noticed that the pool on the roof terrace next door was turning into a small lake. Although he'd eaten a decent breakfast in La Jolla, another cup of coffee wouldn't be a bad idea. He went into the kitchen, lit the gas burner, and put the Pyrex orb on the flame. He finished the article, took his cup of coffee into the living room, lit a Camel, and decided it was high time for a little reflection.

First, he had to reconstruct his idea of Yensid Andress, taking something from all the scattered images he'd collected during the last few hours: the man of the thousand smiles, as the
106

Hollywood press had often called him; the astute gambler who always had an ace in the hole; the public relations expert; the successful man, the most skillful of the acrobats moving above the taut, fine cord strung between the massive movie studios and their often even more difficult and obstinate staffs; the hustler who could put one arm around a highly desirable writer while with the other he clinked champagne glasses with one of any of the inaccessible and feared hierarchs of the celluloid industry. This last was the most widely circulated and stereotyped image Yensid Andress had left behind him and the one that had come to Marlowe's own mind when he read the news of his death. Now he added new elements to the picture: Andress had been one of the founders and in a certain sense the *alma mater* of the Association of Literary Agents. Did this fit in with the other pieces or did it strike the wrong chord? Hard to say. But then he added in Velma's meticulous businessman, the boss respected unto tears by his own staff. And then Andress was also the agent with political convictions, capable of resuscitating posthumous homage from Chandler, a writer with very radical ideas about the dead man's profession. Finally, if the recent deductions were correct, he was also a man courageous enough to risk defying the omnipotent House Un-American Activities Committee, perhaps the FBI itself, and without doubt the persistent, visceral terror that ruled the great Hollywood impresarios—and other industry inquisitors, including the irate John Wayne. If it had actually happened that way, could Andress really have been motivated by nothing but money—by the possibility of selling valuable properties by blacklisted screenwriters who felt obligated to hand over huge percentages of their earnings to the only agent willing to mount such a production? It was possible. But why would Andress take on business that might end up losing him much more than he could possibly gain with his already considerable assets? The puzzle was being assembled bit by bit, piece by piece, forming from the obverse of Yensid Andress's impeccable, reconstructed image in the papers and on TV. You had to turn the whole picture around and look at the other side. That didn't merely change the figure cut by Andress himself; the motive for the crime instantly changed and the entire scope of the investigation pointed in a different direction.

It was time to call Morton. He left the steaming cup of coffee on his desk and dialed the newspaperman's private number.

"Morton here," a voice answered between sleepy yawns.

"Marlowe here. Sorry for pulling you out of the arms of one of Morpheus' vestal virgins."

"Philip? I was about to call you."

"I just read your column in the *Times*. You want to tell me what happened? Did you manage to persuade your bosses?"

"Vincent Starret did all the work," Morton said. "I just vouched for the reliability of my sources."

"What sources?"

"Nulty."

"Nulty again?" Marlowe reflected. "Strange, isn't it? Why this sudden interest in publicity? What's he up to?"

"He's probably angling for a promotion."

"It's possible," Marlowe admitted. "He's playing a dangerous game. I doubt Thad Brown, the Chief of Homicide, is very happy about it."

"This's his territory, isn't it?"

"Not until there's definitive proof a crime has been committed."

"I think we're going to have new developments now; the column demands a response. Or an official denial—otherwise the whole world will interpret it as a tacit admission of the validity of our suspicions."

"Let's wait and see."

"Listen," Morton said. "There's already been one response. I got a call from Jessie Florian, Andress's ex-wife. She says she has to talk to me. I thought it would be a good idea if you came along."

"Okay. Did she give you any idea what it was about?"

"Just that I'd be interested in what she had to say. She read the column, called the paper, and they gave her my number. She seems to be convinced her ex-husband was really murdered. Maybe you have a client now. The paper's offer still stands, of course."

"In that case we'll have more than enough clients."

"Anything new on your end?"

"Yesterday someone offered me a thousand dollars to give up the case."

"You're kidding. You're not trying to blackmail me, are you?"

"I turned it down."

"It's a strange offer, don't you think? Could it be a lead?"

"No. Just a misunderstanding. When and how do we meet Miss Florian?"

"Twelve-thirty, Hotel Roosevelt. She'll be waiting in the bar."

"Perfect. You get there first, take care of the preliminaries, and explain my end of the business. I'll show up fifteen minutes later. Okay?"

"If you feel it's necessary."

"She'll feel more comfortable. If for some reason she doesn't want a detective involved, you give me the high sign and I'll disappear."

"Got it. Then I'll see you at the Roosevelt."

▶ **12:45 P.M.** **Hotel Roosevelt** Marlowe walked through the carpeted hotel lobby toward the bar. The Roosevelt might have been built twenty years before, but it had maintained its original sumptuous elegance. It was one of L.A.'s not entirely contaminated spots, and merely having chosen it revealed something about the tastes and perhaps the personality of Andress's ex-wife. Marlowe's only clues were the few bitter sentences that had passed through Velma's lips. He tried to keep in mind that the moment she'd chosen to hurl them out had been a particularly bitter one for her. He spied Morton chatting with the woman in a strategically located corner table. Morton made a small gesture of approval and Marlowe walked over.

"This is Philip Marlowe, the man I was telling you about," he said.

Jessie Florian raised her face toward Marlowe and her lips half parted in a yawn of a smile. She was a still-attractive woman of about forty. Hard-boiled, beautiful features, loaded with sin. Marlowe pulled a chair over and sat down.

"Mr. Morton told me you're a private detective," Jessie Florian said.

"Mr. Morton is indiscreet," Marlowe observed.

"He also explained to me that you're already working on the case. I didn't know anyone was particularly interested in solving my ex-husband's murder," the woman continued. "Well then, I want to tell you that I am. Your services will be very useful to me, and I'm willing to compensate you generously for them."

A waiter came up to the table and asked Marlowe what he'd

like to drink. He noticed that in front of Jessie Florian was an enormous glass containing a garnet-colored mixture, and Morton had his favorite whiskey, Glen Grant 1953. He ordered a whiskey. The woman lit a Winston.

"Apparently, you're completely convinced Andress was murdered, Miss Florian," Marlowe said. "In fact, Charles's efforts and my own are based on certain pieces of evidence that have yet to be confirmed. It still remains to be proven whether or not a murder has been committed."

"Oh, well, at this point in the investigation..." Morton attempted to clarify.

"I haven't the slightest doubt it was murder," Jessie Florian interrupted. "As soon as I heard the news I discounted the possibility of suicide. I didn't come all the way here from New York just to go to the funeral. Listen to me carefully, Mr. Marlowe. Yensid and I had been separated for almost three years, but that doesn't mean we didn't still feel some affection for each other. Yes," she added, "in a way I still loved Yensid, perhaps in a somewhat maternal way. I knew he would become a victim. My ex-husband wasn't one to sidestep difficult situations. He could bypass difficulties, but he also had the moral resources to confront them head-on."

"Who was your husband a victim of?" Marlowe asked.

"I know what I'm going to say is very serious, but I don't care," Jessie Florian answered. "I came here ready to do everything in my power to bring to justice the person responsible for Yensid's death."

"You mean you have concrete suspicions about someone?" Morton asked.

"Concrete, yes. About the only person who could benefit from Yensid's death. You'll know who I'm talking about."

"As far as we know, your ex-husband was held in high esteem all over Hollywood," Morton ventured. "Who could benefit from his death? That's the greatest challenge of the case."

"Then you probably haven't taken the investigation very far," Miss Florian said sharply. "There is one person for whom his death is very convenient. Even very timely. I'm referring to his secretary and alleged partner. Yensid's disappearance gives her free run of the agency."

"Velma Valento?" Marlowe said, raising his eyebrows.

"Velma Valento or Mrs. Grayle. As far as I know, she's only been separated from her husband for a little more than a year—
110

it happened not long after she'd begun her relationship with Yensid—but they aren't legally divorced. Maybe he made trouble, or maybe she hasn't filed the necessary papers. She didn't want to do that until she was sure she could trap my husband."

"And why do you say Andress's death was convenient for Velma Valento?" Marlowe asked.

"Because Yensid's partnership with Mrs. Grayle was nothing but fiction. In reality, Mrs. Grayle's contribution to the agency didn't go much beyond her presence there. She's very seductive—I'm willing to admit it. At some point in time my ex-husband may have believed there was an advantage to making her look like his business partner and owner of half the business. He must have had his reasons. But that story couldn't hold up forever. Yensid knew that his son's future was at stake. I have my reasons for thinking the partnership was about to be dissolved, and that Miss Valento, or Mrs. Grayle, whichever you prefer, was about to officially return to the lowly position of secretary. Maybe not even that."

"But the partnership wasn't actually dissolved?" Marlowe inquired.

"As I said, the timing of Yensid's death was very convenient for Mrs. Grayle and her interests. A few more days and it might have been too late."

The waiter deposited the whiskey in front of Marlowe, who immediately noted the prestigious smoky odor of Morton's favorite label. Jessie Florian removed the orange slice skewered to the side of her glass and took a sip of her cocktail. She reminded Marlowe of hurricanes and of damp, suffocating New Orleans nights. Mrs. Grayle. What else might the woman say about Velma once she'd imbibed half the contents of the glass?

"Assuming Velma Valento was in a partnership with your ex-husband," Marlowe recapitulated after a mouthful of Glen Grant, "Miss Valento won't get anything on top of what she was given while still your ex-husband's partner. Your son inherits Andress's share. It's just a simple change of partners."

"A change made at the most convenient moment," Miss Florian insisted.

"Do you have any proof Andress was really considering dissolving the partnership, and of whether Velma Valento had made a financial contribution to the company?"

"No, I have nothing a court and perhaps even a good lawyer would consider proof," Jessie Florian answered. "If I did, I probably wouldn't need a private detective to prove someone had very powerful reasons for wanting my ex-husband dead. The proof is what I'd like you to find, Mr. Marlowe."

Marlowe reflected for a moment. Morton seemed bewildered by the turn the whole business had taken. None of it explained the pressure he'd had to put on the newspaper or the caution with which the police were proceeding.

"We don't know very much at all about Mrs. Grayle, or Miss Valento," he ventured to explain. "If there is no concrete evidence, leveling such a serious accusation against her would be risky."

"What arrangements did you make with your deceased husband after the divorce?" Marlowe asked. "According to what you've said, the two of you still had a good relationship."

"Better than what many people seem to think. Every month Yensid sent a generous alimony check to cover living expenses. And a second check for Terry's education."

"An equally generous check?"

"Very. Yensid had great aspirations for his son. He wanted him to have everything. He knew that without anything but the money he sent me, I wouldn't have been able to offer Terry the chance he deserved."

"How old is your son, Miss Florian?"

"He just turned twenty-two."

"And Andress was legally obligated to pay for his education?"

"Until he was twenty-one, yes. It was the arrangement made by our lawyer. Yensid, however, kept it up. As I said, he was always very generous. Especially as far as Terry was concerned."

"Even when your son abandoned his studies and left for Europe? As far as I know, his whereabouts are still unknown."

"Yes, we still haven't had any news of him. Yensid was rather unhappy about Terry's trip. And so was I, to be perfectly frank. It was probably a mistake to interrupt his studies and leave so suddenly. But Terry has artistic leanings; he wanted to expand his horizons. He didn't see the trip to Europe as a postponement—rather, as a necessary complement."

"Did your husband agree?"

"I can't say he completely shared his point of view."

"And yourself?"

"Even less. At heart, I didn't believe Terry's reasons for such a long trip. I think he had other reasons."

"And Andress continued to send you extra money for Terry's studies even after he left?"

"Terry counted on that to make the trip."

"I suppose Terry's money was cabled directly to you?"

"Of course. I was the one who kept in touch with him."

"How long ago did he leave?"

"It'll be six months in a few days."

"And you haven't heard anything from him since?"

"Terry stayed in touch with me until a few months ago, when I got a postcard from Venice describing his itinerary. I wrote to him and wired money to American Express in Venice. After Venice, the next major city on his itinerary was Athens, and then Istanbul. But since I had no further news of him, I didn't wire money to the places he mentioned. I'm afraid something might have happened to him on his way to the Orient. I'm upset with the changes I've discerned in Terry since he's been in Europe. He's spent time with the worst people, living in miserable hostels or those promiscuous guesthouses for young people. I wouldn't be surprised if he's been drawn to drugs, and who knows what else. He was very enthusiastic about the Orient, about Buddhism, mystical experiences. The change in him has been very painful for me, but I think Yensid was the most disappointed."

"You mentioned that Terry might have had reasons other than artistic inclinations for taking this trip," Marlowe indicated. Could you tell us what they were, Miss Florian?"

"That was just what I was getting to," the agent's ex-wife said. Her arm reached hesitantly toward the little box of Winstons. Morton quickly held out his lighter to her. "Before he made this decision, Terry spent some time here, with his father. Until then, he'd never mentioned the idea of going on such a long trip. He was attracted by the idea of getting to know Europe, of course, but it wasn't a specific goal of his, nor an especially urgent one. But while he was in California he met that woman, Velma Valento, or Mrs. Grayle, to be exact. Well, the boy was seduced by the humble Mrs. Grayle. In fact, he was crazy about her—a woman fifteen years his senior. I'm sure you gentlemen will understand why both Yensid and I were firmly opposed to any sort of relationship between them."

"You mean to say Velma Valento shared your son's feelings?"

"I don't think she shared them in the slightest. She was simply skillful enough to keep him interested and fluttering about for as long as she thought it useful. When Terry became a problem, she did what she had to to get rid of him."

"What was that?"

"She made Yensid think Terry was about to be cruelly disappointed. That was when my ex-husband suggested that Terry return to New York, and they had an argument. This hastened my son's decision to go off on that ridiculous trip."

"Did your ex-husband tell you all this?"

"Terry told me everything. And he also told me that what Mrs. Grayle really wanted was to marry Yensid. It was natural, don't you think? To want to solidify their partnership through marital rights. But apparently Yensid was too intelligent to let himself be duped by such a cheap trick. Velma Valento could only deceive him so far. When that woman understood she would never marry my ex-husband, she had to change her plans. So she set her sights on his heir. But first she had to get rid of his father. Now she probably thinks she doesn't have to do anything but wait for Terry to come back and throw himself into her arms as docilely as before. But that won't happen. Not while I'm here to stop it."

Jessie Florian allowed a large mouthful of the garnet liquid to run down her throat. Her nerves were completely shot. Tears of humiliation, fury, or impotence had appeared in her eyes. Morton and Marlowe maintained a prudent silence.

"So you see," the woman murmured when she'd recovered some of her serenity, "now you've got most of the story. You'll excuse me if I leave you now. I don't need an answer right away," she said to Marlowe. "Think it over. In any event, I've resolved to take this thing to the bitter end. I'm going to stay here and wait for my son, and I'll do everything I can to expose my ex-husband's murderer."

"Are you sure your son will come straight to California?" Marlowe asked.

"He will as soon as he finds out what's happened. In any case, I've already made arrangements: I've hired people to find him in Europe, and I've sent telegrams to all the American Express offices, including the main cities on his projected itinerary

114

in the Orient. I'm sure I'll have news of him shortly. He's got to fly back here to take hold of the reins and defend his interests."

And yours as well, Miss Florian, Marlowe thought, although he didn't say so out loud.

Andress's ex-wife extended her hand to both men, repeated that they could find her at the hotel if they needed her, and asked Marlowe to make his decision as soon as possible. The two men stayed on their feet while the woman crossed the bar toward the hotel lobby. Then they sat down again.

"Well, what do you think?" Morton said as he lit a new cigarette.

"That woman is beside herself and consumed with jealousy," Marlowe answered thoughtfully. "It's understandable. After all, her son and her ex-husband fell in love with the same woman. Velma Valento is about to get half of what Jessie Florian thinks belongs completely to her and her son. In addition, it would be in Jessie's best interest if Andress was murdered. If it wasn't suicide, the insurance company has to cough up fifty thousand dollars."

"Was Andress in love with Velma?" Morton asked.

"She thought so, at least. And now, what I'd like to do more than anything is take a stroll through the Doreme Insurance Company. I believe I have an acquaintance there. I want to find out more about that insurance policy and see where the company stands on all this. They might want to go to court if murder is asserted. In any case, they will do everything they can to clinch the suicide theory."

"I was afraid of something like that," Morton said. "I bet after today's article I'm on the persona non grata list at Doreme."

"Very shortly both you and I are going to be persona non grata to a heap of very important people here in Hollywood," Marlowe replied. "I'll call you later to fill you in."

"Wouldn't you like to have something to eat first?" Morton asked glumly.

▶ **7:23 P.M.** *Los Angeles Times* Morton dragged himself into the *Times* newsroom. He felt alienated and disgusted. After all, a newspaperman's life was shit. To be sure, he enjoyed enviable freedom; he spent his time however he wished and went wher-

115

ever he wanted to go—provided, of course, that he filled his two columns every day and maintained his well-known talent for turning breaking stories into interesting articles in the wink of an eye, with no spice but his own imagination and an occasional hand from the insolently loose-lipped, potentially newsworthy members of the Hollywood community. There was no doubt about it: his profession granted him status, plenty of money, a prestigious aura, and the secret password to certain elite circles. Nevertheless, he couldn't stop thinking it was sordid work and the source of the emptiness gnawing at his insides. He had wanted to be a writer, but he hadn't become anything but an automatic-writer with a couple dozen hack formulas that jumped out mechanically onto his typewriter keys and had long ago taken the place of anything that could have been called inspiration. Maybe one day he'd go into public relations, seeing as it was already too late to consider higher goals. Although, he recalled, Chandler had written his first novel when he was fifty-two. He himself was a mature but unsettled thirty-seven. Maybe he should get married; a good part of his existential anguish stemmed from having felt nauseous in bed on Drexell Avenue that afternoon, when after a moderately satisfying orgasm he'd wasted two whole hours recovering from the loneliness both he and his occasional lover endured, before escaping from the hysterical embrace of the starlet who'd never amount to anything. If only he had a magic wand...but he didn't. The depression intensified as once again he realized that the newsroom of Los Angeles's most prestigious newspaper was almost as sordid and disorganized as his own life. Happily, Starret had gotten to his feet and started signaling him from the door of his glass cell before Morton had time to confront that inevitable vacuum, his typewriter.

"Come in, Charlie," said Starret. He slipped into his revolving chair and apparently didn't mind when Morton pushed the door open with the outer edge of his fancy calfskin loafer and collapsed into the chair in front of Starret's desk without even taking off his raincoat. "The picture is beginning to clear," Starret continued, giving him a couple of mimeographed pages. "The official autopsy report; it confirms everything we predicted. Once again the *Times* owes you first fruits."

Morton quickly glanced through the report. "The distance from which the shot was fired (two to three inches) and the bullet's trajectory do not conclusively prove that the case should be treated as a homicide. Although there are unusual details, the
116

possibility exists that the victim could have fired the weapon himself in a way that would explain the unusual relationship between the weapon and the gunshot wound..." Morton kept reading, looking for some mention of how the pistol's safety catch could have slipped shut after the shot was fired, but the report completely ignored that particular point. He raised his eyes to meet Starret's satisfied and somehow expectant smile. He considered mentioning the safety catch and the report's silence on the subject, but decided against it.

"So? What do you say?" Starret said. "I have a green light from the brass to go ahead with this. The ball's in your court, kid. The report is all yours. You fix it, you mess it up, you clear up some of that technical mumbo jumbo, and toughen it up with a little salt and pepper and three or four question marks. All that paraphernalia you use so well. Okay? We were the first to hit gold, and we're going to keep on digging, whether there's anything more underneath or not."

"Okay, Vincent," Morton said, standing up. "It seems to me there's a lot underneath, but for some reason the Homicide Division of our worthy Los Angeles Police Department doesn't want to take the rap."

"You think so? Then we'll make them spit it out. They can't fight the public. The press is still the fourth estate in this country, Charlie. They're passing us the buck, and we're going to give it right back to them."

"I suppose the press is the fourth estate, but you're forgetting that there are three others in line ahead of it," Morton said.

Starret finally divined the crestfallen state of Morton's spirits.

"You got a problem, boy?"

"Nothing special. I'm going to get to work."

Morton stumbled over to a coatrack and hung his raincoat on it, sat down at his desk, and carefully reread the police report. It was a major deployment of technical police jargon, designed to make the whole business dissolve into watery gibberish. He reconsidered mentioning the safety catch, which was the real linchpin of the investigation, but that would compromise the old caretaker at the Andress house. After all, if Nulty had purposely left him on the sidelines, what right did he have to get the man mixed up in all this? He could at least manage to make a veiled allusion to the business, something like... the right construction didn't come to mind. He put a piece of paper in his typewriter and began to draft the article: "As we reported to you exclusively in yesterday's edition of the Los Angeles Times, the circumstances surrounding the death of the renowned Hollywood literary agent still have not been clearly established. In accordance with the police report that has arrived at our offices..." He went on, minutely reconstructing the autopsy report, inserting ellipses and an occasional veiled innuendo into his description of the contortions Andress would have had to twist himself into for the bullet to enter his cerebral cortex and land in the marsh of his encephalic mass at a slant. Morton was in the thick of this jolly verbal fireworks display when the phone rang.

"Morton," he said, balancing the receiver against his collarbone.

"Listen," it was Marlowe's voice. "Are you working on the Andress case by any chance?"

"That's what I'm working on, but it's not by chance," Morton answered.

"I'm glad you haven't turned in the copy yet. I have something that could be interesting. I'd like you to fix things so you can get it in your column. You decide how."

"Out with it," Morton said. "I could use something earth-shattering to cheer me up."

"I went to Doreme Insurance. I managed to see the Andress policy. Surprise: the recipient of the fifty thousand dollars isn't his son, Terry, it's his wife."

"Jessie Florian?"

"Exactly. I meant to say his ex-wife."

"How's that?"

"Andress acquired the insurance while he was still married. After the divorce he indicated a couple of times that he wanted to change the name of the beneficiary, but he never finalized arrangements. This proves at least one thing: Andress had no intention of dying in the near future, unless it was a sudden inspiration. He would have at least made sure that that money, if the company paid it, would go directly into his son's hands."

"Your logic is flawed in one respect: if Andress had decided to kill himself, no one would get the insurance money. Not his son or his ex-wife. The company would pocket it, case closed."

"Very true, but we know that Andress didn't kill himself. What I actually said was that the guy apparently had no idea his life was in danger. You know how a Hollywood agent's mind
118

works—just like his business does, he's required to deal with all the variables and unknowns of any given case way in advance. He would have modified the terms of the policy immediately if he thought he was in any kind of danger."

"And what if he really had wanted to give his ex-wife all the dough? You know, that strange guilt complex that sometimes feeds on divorced husbands. When all is said and done, Jessie Florian was responsible for his son's education."

"I'm telling you, Andress had already told Doreme that he intended to change beneficiaries. But doing that requires a certain amount of paperwork and lost time, and Andress didn't go to the trouble of doing it."

"And you think Jessie Florian knew that?"

"I don't have the slightest doubt."

"Why not?"

"Does the name Howard Melton mean anything to you? He's the director of Doreme, and I did some work for him once. As you can probably imagine, these types of documents are confidential —no one but the parties directly concerned can get access to them. But Jessie Florian periodically became concerned about whether or not the insurance continued in her name."

"Periodically?"

"Until very recently. She called from New York a week before the murder to see if there had been any 'change.'"

"Holy moley! That's food for thought."

"Why do you think she called?"

"And is Doreme going to pay the insurance?"

"Not unless it's officially proven there was foul play. And even then they'll investigate to determine whether any of the direct or indirect beneficiaries of the policy are implicated."

"So—what do you want me to do?"

"Just mention in passing, as if you weren't giving it any importance, that Yensid Andress left an insurance policy for fifty thousand dollars, whose beneficiary, 'according to what has become known' or something of the sort, is his ex-wife, Miss Jessie Florian, who has been divorced from the agent for two years or more. And then remind them that only in the case that Andress's death is proven to have been a homicide, etcetera, etcetera, okay?"

"Okay, but I'm afraid that you're not going to end up with a client this way."

"We'll see. I'm planning on having another chat with Miss Florian."

"I'll take responsibility for the information, if you like. This will give my column a good deal of flavor."

"Another thing, Charles. I forgot to ask you this morning. Have you had any suspicions that someone has been following you for the last two days?"

"What do you mean? Someone tailing me?"

"Exactly."

"No...I haven't noticed anything unusual."

"But there was. On Monday, after the visit I paid to the Andress house, a car followed me for half an hour. I managed to shake it, or at least I thought I had. You came to my apartment that night, remember? When you left, a car parked about fifty yards down Shetland Lane started up and followed you. It was a dark gray or brown Plymouth sedan, I'm not sure on account of the fog. I think it was the same car that was following me."

"The police?" Morton asked.

"It's possible. I haven't seen the car since."

"Now that you mention it..." Morton hesitated. "Yes, during Andress's funeral, while I was talking to Nulty, the Lieutenant picked up on two suspicious characters who were keeping their distance. Evidently they weren't there to pay their respects. I thought they were a couple of police bloodhounds, you know; they had all the trappings. But Nulty assured me they weren't from his department."

"Which doesn't mean they couldn't have been from another division. Thad Brown's, for example. Anyway, it would be a good idea to keep on your toes."

"Who could possibly be interested in us?"

"Anyone who's bothered by the fact that the Andress case is still open. For the moment, we're the ones visibly responsible for making waves."

"I'll admit I don't understand any of this. And Jessie Florian?"

"That's a different angle."

"You've discounted Velma Valento?"

"I'm meeting her in half an hour. I'll try to find out what truth there is in Andress's ex-wife's accusations."

"Good luck. Keep me posted."

Marlowe hung up, and Morton began working frantically on his column. He'd received a new little halo of inspiration, and felt satisfied with the result. He brought Starret the draft; he read it, whistled, and made an emotional pronouncement.

"This keeps on picking up color, Charlie," he said. "When we get to the bottom of it, I promise to put in for a raise for you."

For an instant, Morton thought it might be the right moment to mention Marlowe's honorarium, but decided to put that off until later.

He left Starret rereading and marking the piece, picked up his raincoat, and deserted the newsroom in high spirits. He decided that journalism had its creative side, too.

It was still cold out, and the night was saturated with a fine, almost dusty, drizzle. The neon sign at Shamey's coffee shop on the other side of the street was pulsing red lightning onto the asphalt. Morton turned the corner of Sixth Avenue and walked quickly toward the parking lot. West 54th Place was deserted, and the wide cement inlet of the parking lot contained just a few scattered vehicles. Starret's car was parked next to his Jaguar, and a dozen jalopies were visible in the area reserved for the print-shop boys. The boss's Lincoln Continental shone under the powerful cross section of streetlamps lighting the lot.

Morton took his key ring out of his raincoat pocket and opened the Jaguar's door. He hadn't even settled in behind the wheel when the door flew open again. Before him stood an unusually tall man wearing a raincoat whose collar was turned up to hide his face and a rain hat that was pulled down over his eyes.

"What the hell...?" Morton managed to get out before he noticed the individual was holding a gun in his right hand, and that the strange cylinder fitted to the mouth of the barrel was a silencer.

He didn't have time to say anything else. The shot rang out with a dry report that put a hole into the night silence. Morton felt the impact near his stomach and instinctively lifted his left arm there, as if to ward off the pain or other shots that might follow the first. The pistol coughed two more times. Morton's body shook convulsively and one of the bullets bounced off the steel surface of his Rolex, instantly immobilizing its hands. Morton's torso slumped across the steering wheel. The man in the raincoat fired one more time, this time taking careful aim at Morton's head. He sealed the Jaguar shut with a slam. The Rolex's hands read 10:07 P.M.

•••

▶ **10:07 P.M.** **Lucey's** "If it's all the same to you," said Velma, "let's not mention it for the rest of the evening."

I interpreted that "rest" as a tacit and promissory agreement between us. We walked into Lucey's, a Melrose Avenue bar and restaurant across from the Paramount studios. The foyer was done up like an MGM soundstage readied for the shooting of a musical comedy. A glittering hallway led down from it to the main dining room, and a staircase shielded by a white railing insinuated access to the booths on the second floor. The flat ceiling appeared to be speckled with twinkling stars. Next to the dark, purplish bar was a little artificial cave containing a black marble table and an oval-shaped mirror. The nook looked vaguely Egyptian, and a woman in a midnight green gown and strass appliqués was inside touching up her platinum bleach job. Our eyes met briefly in the mirror. It wasn't exactly the kind of place where I'd choose to spend my time. Too sophisticated for my tastes. If you wanted to make sure you'd eat you had to reserve a table ahead of time or resign yourself to a wait. I approached the maitre d', who was posed like a statue at the dining room entrance, a fixed smile on his face and a set of leather-covered, golden-tasseled menus under his arm. He promised to see what he could do for us. We plunged into the shadows of the bar and managed to clear a path to the counter, where I ordered two old-fashioneds.

Velma and I had spent all day going over Andress's coded list, his personal papers, and the company books. We were exhausted. Little doubt remained that the secret list referred to the Group of Ten, and that the initials d.t. and a.m. stood for Dalton Trumbo and Albert Maltz. A rumor making the rounds of certain inner circles said that the anonymous screenplay for *El Bravo*, which had a good chance of winning an Oscar, showed unmistakable signs of Trumbo's hand, but the topic was taboo among the Hollywood big shots. It was difficult to imagine someone risking his money and maybe his head to film a script by one of the prohibited authors. I suggested to Velma that perhaps Andress had just finalized arrangements with those two writers, and that was why nothing had been noted but their initials. The rest of the information on the list might be nothing more than skillful camouflage designed to make any investigation difficult. The hypothesis seemed plausible to her and it fit in Andress's bag of dirty tricks. That made everything more complicated; only an accountant or a bookkeeping expert would be able to tell, after a thorough study, whether something had been buried in the over-all finances of the agency. There were various lists, accounts were kept separately, and a single transaction might be recorded in any of two or three different books, according to the chosen criterium: the medium, the studio, or the client. Velma obstinately clung to her belief in Andress's complete credibility and honesty, and eventually convinced me we shouldn't bring in a third party; she herself would go over the books once she had a little peace and quiet. For my part, I wasn't convinced that Andress wouldn't have considered his dealings with the Hollywood "damned" strictly personal business. His neck was the one on the line and so he might have considered it a private investment, a legitimate compensation. In any event, I deferred to her and dropped the subject once we were inside Lucey's. We were sitting at the bar casually sipping at our drinks when the maitre d' approached to tell us our table was ready.

"I saw Jessie Florian this morning," I finally said, approaching the subject I least wanted to touch. The atmosphere, the candlelight, the china, and the bottle of champagne didn't offer the most appropriate setting for this sort of conversation. Velma raised her eyes and waited expectantly. "Are you interested in the details of our meeting?" I insisted.

"I leave that up to you. Did she make the appointment or was it your idea?"

"Half and half. Miss Florian got in touch with Morton; Morton got in touch with me. She was interested in hiring a detective."

"I don't doubt it in the least. I thought you were working for her from the very beginning."

"Granted, but I wasn't."

"And now?"

"Not now either. Jessie Florian isn't my type."

"She's a little old for you, dear. It's been years since she turned forty, even though it may not look that way."

"More specifically, what I meant was that she isn't my type of client. Maybe under different circumstances we could have found areas of mutual understanding."

"Is that so? And what do you have against her as a client?"

"In the first place, she's bossy and has preconceived notions about things. Hard to handle. I never agree to work for anyone who tells me what I have to do or who I have to look for first. The beginning of an investigation is like the beginning of a chess game. All the pieces are on the board. If someone tells me before-hand how I have to play to get to checkmate, I lose interest."

"And apparently Jessie Florian had everything figured out?"

"Point by point."

I deliberately fell silent. I raised my glass of champagne and waited for Velma to do the same. There was a small, light per-cussion of crystal and for an instant the candelabra flames shiv-ered. I attacked my lobster.

"Well, now I want to know the rest," Velma said.

"This is the gist of it: Miss Florian says she came here from New York convinced that her ex-husband had been murdered. Who could have done it? You, or someone in cahoots with you. Motive? The most obvious: you wanted to have the agency all to yourself. You tried to land Andress, unsuccessfully. Andress wanted to get rid of you; you bought him a ticket to the other world first. Now all you have to do is wait for Terry to come back—he'll fly in from somewhere like Katmandu or Karachi to spill tardy tears on his father's tomb and then hurl himself joy-fully into your arms. By the way, did you and Terry have a little thing going on the side at his father's house when the pup was in town?"

"I don't know if I like this other side of yours. You can be very cynical."

"It's just gloss. Let's leave cynicism out of this."

"I suppose what Terry and I had is what Jessie Florian would call an 'affair.'"

"No, not really. She was very objective on this point. You threw Terry out on his ear, and the kid ran away all disillu-sioned. But of course, she figures you must have done something to give the kid some hope for a while; then you broke it off, so he woke up one morning and left on that crazy trip through Europe and the Orient, offering himself up to drugs, vagrancy, and Bud-dhist contemplation."

"Yes, I did something. I certainly did do something. I made two mistakes. The first was to try to be his friend; the second was to allow Yensid to become jealous to the point of pettiness, until he even regarded his own son as a potential rival."

"With good reason?"

"Jealousy always has some foundation, doesn't it? Yensid

124

had asked me to marry him twice, and I'd declined; that was a good reason. And then, between Terry and me...how can I explain it to you? Terry is a cheerful and sensitive boy; we probably shared a sort of intimacy that never existed nor ever could exist between Yensid and myself. After Terry left I thought it all over; I think Yensid must have interpreted our friendship as a sort of youthful conspiracy. Although I've got a few years on Terry, Yensid felt much older than both of us, excluded from the sort of things his son and I could enjoy: modern music, dance, poking fun at or feeling indifferent toward certain kinds of conventions. Yensid was very formal, too formal about everything. And he exaggerated his remonstrances against what he called our lack of seriousness, our youthful excessiveness. He and Terry fought, and I felt quite badly that I'd been the cause of their misunderstanding; I tried to put a stop to things, and that was when Terry decided to leave—or better put, when Yensid suggested he go back to his mother."

"But you couldn't marry Andress anyway, could you? Legally you're still Mrs. Grayle."

Velma's eyes studied me for a few seconds over the champagne bubbles.

"Did Jessie Florian tell you that too?"

"Everything I know about you comes from you yourself or Jessie Florian."

"Then I'll let you make your own confirmations. After all, it's your job, right?"

"Only when someone is paying me; so far no one has hired me to investigate your civil state."

"Jessie Florian would compensate you very well for that information."

"Apparently she's not interested. She takes it as a given that you still haven't divorced that lucky—although from my point of view slightly hard-to-get-a-handle-on—Mr. Grayle."

"I'm surprised Jessie Florian didn't suggest I'd planned two murders. First my husband's and then Yensid's. And the next would have to be Terry's, I suppose."

"Perhaps she suspects that one of the two could have been your accomplice."

"One of the two?" There was a sudden, hostile, and wary contraction of her eyelids. Suddenly we were miles apart.

"Mr. Grayle or Terry himself," I said, as if we were playing a game that couldn't be interrupted once it had been begun.

125

"I think I lost you," Velma said.

"Jessie Florian is skeptical about the validity of your cash investment in her ex-husband's agency. She believes the partnership was nothing but a cover story."

"And therefore?"

"How do I know? Were you really Andress's financial partner?"

"I was."

"And this money came from Grayle."

"Absolutely not. I invested my own capital: my portion of my father's inheritance. Satisfied?"

"Was your husband or ex-husband a rich man?"

"Why don't you look into that too?"

"Perhaps it would interest you to know that Andress's insurance policy wasn't in Terry's name. Jessie Florian is still his beneficiary."

Once again she observed me incredulously.

"Who told you that? Did she?"

"Doreme, Inc. Andress never officially changed the name of the recipient of the fifty thousand dollars."

"I'm sorry for Terry's sake. Now he'll never get out from under his mother's thumb."

"He still has Andress's personal assets—plus rights to half the agency."

"Jessie Florian will manage to get her hands on that too."

"You two don't have any great love for each other, do you? Who's the reason? Andress or Terry?"

Velma dropped her fork and knife on her plate.

"I think I've lost my appetite," she said. "This conversation is ruining everything. I'd be grateful if you'd ask for the check and take me to my car."

"And abandon this splendid lobster?" I said.

"Please," Velma insisted.

I'd gone too far. I tried to establish how much of the damage was irreparable.

"I hate attracting attention," she went on. "I could get up and leave you flat at the table, but I don't want to. Tomorrow everyone will be talking about it. Don't force me. Call the waiter and let's leave as discreetly as we possibly can."

I understood I'd been hitting a very sensitive place or even an open wound. I started looking for the waiter and just then someone who looked vaguely familiar approached our table and

126

shot me a forced smile. He nodded courteously and turned toward Velma.

"Will you excuse me if I interrupt you for a moment?" he said. "Velma, darling, I wanted to tell you before how sorry I am about what happened. I couldn't find you at the office when I called. I'm deeply saddened by the Andress thing."

"Hi, Rog," Velma responded. She limply abandoned her hand in his and he raised it to his lips with a courtly gesture. He was an individual whose hair, once thick and black, was now going seductively white along the edges of his temples; he wore thick glasses with tortoiseshell rims that gave him an unmistakably intellectual air. "Do you know Mr. Marlowe?" Velma added.

"Philip Marlowe, by any chance?" the man said, holding his hand out to me.

"Precisely."

"Chandler used to wear me out talking about you," he replied. "You don't mind if I join you for a few minutes?" He pulled up a chair and sat down without waiting for a reply. "My name is Roger Wade," he told me. "I work for 20th Century–Fox and I'm a Chandler fan. Actually, I can say that I was the one who welcomed him to Hollywood, back around 1943."

"Roger is now one of the most important producers at Fox," Velma explained.

"Not so fast, not so fast," Wade laughed. "I'm still nowhere near the level of *The Last Tycoon*. I admire that book of Fitzgerald's—all of his work, actually, as I do Faulkner's. And the work of that sacred monster who has never wanted to get near us, the incorruptible Hemingway. Although the company hasn't given up all hope of luring him here at some point, locking him up in one of our cubicles, and forcing him to write a screenplay. Andress would have gotten him to do it, if he'd put his mind to it, don't you think?" he added, turning toward Velma.

"I doubt it," she replied freely.

"I see a pronounced resemblance between Chandler's style and Hemingway's," Wade continued. "Of course, Raymond would never forgive me for insisting Hemingway might have a certain influence on what he writes. He hates being compared with any writer who's a possible Nobel contender, and Faulkner and Hemingway already won theirs."

"Isn't Hemingway one of the authors forced out by Hollywood?" I asked casually.

"Hemingway? Of course not," Wade said severely. "There

aren't any forbidden writers in Hollywood anymore. That whole story is a thing of the past now. When someone writes something that's really worthwhile, there is always a way to get it produced. But Hemingway? Really, no. Every door in town would open up for him."

"Something I don't think would happen for people like Alger Hiss or Albert Maltz," I indicated. "They say around here that Frank Sinatra has tried many times to film a Maltz screenplay, with no success."

"Just bad inside jokes," Wade hastened to reply. "You shouldn't pay attention to everything you hear murmured in the industry. There is a lot of envy, jealousy, and self-interest. I've never known another guild that's as afraid of competence as the writers' guild."

"And Dalton Trumbo?"

"Oh, Trumbo..." Wade spread his arms in a gesture of powerlessness. He turned toward Velma and quickly changed the subject. "What is this I read this morning about Andress's death? Is somebody interested in having people believe Yensid could have been murdered? Who would want a man like Andress dead when everyone in town owed him a favor? I think all this sensationalism is pure infamy. It's obvious the press is going to try to get as much as they can out of it."

Velma slipped in an ambiguous comment that partially appeased Wade's protests, and in a few minutes he stood up, effusively made his good-byes to me, and said good-bye to Velma with another bourgeois-gentleman kiss. His unexpected interruption had banished our earlier tension. Velma seemed to have forgotten her fury and we finished dinner comfortably in spite of the chilly atmosphere that was still floating between us. It was way past midnight when I paid the padded check, leaving a generous tip, and we began to make our way toward the coat check. I picked up the coats and glanced distractedly at the television screen while Velma went to the restroom. Suddenly the pale face of an announcer for the Los Angeles station broke in on a variety show. When Velma returned, stern but apparently calm, I knew Morton was dead and where I'd better go in a hurry.

▶ **12:45 A.M.** *Los Angeles Times* **Parking Lot** Two prowl cars with dimmed headlights were blocking the lot entrance, and from way in the back of the lot an ambulance pulsed dramatic purplish flares through the soupy damp.

I parked on the sidewalk on the right side of West 54th Place, and insisted that Velma wait for me there. She refused.

"You can't go in there," one of the policemen posted next to the prowl cars told us. I could see people moving and talking inside the lot. Two orderlies rolled a stretcher that probably contained Morton's lifeless body into the ambulance. I took out my wallet and flashed my license in hopes of impressing the officer.

"What's that?" he asked, throwing a suspicious glance at the certificate. "Private detective. You've got no business here, friend. See this uniform? This represents public might. We have to be first sometimes."

"Who's running this operation?" I asked.

"Inspector McGee, I believe." He turned toward another officer, who was watching silently and impatiently, as if waiting for the right moment to join the fray.

"It's McGee, right? I just drive the vehicle," he explained to me.

"Yeah, McGee," the other said.

"And isn't that Lieutenant Nulty?" I asked. The official's enormous shoulders rose above the rest of the small crowd gathered around the ambulance and two cars still parked in their usual spots. Reluctantly, the policeman turned around.

"I won't tell you it isn't," he said. "He's hard to keep hidden."

"Do me a favor," I implored. "Tell him Marlowe is here. I promise you he's going to want to talk to me."

He held out his hand for my license and moved off toward where Nulty was standing. He came back just a few minutes later.

"Come on," he said, returning my wallet to me. I took Velma by the arm. "The lady stays here."

"She's the dead man's wife," I spat out quickly. I dragged Velma toward the back of the parking lot. We rushed over to the ambulance. The orderlies had settled the stretcher on the floor of the ambulance and a sheet completely covered Morton's body. I climbed inside and before anyone could stop me I pulled the top edge away to see his face. A trace of coagulated blood ran down his left temple to the top of his cheekbone. There was a violent purple bruise in the middle of his forehead.

"He has two more bullet holes in the abdomen," said the rough voice of McGee, who had slipped behind my shoulders. "Another bullet destroyed his watch. That wasn't anything but the coup de grace. A merciful piece of work—no one would have been able to save him anyway. He died instantly. No one found him for two hours."

I smoothed the sheet over Morton's head again. I climbed out of the ambulance and McGee followed me.

"What were you and Morton up to, Marlowe?" he asked.

I lit a cigarette. I heard McGee's deep voice droning in my ears, but I couldn't make heads or tails of what he was saying.

"What happened, exactly?" was all I managed to ask.

"Do you think somebody was here to film it?" McGee replied caustically. "All we know is that it happened at seven minutes past ten, according to the watch that was hit by the shot. And that they shot him while he was in his car."

Nulty and a few others came up to us. I glimpsed Velma's terrified face—she was bundled up in her coat behind the ring of policemen and photographers.

"Hi, Marlowe," said one of the individuals with Nulty. I recognized Vincent Starret. "It was my bad luck to find Charlie's body. There was nothing to be done, you can take my word for it. He'd been there a couple of hours already, slumped over the steering wheel."

"What happened?" I asked again irrationally. I heard the echo of my own voice, resonating like a lunatic's singsong. Sound and fury signifying nothing in the middle of an incoherent dreamworld.

"It must have been five minutes after he said good night to me," Starret said. "He left the newsroom around ten and must have come straight here. Evidently, someone was waiting for him. They let him get in the car and then they pumped him full of lead. I left the newsroom a little past midnight. It struck me as strange that Charlie's car was still parked there, but at first I thought he could have dawdled at Shamey's. I know he ate dinner there sometimes. And then, I don't know what happened first: if it was a feeling I had or if I saw the lump slumped over the steering wheel. I never even opened the door to my car."

"Got any ideas?" McGee asked again. "Come on, Marlowe, you're the genius. Who'd want to get rid of Morton?"

"Whoever suicided Andress," I answered.

"What?" He looked at me as if I were from another planet

and speaking some galactic dialect. "What the hell are you talking about?" He turned his head from one side to the other, looking for support which was not forthcoming. "You in the mood to complicate matters? Tell me what the hell your buddy's murder has to do with Yensid Andress's suicide."

His words may have been stinging, but he'd prudently lowered his voice to pose that final question.

"If you don't know what I'm talking about, reread the first page of yesterday's *Times*. Morton wrote the column about Andress," I explained. "That'll probably put you on the right track."

"So that was what you and Morton were up to?" he insisted. He seemed willing to be reasonable and studied me carefully as he took his tobacco pouch out of his raincoat pocket and got ready to roll a cigarette. "This is what happens when amateurs get mixed up in things. When will you guys learn to toe the line? What did you think? You could get the edge on the Andress case? You can't go any faster than we do, Marlowe. I hope you've learned your lesson. I'm almost tempted to book you for Morton's murder."

"Whoever killed Morton wasn't an amateur," I responded.

"Let *us* answer that question!" he shouted. He lit the cigarette and observed me one more time. "So you have nothing else to say?"

"What else do you want me to say? You did all the work, this time."

"Who hired you for the Andress case?" he asked.

"Morton did."

"Oh yeah? And who hired Morton?"

"Why don't you ask him," I answered.

"Calm down, Marlowe, don't exasperate me. Anyway, you don't have a client anymore. Stay out of this mess. I'm no corpse collector, and there are times when you turn out to be a useful guy. I wouldn't like to find you in this condition one of these nights." He glanced toward the ambulance, which at that moment began to move. "Well, I'm off to the morgue." He turned to Nulty. "Have the guys do the usual," he added. "Look for trails, footsteps, cigarette matches. As if we were going to get something out of all this." He turned around and left without saying good-bye.

Nulty, Starret, and I were silent for a few seconds.

"Charles wrote another column on the Andress case," Starret finally said. "I already handed it in for today's edition. It adds a few new elements, but there's still time to pull it. What do you think I should do, Marlowe?"

"Run it," I answered without thinking about it too long. "It'll be a sort of posthumous homage to Morton."

"Maybe." Cautiously he raised his eyes toward Nulty and then risked asking me, "Are you mixed up in this thing too? It wouldn't compromise you too much if we published that column?"

"Nothing Morton could have written can compromise me any more than I already am," I replied. "The real nuisance was the publicity Charlie was giving the Andress case. That's why they knocked him off."

"Maybe," Starret said. He meditated for a few seconds and then added, "As far as homage to Charlie's concerned, I'm personally going to be responsible for writing the farewell. I have a real knot in my stomach; I don't know where I'm going to get the strength to sit down and write, but I feel like I'm the one who has to do it. I'm going to get started right now."

Our eyes met and I nodded silently.

"I'm off, then," he said. "Will you be needing me for anything else, Lieutenant?"

"Not for the moment," Nulty said. "They'll probably call you later for your statement."

"Okay. I'll be in the newsroom or at home."

He took the key out of the door of his car and walked off slowly across the parking lot. He was a slim man; now his shoulders slumped as if he were carrying all the night's horror on his own back.

"Listen, Marlowe," mumbled Nulty as soon as we were alone. "You knew that they were following Morton, didn't you?"

"Dark gray or brown Plymouth sedan," I answered. "They started out after me. I was the one who put them onto Morton."

"Don't start stirring up the ashes," said Nulty drily. "It was the publicity that was bothering these people, as you know. That doesn't mean that eventually they wouldn't have gotten interested in anyone digging around in Andress's grave. You better be very careful. McGee can be a little harsh sometimes, but the warning he gave you was for your own good. Keep it in mind."

"Morton told me that you might have picked out the Plymouth's occupants at the Andress funeral," I commented.

"I picked them out at the funeral and later I identified them," Nulty admitted. "I've got an elephant's memory for cer-
132

tain faces. I spent a whole night going through the Department files, but they finally turned up. Listen well, Marlowe: those two characters are hired guns. They kill without asking questions and they don't leave time for anything. There are no charges pending against them in the state of California, but the FBI would be very happy to be able to put them in handcuffs, regardless. This is turning into a Federal case. When people of this caliber get in on the action, you never know what's behind them, but the very least that can be said is that it's real big. They got rid of Morton and they won't be exactly sorry if they have to get rid of two, three, or ten more people who insist on annoying them. Do we understand each other? Fine, I just want you to keep that in mind. This isn't a job for one man on his own; we may have to call in the whole army to stop these people."

"I'm not in a joking mood, but sincerely, no one ever said anything that moved me more, Nulty. Don't think I don't appreciate what that means."

"Take it however you like. Remember: keep on your toes; and if this thing doesn't have a very personal meaning for you, leave it in our hands. It's the best advice I can give you."

"Until a few hours ago there wasn't anything personal about it," I reflected. "Now there is. Morton and I got mixed up in the thing together. I always have trouble with abstract concepts," I added. "But I think what we had in common was something along the lines of what's known as friendship. If you think I can leave a bouquet of flowers on Morton's grave and go on sleeping with a clear conscience for the rest of my life, I think you know very little about human nature, Lieutenant. Anyway, don't think I don't appreciate your advice. I suppose we'll be seeing each other around."

It was a farewell of sorts.

"Damn it, I don't have the slightest doubt that we'll be seeing each other around more often than I'd like," Nulty grumbled.

Waving good-bye, I walked away from him, leaving him lost in thought. Velma, who'd been left all alone, looked as though she'd been stripped of her cool exterior by the penetrating night dampness. She was leaning against Starret's car. I walked up to her and took her by the arm. As she pressed against me I felt human warmth and compassion for the first time during those dark, implacable hours.

There was still a bitter taste in my mouth.

▶ **5:07 P.M.** **La Jolla** In the middle of 1956, one month after wrapping up his second turbulent sojourn to London, Chandler moved to La Jolla. He stayed at the Del Charro Hotel and then rented an apartment at 6925 Neptune Place, just a few blocks from his old house. The building consisted of a series of apartments with a central patio, and his apartment faced the beach that sheltered the Pacific. It had two bedrooms, but the major attraction was a large attic where he could keep his papers when he embarked on his next trip to England, perhaps in the spring of 1957. He furnished it with some of his old pieces and a carefully edited selection from his library. "Dear God," he wrote at the time, "what on earth shall I do with books that over-flowed a large house? I guess you have to be ruthless with pos-sessions."

He tried to be as merciless as his devotion would allow him to be, but the ultimate limit was determined by the dimensions of the new apartment. Naturally he felt bored and nostalgic for London. MacShane quotes him during that time: "I'm not anti-American, but there just isn't any life here for people like me. Four days a week I have someone to go to dinner with, but the other three are hell. I am already sick to death of skins like burnt orange and smiles like gashes. I am sick of people who never put a glass down and cocktail parties where no one (but me) can sit down. Alas, not all my country is hopelessly vulgar, but this part of it certainly is."

Loneliness and excessive drinking, either alone or with guests, landed him back in the Chula Vista clinic where he'd already spent some time in 1955. In the middle of July he was given the green light and decided to spend a while in San Fran-cisco at the home of Louise Landis Loughner, an admirer who had effusively written him after his suicide attempt. Louise's protection didn't take him away from his bottle. This time it was a clinic in Pasadena. The treatment mustn't have lasted very long, because when he got out of there he proclaimed his desire to marry Mrs. Loughner. Said pretensions to domesticity didn't last more than a week. "I can't stand quarrels," he explained, again according to MacShane. "I don't quarrel myself; they say it takes two. It doesn't. I'm very sorry and very lonely, but I know the same sort of thing would happen periodically."

Presumably he returned to Los Angeles, and he must have spent a relatively tranquil period in his La Jolla apartment. Some of his old friends in the area, the writers Jonathan Latimer, Max Miller, and Ronald Kaiser, came to visit from time to time. The three of them were there when Chandler's old buddy Roger Wade, a 20th Century–Fox producer and also one of the company's top executives, dropped by out of the blue. It was Thursday, the 26th of September, at about five in the afternoon, a time when writers and movie producers have usually stopped working and haven't made any definite plans for the evening. Their glasses weren't even close to empty, but Chandler refilled them with whiskey almost to the brims, with the exception of Wade's chalice, which had been prudently and uncharacteristically marked off by its proprietor's inflexible index finger.

"An evening promising much liquid awaits me," he explained. "Dinner at Romanoff's with the company staff."

"At Romanoff's?" Latimer echoed. "Well, at a place like that you can have the pleasure of putting down a solid foundation before you load up on drink."

"That's what I'm hoping," Wade said. He raised his glass to his mouth, sniffed it, tasted it, and expertly assessed its color while he swirled its contents. "Good whiskey," he observed. "I thought you were a bourbon drinker."

"I've always been a closet scotch addict," Chandler confessed. "Talisker. Remember that label—a discovery I owe to Marlowe, like various other ingredients that cemented together the cinder blocks of my celebrity."

"Marlowe?" Wade repeated. "By coincidence I had the pleasure of meeting him last night. Keeping very good company, by the way."

"Marlowe isn't an individual who is exactly known for the quality of the company he keeps," Chandler said.

"Then it must have been an exception. He was with Velma Valento, Yensid Andress's former secretary."

"Ah, yes. A credit to her race. She's one of my neighbors here in La Jolla, but she doesn't show herself in the area as often as one would like. I'll have to go see her one of these days, anyway. Now all Andress's business is in that lady's hands, and if our accounts don't conflict there is still a balance in my favor at the agency."

"Do you really think Andress went bankrupt?" Kaiser asked.

"What's this I read in the *Los Angeles Times* about the possibility that it was murder?" Max Miller noted.

"That's just the press," Wade said. "Sensationalism and violence."

"And Morton's death?" Miller replied. "That was no sensationalism. That was pure violence. I'd like to know just what the hell for."

"Whose death?" Chandler choked on his whiskey. "Which Morton is this?"

"You're not up on the news, Raymond," Latimer explained. "Charles Morton, the *Times* columnist. He was the one who wrote the column insinuating the Andress business might not have been suicide."

"My God, Charles Morton," Chandler repeated incredulously.

"They gunned him down in his own car: three shots in the stomach and one in the head. It's in today's papers. Practically the whole first page of the *Times* was filled with it."

"Well, tell me that isn't useless sensationalism," Wade reiterated. "Why rub our faces in that spectacle? The flaw is in how they treat the news; they could have done things more carefully."

"Like you do in the movies," Roland Kaiser said sarcastically. "Why the violent spectacle? Because violence sells well, that's why."

"But movies are fictional," Wade alleged. "More precisely, they're a method for sublimating real violence. We remove it from reality and wrap it up in celluloid. And so it becomes inoffensive. We work with specialists to evaluate the stuff—psychologists, sociologists ... we don't put out just anything."

"And marketing analysts," Kaiser added to the list.

"And marketing experts, of course. It's only logical. I can't think of a modern company that doesn't carry out a solid study of its target market before launching a new product."

"Let's agree then: violence is a product that is in high demand."

"I admit it. Don't the critics talk about something like a poetry of violence when they talk about the novels you gentlemen write?"

"What I was asking myself," Latimer interrupted, "is what Morton and Andress's deaths might have in common. It's rather curious, don't you think? Morton charges a murder may have

136

taken place, he starts digging around in the dung, and they wash their hands of him. Before he can dig too deeply."

"Write me a script with that," Wade proposed. "I promise you Fox will pay you well for it."

"I can't believe it," Chandler repeated from his own private, alcoholic, sentimental world.

"It's nothing to get depressed about," said Miller supportively. "Morton was a good guy—they killed him. Andress, in his own way, wasn't such a bad guy either—he killed himself. At heart, I think, everyone chooses his own death. It has a lot to do with the style in which one lives, with the sort of occupation, activities, interests, scrapes, and problems you get yourself into. It's not that I believe in fate or Greek tragedy. But I do believe that in the long run everyone chooses how he's going to make his entrance into immortality."

"That's nonsense," said Chandler. "If there is anything I have absolutely no faith in whatsoever it's that stupid fairy tale about personal immortality. I don't see the least need for it. God probably finds something to preserve, but I frankly don't know what it is. He could even find in me, a sensual, sarcastic, and progressively more cynical man, something worthy of preservation—but I have no idea what it is. Therefore I prefer to be perpetually drenched in alcohol. That's the best form of self-preservation I can think of."

"You can't have clear ideas on the subject when you're as skeptical and depressed as you are right now," Latimer said.

"Bah, I say. Why does a man work? For money? Yes, but in a purely negative way. Without a little money nothing is possible, but once you have some (and I don't mean a fortune, just a few thousand a year), you sit down to count it and ask yourself what you can or want to do with it. Each item it can buy eliminates one reason for wanting something. Once upon a time I wanted to be a great writer. Then I realized that if the good Lord had wanted to make an important writer out of me, he wouldn't have let me waste twenty precious years of my life in offices. There are things I like about being a writer, but it's a lonely and unappreciated profession. Personally, I would have preferred to be a lawyer, or even an actor."

"Come off it, you're a good writer and you know it," Roland Kaiser said. "Leave the complaining to us, the illustrious as-of-yet unknowns: Latimer, Max, myself. Hundreds of thousands of

137

copies of your books are printed here, in England...you're translated into other languages. You're as well known as Hemingway or any of the so-called 'greats.' Only they give some of you the Nobel prize and not the rest. Well, mystery writers aren't usually Nobel candidates; you'd have to have written about one of the world wars, or about a minor epic like the Spanish war at the very least. It's so colorful and ostentatious that whatever you wrote about it would take on enormous importance."

"Or about an old man who goes fishing and sharks eat his prize catch. That's not grandiloquent, but it has grandeur," Latimer said.

"Solitude," Miller corroborated. "Solitude and the fight for survival—that's how you push to the very edge of human existence, so what you write achieves a kind of ultimate meaning. It's as if you'd given a set of keys to the reader, keys to self-awareness—to understanding himself, humanity in general, the very essence of life as we know it."

"The mystery novel reaches those very same boundaries," Wade intervened, "and in my judgment reaches a much greater number of readers than the books that usually win Nobel prizes. The same thing happens in the movies, if they're applicable to this instance. On a daily basis, film is the only true mass art form. One single production shown simultaneously all over the country reaches a larger audience than ten or twenty first-class novels. But there still isn't a Nobel for the cinema. We have our 'Oscars,' to be sure. Little by little they're gaining prestige."

"Nobel, bah," Chandler grumbled. He took advantage of his brief fit of rage to refill all the glasses to the rim, despite Wade's preventive, if tardy, index finger. "More than once I've asked myself if I'd want to win another Nobel for the United States. Quite honestly, no—it's too much work. You have to go to Sweden, get all dressed up, make a speech. Is the Nobel prize worth all that? Hell, no. They give that prize to too many mediocre people for me to get all excited about it. And then that distinction between the mystery novel and the serious novel makes me suffer as much as the measles. There's that book by Haycraft, for example, *The Art of the Mystery Story*. A collection of articles called criticism of the mystery novel. They're all so mediocre! The whole business is built on a foundation of lowered values, the critics hastily excluding the mystery story from literature for fear that the authors of such tales think they're important prose. That's the result of the decline of the classics, a sort of narrowing

138

of intellectual vision that lacks historical perspective. People spend all day making suggestions to writers such as myself: 'You write so well—why don't you try a serious novel?' Meaning novels written by authors like Marquand or Betty Smith. They'd probably feel insulted if I told them that the esthetic difference, if it indeed exists, between a good mystery novel and the best serious novel of the last ten years can hardly be measured on the same scale that's used to measure the difference between the serious novel and any representative work from the fourth century B.C.: any old ode by Pindar, Horace, or Sappho, any old Sophoclean chorus—you name it. There can be no art without popular taste, and there can be no popular taste without a uniform sense of style and quality. The curious thing is that this sense of style has so little to do with refinement or even humanity. It can exist in the age of Milton Berle, Margaret McBride, the Book-of-the-Month Club, Hearst Publications, and the Coca-Cola machine. You can't create art if you try to, obeying demanding rules, talking about quibbling details, using the Flaubert method. It's created quite easily, almost by accident, and without setting your mind to it. You can't write just because you've read all the books."

"You said too many things all at once," Latimer reflected. "But I'm inclined to agree with almost all of them."

"Perhaps," Miller objected, "but you can't mention Marquand and Betty Smith and deliberately omit writers like Hemingway, Faulkner, or Scott Fitzgerald."

"Hell, I haven't forgotten about any of them," Chandler protested. "Back around 1932 I wrote a story that I titled, in its second draft, 'The Sun Also Sneezes,' to show my admiration for the practically homophonous Hemingway novel; and in case there was any doubt, I dedicated it, for no good reason, to the man I considered the best American novelist of the period."

"In my opinion critics always tend to establish an inversely proportional relationship between the number of readers of a book and its literary value," Wade said. "At heart, it's an elitist concept of literature, the evidence being the scorn the elite critic feels for the masses, for the general public. Well, in that sense the movie business is also being obliged to revise its traditional ideas. Film is an art but it's also an industry, and an industry needs a public, consumers. But we're arriving at the surprising conclusion that the films most widely consumed aren't necessarily the most mediocre—the ones with so-called mass appeal;

139

many of our best dividends have been earned off high-quality films. Why can't the same thing happen with literature?"

"It does, in fact," Latimer maintained. "I doubt any mediocre writer has more readers than Hemingway, Fitzgerald, or Dos Passos, here in this country. I exclude Faulkner, because I know he's particularly difficult. And that's also Raymond's case, as it was Dashiell Hammett's in his day. They are genre mystery writers, but they are essentially just good writers; that's why people read them, and for no other reason."

"You may be right, as far as the public is concerned," Chandler accepted. "But not as far as the critics are concerned. Neither here nor in England has there been the least critical acknowledgment that there's more art in the best examples of the mystery genre than in many fat volumes of historical fiction or in the foolishness called social commentary. A good study has yet to be done on the psychological basis of the immense popularity which novels of murder, crime, or mystery enjoy among people of every class. There have been a few superficial or frivolous attempts, but nothing carefully thought out. The genre offers much more than people think it does, even people who are interested in it. People think, and quite wrongly so, that because murder mysteries are easy to read they have to be superficial. I don't think they are any easier to read than *Hamlet*, *King Lear*, or *Macbeth*, which, by the way, also contain a lot of mystery and more than one murder. The modern police novel verges on tragedy and yet it's never completely tragic. Its form imposes a certain clarity of structure that's only found in the most accomplished of those books called 'great novels.' And in truth, a large proportion of universal literature deals in some way with violent death. If you were to ask me what that means, I'd say it's the inevitable stamp of a culture like ours; it's very possible that the tensions in a murder novel provide the simplest and nevertheless most complete model for the tensions we are living through in this generation."

"Sounds convincing," Roland Kaiser replied. "We live in a culture of violence and terror—that's undeniable. Especially in a society like ours. A good mystery novel reflects that, without any doubt; your novels contain the essence of Los Angeles and the essence of the state of California, and in a way they also reflect the essence of the United States. However, I don't completely agree with something you just said about the novel's social consciousness. Your novels have one—although perhaps you didn't mean to give them one, and perhaps that's precisely why they do. Since your work doesn't make any outright accusations, the implied ones take on more power and objectivity."

"I agree," Max Miller added. "Probably the biggest difference between what the critics call serious literature and the popular novel is a question of language—the pains the author takes to polish it."

"It's possible," Chandler admitted. "Nevertheless, for me all language begins with the spoken word, and more specifically the words spoken by the common man. All language begins with speech, and the speech of common men at that, but when it develops to the point of becoming a literary medium it only looks like speech. That's why I don't tire of praising what Dashiell Hammett did. Hammett's style, in its worst moments, was as formal as a page of *Marius the Epicurean* at its best. What Hammett did was to take murder out of the Venetian glass vase where it had been put and throw it in the alley. In the English stories, murder is an upper-class affair, something out of weekend parties and the vicar's rose garden. Hammett gave murder back to the people who commit it for a reason, not just to provide a dead body. He moved these people onto paper just as they were, and he made them talk and think in the language that's currently used for such purposes. And that's what I learned from him, and what I tried to do in my books."

"Good thing that's all," Jonathan Latimer said. "Hammett's example isn't the most highly recommended. He was a good writer, but he burned out too fast. There are those who think alcohol finished him off and those who think Hollywood did it to him. Hammett didn't have very much to say; he was unrolling the skein he'd gathered so carefully during his years at Pinkerton. Then one day he woke up and there was nothing left. The drinking came later."

"And why don't you add the Un-American Activities Committee into our theory?" Kaiser scolded him. "Five months in jail and the Hollywood blacklist can also finish a writer off—and he wasn't the only one."

"Hammett's career was over before that. Senator McCarthy wasn't provoked by the d.t.'s—it was more Hammett's affiliation with the Communist Party. That's what Max said a while back; everyone chooses his own death, and also his own way of leaving the scene. That was the one Dashiell chose. Why? I think it was a kind of desperation; he knew he was all washed up as a writer,

141

so he looked for excuses: politics, wartime heroism, persecution, and prison. He lived intensely and his name is still on everyone's tongue, but he has nothing else to say."

"I still think in this country the FBI is powerful enough to put a gag in your mouth or render your hands useless with a pair of cuffs," Kaiser rebutted. "That's what happened in this case. Hammett ended up on the blacklist; he couldn't manage to publish any more books or write for Hollywood. That was the real end of his career."

"Although you may not know it," Chandler said, "I had my own problems with the FBI. At one time there was a restaurant around here called the Plaza, run by one Moe Locke. "I told you about that, Rog, didn't I?" he asked, directing himself to Wade. "They had an open grill, and I can't say I ate badly. Well, one night the waiter approached our table and told me that the gentleman nearby was J. Edgar Hoover, accompanied by his friend Clyde Tolson, and that he wanted me to join them. I told the waiter to tell Hoover to go to hell. It seems he became furious and swore he was going to have me investigated by the FBI, but I think Tolson managed to calm him down."

There was laughter and Wade said he remembered Chandler's account of the incident.

"This is delightful, and the conversation was one of the most stimulating I've had in the last few months," he added. "But I have an engagement at Romanoff's with the rest of the junta that I can't put off any longer. They're the sort of people who don't usually accept excuses. It's at least two hours by car to Hollywood, isn't it? Why this mania for moving farther and farther south, Raymond? A little farther, and you'll be conclusively exiled in Mexican territory."

"Bah, Los Angeles's breath still smells stronger than Mexico's from here," Chandler said. "And that's no advantage. San Diego is even farther south from here and then you have to go a few miles more to get to the border."

"Anyway, rush hour is over," Latimer observed. "At this time of day the problem is the southbound traffic from Los Angeles. But if you take the Coastal Highway and maintain a good speed you can get to Hollywood in a little over an hour."

Wade finished off his drink and stood up.

"Listen, Raymond," he said. "Before I go I'd like to talk to you privately about a small matter. You won't be offended, will you, gentlemen?" he added with a smile to the others present. "After so many years of mutual confidences, Raymond and I have our little secrets."

"Come on," Chandler said.

They went into one of the two bedrooms in the apartment. Chandler had converted it into a personal study, although he kept a guest bed in it, too. The solitude of the old, almost resigned man showed through here. Here were his desk, the library containing the books he still hadn't given up, an enormous collection of pipes, and the silent typewriter. The windows looked out over the beach, and the far-off, blurred dusk spilled its leveling bagasse over the immense Pacific.

"What's this about?" Chandler asked.

"It has to do with that accidental meeting I mentioned to you before," Wade answered almost hesitantly. "Velma Valento and Marlowe. They were having dinner at Lucey's, which isn't exactly the kind of place you go when you don't want to be noticed. Do you think they're old friends, or might it have something to do with this Andress business?"

"What's all this about Velma Valento?" Chandler replied. "Are you interested in the lady? You don't have to worry about Marlowe. His lady friends never stick around for long."

"I'm interested in Velma, but not in the way you think. Nothing very personal. I'd just worry if Marlowe got her mixed up in something shady. You can already see all the ruckus being kicked up about Andress's suicide; now there are people who are trying to connect Morton's murder with that death. Latimer isn't the first guy I've heard say that. I don't like it for Velma's sake; I know how much the Andress thing affected her."

"Marlowe can help distract her from it," Chandler said. "The man has his charms, don't underestimate him."

"You think Marlowe is digging around in the Andress case?"

"He is. And now he'll continue with the Morton case. And he'll end up clearing things up. I'm willing to bet ten to one in favor of Marlowe."

"Well, that's exactly what I thought. And I'd like to do something to get Velma Valento out of this business."

"You can't get Velma Valento out of it," Chandler said severely. "She was Andress's partner, wasn't she? Whatever may come to light out of this mess will affect her one way or the other. If I were you I wouldn't worry. Let Marlowe do his job."

"I don't like it," Wade mused. "But maybe you're right. To sum up, perhaps what I should do is talk frankly and directly with Velma."

"And warn her off Marlowe?"

"I didn't say that. Just warn her that if she follows through on this investigation things may come out she won't necessarily like. It seems Andress tended to go over the line in his business dealings. That's what ruined him. Now Velma is running the agency, but she doesn't have any reason to risk her own professional reputation on account of any shady dealings her former partner got himself into."

"I'd pay money to know whether you're talking out of your supposed personal interest in Miss Valento or as a 20th Century–Fox executive," Chandler observed caustically.

"20th Century–Fox?" Wade disdainfully waved away the insinuation. "The company doesn't have anything to lose by this. Andress is the one who'll go on losing; he had more to lose than his life. His reputation, the thing he was trying to salvage with his suicide, is all that's left of him. I'd like to get Velma out of the path of the looming tidal wave, but with Marlowe in the game, that looks pretty tough." Wade had approached the window and suddenly he turned around. "Listen, Raymond, why don't you talk to Marlowe? I suppose you still have some influence on him?"

"And convince him to drop the case?"

"To do everything in his power not to get Velma mixed up in it. Interpret it as a very personal favor."

Chandler closely observed the man facing him. They were approximately the same age, and they'd known each other for some thirteen years. Wade, nevertheless, had managed to keep his slim athletic figure, firmly squeezing his belly under his elegant dark suit. His tanned skin and the white streaks at his temples suited him quite well, and he still wore the thick tortoiseshell glasses that had always given him more of an intellectual look than an executive one. Chandler became aware of his own limpness, the way he'd let himself go, and of the hopeless bonhomie with which he had accepted the latest events of his life. He'd resigned himself to growing old and preparing his discreet exit from the scene, while Wade was still in the thick of things, in full possession of his vigor, as aggressive and ambitious as he had been when Chandler had met him over a decade ago. Wade had risen almost to the top, and now he was a key
144

man at 20th Century–Fox, the sort of studio executive with almost unlimited resources who'd made him hate working for the movies in the first place. Could he really believe that this mature, cold, skillful, and calculating man could be so youthfully enthusiastic about Velma Valento that he'd come all the way to La Jolla just to ask for help in interceding with Marlowe? The hypothesis suddenly seemed so obviously absurd and inconceivable that the whole scene made him sick to his stomach.

"Didn't it occur to you that Marlowe is probably working for none other than your beloved Miss Valento?" he finally said, choosing a pipe from his desk and calmly beginning to fill it. "Who else would have been interested in using his services? Marlowe needs a client to operate, and Andress's ex-partner is probably the person most interested in clearing up the facts. Especially if that suicide turns out to be as improbable as everything coming to light implies it will be. Don't you see it more or less that way?"

"Velma contracting Marlowe's services? No, frankly, I don't see it. No doubt someone got Marlowe involved in this, but Velma isn't his client. More likely I'd say she's his prisoner, a very highly valued prisoner in the Hollywood jungle." Wade glanced quickly at his watch. "Well, I have to force myself to leave. Then you won't do me this favor?"

"I can talk to Marlowe. I don't promise you I'll convince him of anything."

"For the moment I'll settle for that. You'll keep me posted?"

"As long as you're within reach of a telephone."

"You won't have any trouble finding me."

They went back to the living room. Latimer, Kaiser, and Miller were ready to go. Chandler watched from his second-story window as the men disappeared into their respective cars and vanished into the deserted night. He absolutely hated La Jolla. It lacked the noise, the movement, and the bright lights and glitter of Los Angeles or Hollywood, and at the same time it wasn't isolated enough for him to be able to thoroughly enjoy his solitude and throw himself wholly into his new novel. He thought of that bungalow up in Big Bear, near Arrowhead Lake, an absolutely primitive spot lost in the San Bernardino mountains, where for a time he had believed himself to be happy with no company but Cissy's. Yes, it wouldn't be a bad idea to go back and settle for a few weeks. However long it took to finish one more book, perhaps his last. And to make sure no one would fuss

145

over him if he decided to tie on one last good one; the kind that took you all the way until you touched the absolute bottom of things. What doubt could there be? These were the three things he most urgently needed: one more novel; an enormous, endless drunken binge; and an immense solitude on which no one would be able to intrude, once in a while or forever.

▶ **8:11 P.M.** **Los Angeles Police Department** Just after eight o'clock Lieutenant Nulty arrived at the Los Angeles Police Department Homicide Division. It had occupied the same street-level City Hall rooms for a number of years. The outer room was about twenty yards square, but the department never stopped growing. The floor was covered in brown linoleum and a wooden railing divided the office in half lengthwise. There were a large empty table, its edges scorched with innumerable cigarette scars; half a dozen worn oak chairs; a telephone; and some fifteen plainclothesmen. They sat there watching television or listening to the radio when they didn't have a job to do. Almost all of them bought their suits in places like Hart Schaffner and Marx, smoked a lot, and didn't have enough ashtrays. Once in a while a kid pushed a broom around to get matches off the floor. The Department chose its men with great care. In general they were at least six feet tall; they were tough-looking, but only acted rude or vulgar when circumstances forced them to. Nulty greeted them routinely and somewhat abstractly, and he received a few stray responses. It wasn't exactly an Aeschylean chorus, but he hadn't been expecting one, either. He crossed the room and stopped in front of a door with a large green glass window. He didn't bother to knock. Captain Thad Brown was in his revolving chair with the moth-eaten headrest, in front of his glass-covered desk and two telephones. Inspector McGee was there too. His desk was pushed off to one side, near the door. In the back, half hidden behind a wood and glass divider, a secretary with unnaturally orange hair typed incessantly, completely oblivious to anything happening in the room as long as her name wasn't mentioned. There were two green metal file cabinets, a closet, a coatrack where the Captain's and Inspector's overcoats were hanging, and a couple of armless wooden chairs. Nulty dragged one of them over to Thad Brown's desk and lowered his two hundred twenty pounds into it, making the wood creak.

"These are our customers," he said, throwing two white

cardboard dossiers onto the glass. There was a double photo, full face and profile, in the upper right corner of each.

Nulty smoothed his hair back in a gesture of fatigue or disgust. Captain Brown picked up the dossiers and began to look them over. McGee approached and gazed over his superior's shoulder.

"Steve Skalla, alias Lou Lid; and Arizmian Soukesian, Armenian, naturalized, alias Moose Magoon," Thad Brown read. "L.L. and M.M.—you can't say the boys don't have any imagination. There's enough in their records to write a two-volume biography." He looked at Nulty. "Are you sure these are the men?"

"How can I be sure of anything? I wasn't there when they shot Morton full of holes. These are the characters from the Andress funeral—I admit a ten percent margin of error. They had their raincoat collars turned up over their faces and their hats turned down. But that one, Skalla, is six feet six; that fits with the guy I saw. What's more, it wasn't the first time I'd seen their exquisite hatchet faces. They rang a bell. I went to the files, looked around for a pretty long time, and they showed up."

"And what makes you think they were at the cemetery to tail Morton?" McGee asked.

"They sure didn't come to pray. Later Marlowe confirmed someone had been following them—first him, then Morton."

"And the car?"

"Marlowe thinks it was a Plymouth sedan—gray, maybe brown. He only saw it at night. He couldn't read the plates or get any other information."

"Magnificent," McGee harrumphed. "All we can do is put roadblocks on all the roads out of Los Angeles and a few especially foul-smelling suburbs and stop every gray or brown Plymouth, made, let's say, in the last five or ten years. And politely ask the occupants if by any chance their names are...what are they?"—he leaned over to read the files—"Mr. Skalla or Mr. Soukesian, even though their friends may have baptized them with more picturesque nicknames. And whether they attended Yensid Andress's funeral, and if by chance they'd been nursing any special resentment against a newspaperman by the name of Charles Morton. Isn't that more or less the way you see it, Nulty?"

"Those two characters are already well out of our jurisdiction," Thad Brown said serenely. "If what they wanted was to hunt down Morton, they've already done it. I know how these

147

people work; they do their jobs and then they make tracks." He reviewed the facts recorded in each file. "There are charges pending against them in Nevada, Colorado, Arizona, Illinois, and Michigan. Now they've made inroads in California, or at least it's the first time we've caught them at something. This is FBI business. I don't think we're going to have to work very hard on this case."

"What makes you think they've finished their work in Los Angeles?" Nulty asked.

"And what makes you think they haven't?" Brown replied.

"Those people are guns for hire. The first job was probably Andress; Morton began to dig around and they had to get rid of him. They're going to keep renewing their contract until there aren't any stray Boy Scouts who feel like investigating left around."

"Who's renewing their contract?" McGee inquired.

"I guess that's what we'll find at the very end of the skein," Nulty said. "But now we've got hold of one end. To find that out, we've got to unravel the whole tangled mess. Three days ago we were groping around blind on the Andress case. Now at least we know where to start pulling."

"Suppose we do. Who are the other Boy Scouts in this mess?"

"Marlowe's the most obvious. I don't know if he's working for someone, but the Morton business turned this into something personal for him. Then there is a certain Miss Valento and Andress's ex-wife. For different reasons, both may be interested in proving that Andress's death was murder and not suicide."

"Andress's widow is still here?" Thad Brown asked.

"She's staying at the Hotel Roosevelt," Nulty said.

"Okay, let's keep them both under surveillance. As far as Marlowe is concerned, we've got to make him sit tight. I'm not willing to waste men following him all over the place. That man's got ants in his pants. Convince him, Nulty, to leave this to us."

"I already tried," Nulty answered. "But frankly, I don't think I got very far. On the other hand, Thad, I think Marlowe may be our best lead. As soon as he makes his first move, the two hounds are going to throw themselves on his trail. And that may be our chance."

"Exactly. But I don't want any more murders on this case." Thad Brown passed judgment in an arid voice. "Two deaths are

148

more than enough to complicate matters. McGee," he added, looking over his left shoulder, "have Marlowe followed discreetly; keep a car on him round the clock. And if things begin to smell bad don't think it over too long. It doesn't pay to lose time with these sorts of people."

"But if we get rid of them, we also cut the thread of the skein," Nulty observed.

"And do you think you're going to be able to get to the other end? Don't be naive, Nulty." The captain executed a forty-five-degree turn in his chair, leaned back, and began to fill his pipe. "There must be an endless number of intermediaries between those two butchers and whoever is way up on top of the mountain. These people don't sign guys up at the conference table, you know. And they probably haven't the slightest idea who they're working for. Some anonymous corporate lackey meets them in some well-chosen and never-repeated place. They collect a previously negotiated price, receive new instructions if necessary, and scram. Not even they know who called them, nor do they have a way to find out."

"All I'm saying is that one thing will lead us to the next," Nulty insisted. "If we hold on to one of the ends, we may get to the next link. And once we have the next link . . ."

"Someone will make sure to cut the chain," Thad Brown punctuated drily. "It will be some venerable representative of the state of California—the senior mayor, the Municipal Council, the Chamber of Commerce, a judge, the D.A. himself, or some corporation." He handed McGee the two folders with an impatient gesture. "Let's go put a lid on this business. Andress wasn't just any guy, and the whole package smells real bad but also very big. It's not my job. Let the D.A. take care of it, if he has the guts. We have two murders on our hands, and also the identity of the murderers. Make about fifty copies of those mug shots," he ordered McGee. "A twenty-four-hour guard on Miss Valento, and the same goes for Andress's widow. And you, Nulty, on Marlowe. And check out the mood in the city a little. Those two guys have to have some underworld contacts. I don't think they're staying at the Roosevelt or the Sheraton. Someone has to have put them up. If they're still in our jurisdiction, we're going to find them. And if not, we'll hope you're right, Nulty, and that they take the bait. Warn Marlowe if you have to."

"If I drop the slightest hint, we'll lose them all," Nulty grumbled. "First Marlowe, and then our little couple."

"Very well, I leave it to you. But I'm holding you responsible for whatever happens. Not a single murder more." He fixed his gaze on Nulty's face. "And not one moment's hesitation with them."

Nulty straightened his immense bulk with visible annoyance.

"Understood. Is that all?"

"That's all. Pick out a couple of men to your liking. And you, McGee, start poking around the city waste heap on the double."

▶ **8:50 P.M. Brentwood Heights** The telephone rang in the living room. Five, eight, ten rings. Then it stopped and started ringing again. I threw myself out of bed and crossed the bedroom in my bare feet.

"Marlowe," I answered.

"I've finally found you, Mr. Marlowe. Why didn't you get in touch with me?" It was the voice of Jessie Florian. "I read the terrible news about your friend Morton. Who do you think it could have been? Why him, exactly?"

I tried to clear the sleepy fog out of my head. The darkness softened the shapes of things. I managed to turn on a lamp.

"Listen, Miss Florian, those are too many questions all at once. We'll talk about that when the time comes."

"I'm terrified," she confessed, and I heard a pathetic note of sincerity in her voice. "I was hoping to hear something from you quite soon after our meeting yesterday, and instead, that terrifying announcement in the papers. Do you think his death had something to do with Yensid's?"

"I told you, we'll talk about it later. Where are you now? At the Roosevelt?"

"Yes. And I urgently need to talk to you. I've received a cable from my son, Terry. He'll be in Los Angeles tonight."

"Tonight?"

"TWA flight 632. I just called the airport. It's expected in at ten forty-five."

"Fine. What do you want me to do about it?"

"Are you going to take on my husband's case or aren't you? I've been waiting for your answer. I didn't leave the hotel all day because I was waiting for your call."

"We have to talk about that too. Actually, I'm already working on your former husband's murder. But I don't know if I want

150

to do it for you—not on the basis of the presumptions you made yesterday. I'm not going to investigate Miss Valento. I consider her above suspicion. I'm following a different lead. If you accept those conditions, we can discuss the matter again."

There was a brief silence on the other end of the line.

"I understand. Maybe I was too vehement yesterday afternoon. I still have my doubts about Mrs. Grayle's behavior and the role she has in all this, but what happened to your friend made me think things over. I know the two deaths are related. Tell me, Mr. Marlowe. I'm beginning to be afraid. I need your protection. I'm willing to hire you just to provide me with a certain level of security while I'm in Los Angeles. Would such an arrangement suit you?"

"I'm sorry, no," I answered. "I'm not a bodyguard. I can recommend someone, if you think it necessary. I require complete freedom of movement."

"Could you come with me to the airport to meet my son at least? I don't want to leave the hotel alone."

I glanced at my watch.

"Ten forty-five, you said?"

"Yes. A TWA flight from New York."

"Fine. I'll come pick you up at the hotel at ten. We'll have plenty of time to get to the airport."

"I won't move until you get here."

I hung up and went back to the bedroom; I'd been asleep since about two in the afternoon and I still felt groggy. The night before, neither Velma nor I had managed to close our eyes until almost dawn. I reconstructed the fragments of that torn and shredded night—the hallucinatory scene in the *Times* parking lot, later our trip back to the house in La Jolla, both of us submerged in thought and an intense, communicative silence. We'd stayed up late drinking, and by the time we buried ourselves in bed, all the passion had fled through our pores or with our cathartic alcoholic confessions, strings of words dropped almost at random like some hesitant, foggy religious recitation. When I left around noon Velma was still sound asleep. Under the telephone on her bedside table, I left a note that said I'd call her in the afternoon or she could call me, and went home to put my thoughts in order, to take in the fact that Morton had been murdered and I couldn't even count on him for a drink in some Santa Monica nightclub when we both happened to be alone and depressed. And on top of everything, I had to decide what direction to go in next. Charles's death took top priority, but I was more convinced than ever that his death and the Andress case would lead me down the same path. I recalled the uneasiness and clamoring emptiness I'd felt upon my arrival at the apartment; I'd lit the last Camel left in the twisted packet I'd felt in my pocket, then I'd undressed and thrown myself in bed. Bitter anguish had coursed through me and stirred up images buried somewhere deep in my subconscious, that most elemental region of the brain, propelling me backward in time to the limits of my own existence and beyond, into the mists of some primitive, larval life form, the first deaf and blind awakening of humanity fighting nature for its life. Awake, my mind was still filled with unsettling dream images. It would take a hot shower to give them the slip. I looked at my watch again. Velma had told me she planned to go over some files with Mrs. Prendergast in the evening, but I had to leave immediately if we were to catch the plane. It would have to wait until later.

Shetland Lane. There were several cars parked along the street. The Triumph was pointing toward Sunset Boulevard. I parked myself behind the wheel and started it up. I switched on the parking lights and let the motor warm up for a few minutes, keeping my eyes in the rearview mirror. None of the headlights of the parked cars lit up. Nothing moved. Then a car came toward me from Brentwood Heights. I threw myself back, away from the window, and waited. It wasn't the Plymouth—as it zipped past I caught a fast glimpse of a long platinum bleach-job in the passenger seat. I pulled away from the curb, turned south on Sunset, and sped toward downtown Los Angeles.

Jessie Florian was still in her room. She was in the lobby in five minutes.

"Thank God," she said. "I don't know why, I thought you weren't going to keep your promise."

"Why?" I asked.

"You don't have any great sympathy for me, do you, Mr. Marlowe?" she asked succinctly.

"What makes you think that?" I asked. "I'm not what they call the demonstrative type. Anyway, if we're going to discuss our personal feelings about each other we'd better do it on the way to the airport."

The doorman opened the car door and that meant a fifty-cent tip. We had an ample forty minutes until the flight arrived, plenty of time. The evening traffic was reasonably heavy. I took

Franklin Avenue, turned onto Spring Street a few yards from Chateau Bercy, and buried myself in the three-lane wave going north on Sunset Boulevard. I felt my pockets, just to discover I'd forgotten to buy a new pack of Camels. Jessie Florian offered me one of her cigarettes. Neither of us broke the tense silence.

"I had a somewhat unexpected telephone call this afternoon," she finally said. "That was another of the things I wanted to talk to you about."

"Your son?" I conjectured.

"No, Terry cabled me from London. That was last night, and by then he was already on his way to New York. I thought he might call me from there, but I think he had to make the TWA connection right away. He probably didn't have time."

"Do you have any idea how they found him?"

"All I know is what he said in the cable. I have it here, in my bag, if you're interested."

"That won't be necessary. Within an hour I'll be able to talk to him. That is to say, if he's interested in talking to me."

"He will be. He'll want to know how his father died."

"Who was the phone call from?"

"A reporter from the *Los Angeles Times*. The managing editor, in fact. One Starret. You know him?"

I nodded and she continued.

"He told me he wanted to talk to me, about something that had to do with me. I believe your friend Charles Morton had written a second column about Yensid's death before he was... before it happened. This Mr. Starret said Morton mentioned something in this column that involved me indirectly. The *Times* was considering publishing it posthumously but he wanted to ask me first."

"Did he tell you what it was about?"

"No. I wanted to talk to him in person. I told him I couldn't leave the hotel, because I was waiting for an important phone call, and he didn't have time to come to the Roosevelt, either. So he decided it wasn't that urgent, and that he'd get in touch with me later. He never called back."

"That column will probably never be published. But if you're interested, I can tell you what he wanted to talk to you about."

"Please do."

"Your ex-husband's insurance policy. You knew you were still the beneficiary of the fifty thousand dollars."

Her lips pressed together in an involuntary sneer. For a few seconds she was buried in an obstinate silence.

"Whatever gave you that fascinating idea?" she asked finally.

"I can't help you unless you level with me," I said. "That's one reason I can't take you on as a client. Not only do you have many preconceptions about the motives of your husband and the people who surrounded him, you've also kept me in the dark about a lot of things, Miss Florian. I can give you the exact date of the last phone call you made to Doreme, Inc., from New York to determine whether Andress's insurance policy was still in your name. Will that be necessary?"

Again, she thought hard before she answered me.

"Whose side are you on, Mr. Marlowe?" she asked. "Are you working for Mrs. Grayle?"

"No," I said.

We'd reached the turnoff for the airport. I let up on the gas pedal, flicked on my turn signal, and got in the right lane. We left the Boulevard, and I followed the cloverleaf to a red traffic light, stopping once more before I could cross Sunset toward the ocean. West Doheny Drive was a bracelet of light snaking through the night. Two or three neon clusters of motels and shopping centers blinked in the dark, and in the distance the revolving airport searchlight intermittently swept through the thin curtain of drizzle. I slipped the window down and threw out the scorched butt of the Winston. The light turned green and we went on toward Sunset.

At long last Jessie Florian decided to answer my question.

"Very well, I certainly did call Doreme a number of times," she said. "But you're mistaken if you think my motive was to make sure Yensid's insurance policy was still made out to me. I just wanted to be sure he replaced my name with Terry's. I was afraid Miss Valento, as you prefer to call her, had also managed to get herself made the sole beneficiary of Yensid's life insurance and his will."

I wondered how much truth her defense might contain.

"Normally one doesn't worry about those things when they concern a person who's still relatively young, like your husband," I observed. "He gave every indication of being in excellent health, and no one had any reason to think he was in danger of coming to a tragic demise in the near future."

"Maybe you didn't," she replied. "I had reason to believe

154

Yensid was capable of arriving at some desperate decision at any moment. He was a haunted man. But I didn't think his life would end as abruptly as it did, either. It was really very simple. I called Doreme because I had no other way of finding out how far his relationship with Mrs. Grayle had gone. I tried to talk to his lawyer about his will, but he wouldn't tell me anything. He said he could do so only with my ex-husband's consent. It goes without saying, I didn't want Yensid to know about any of this. It would have created even more tension between us."

"I understand," I said. "Do you realize what a tough spot this excessive worrying of yours has landed you in? Some very suspicious and highly motivated person might consider you a suspect in your husband's murder."

"It's such an absurd idea, it hadn't even occurred to me," she said.

She nervously extracted another cigarette from her wallet. I'd noticed she chain-smoked when she was nervous during our first encounter back at the Roosevelt. Now she was so shaken up she forgot to offer me one. So I asked her for it instead.

"Forgive me," she said, holding out the box of Winstons. I lit the electric lighter on the dashboard; a few seconds later the spring jumped out and I reached for it, lighting both our cigarettes. She inhaled anxiously and hurled the smoke out again violently. She couldn't decide where to rest her eyes. Apparently she hadn't been in the least seduced by the wide-angle panorama visible through the windshield, the night dilating itself until it embraced the ocean somewhere in the far distance. A dizzying parade of illuminated billboards and posters for Coca-Cola, Pan American, and Western Airlines filed by the window. *Put a tiger in your tank,* Esso announced ferociously.

"Calm down," I told her. "I was only pointing out a mere possibility. Just to make you see how wrong our own attitudes can appear to others. I don't think you have anything to be afraid of."

"I didn't know you were a psychologist too," she said sarcastically.

I decided not to answer that.

"It's completely ridiculous," she went on, now entirely in control of herself again. "Who could be suspicious of me? I don't think the police here would be stupid enough to waste their time interrogating me. They haven't even called me. As far as they're concerned, my relationship with Yensid was over a long time

155

ago. I could have left for New York already without any trouble. You know why I didn't."

"They'll start asking questions once they throw some light on this insurance business," I told her. "But first they have to prove your ex-husband was really murdered. Doreme Insurance, on the other hand, could get very interested in you. As you know, insurance companies have their own investigators. They play every possible angle before they pay out on a policy. Since your repeated calls are on file with the company, they will take special pains to harass you. Perhaps with the idea of obliging you to go to court or, at the very least, to make a deal with them—for, let's say, some figure nowhere near fifty thousand. If I were you I'd talk to my lawyer right away. And if you don't have one, find one as soon as possible."

"So I'm between a rock and a hard place," Jessie Florian said bitterly. "If I go out of my way to demonstrate my husband was murdered, the insurance company will amuse itself tormenting me; and if I don't, neither Terry nor I will ever see a cent of that money."

"That's it in a nutshell," I corroborated.

This latest discovery didn't exactly help calm her nerves. Meanwhile, we'd arrived at the airport. I looked for a place in the lot, put the car in a space near the terminal, and we got out. I put a coin in the meter. The needle swung abruptly to the end of the scale and awarded us with half an hour. Before that half hour ran out Terry would be back with us. I took Jessie Florian's arm and slowly we walked toward the arrivals terminal. I felt her tense and vulnerable body under the light pressure of my hand.

It turned out that the TWA flight was delayed forty-five minutes on account of an unscheduled landing in Denver. We went to the coffee shop. Since I hadn't eaten anything since morning, I ordered myself a club sandwich and a beer. Jessie Florian didn't want anything but a cup of coffee. I remembered I was out of cigarettes, made my excuses, walked to the cigarette machine, and got two packages of Camels. It occurred to me it wouldn't be a bad idea to try to get in touch with Velma. I dialed the office number. It didn't ring. I tried again. It seemed like the line was dead. Then I dialed the operator. I explained what had happened and asked her to call Haaldale 9-5033, Hollywood.

"I'm sorry, sir," a woman's voice announced. "The line seems to have been disconnected."

I couldn't shake the feeling that this was odd. I knew Velma had dismissed the staff until the following Monday and that for the time being the agency offices were officially closed. But Velma and her most trusted employee were supposed to be at the office putting Andress's affairs in order. I couldn't think of any logical reason for the phone to have been turned off.

Something wasn't right. I decided to try to find Nulty. He wasn't at Headquarters, but I found McGee in the Homicide Division.

"Now what, Marlowe?" he grumbled with the unmistakable peevishness of a man who would doubtless prefer to be sharing his conjugal bed to working the night shift.

I briefly explained what had happened.

"And you think we're the telephone company?" he answered. "I can give you the number for twenty-four-hour service."

"I'm not joking, McGee," I insisted. "You know as well as I do this could mean something. The guys who finished off Andress might also be interested in Velma Valento, his partner, or in giving his office the once-over for something they couldn't find at his house."

There was silence. McGee was chewing the idea over.

"Where the hell are you now, Marlowe?" he inquired.

"At Los Angeles International, but I can't go anywhere for a while. I'm with Jessie Florian, who isn't exactly wild about being by herself, either."

"Andress's ex-wife?"

"Exactly."

"What's going on? Is she going back to New York?"

"No. We're waiting for her son to get here."

"Well, stay put. The boss just said to put Florian and Valento under twenty-four-hour surveillance. When you bring her back to the Roosevelt, there'll be an officer there to attend to her. Meanwhile, we're going to take a look at the agency. Do you know the address offhand?"

"Avenant Building, corner of Vine and Sunset."

"Vine and Sunset, I wrote that down."

"Can I call you again, let's say in half an hour?"

"You can call here as often as your heart desires, but that doesn't mean someone will always pay attention to you."

He hung up without waiting for a reply.

I returned to the bar, where Jessie Florian was waiting impatiently.

"Is something wrong?" she asked.

"I don't know. The telephone at the Andress Agency was disconnected. Something might have happened there."

"You're very worried about Velma Valento too, aren't you?"

"She's mixed up in this case, too," I responded elusively.

I glanced at my watch. 11:10. I realized I'd have to put another coin in the meter if I didn't want to get a ticket. I told Jessie Florian, who looked more tolerant this time. Despite the late hour, there was a lot of commotion in front of the terminal. Not far from where I'd parked the Triumph, a Traffic Department tow truck was beginning to drag a car out of its parking place. I put a quarter in the meter and went over to the truck.

"What's going on?" I asked the officer who was watching the lot.

"We're towing away that car," he answered. "Someone left it here last night. It happens sometimes. People take a plane for a day or two and want to avoid paying for long-term parking in lot C. This is going to end up being a lot more expensive."

I got a little closer and noticed that the fuss was over a lead-gray four-door Plymouth. The plates read Nevada 6330.

"You say it's been here since last night?" I asked.

"Since about ten-thirty. The twenty-four-hour grace period just ran out."

The tow truck ground to a start. I caught a quick glimpse inside the Plymouth through the windows. Nothing I saw struck me as particularly unusual. The car had been parked there approximately twenty-three minutes after Morton's death. It could have been a coincidence, but I'd stopped believing in coincidences a long time ago.

▶ **11:25 P.M.** The Avenant Building   A wailing prowl car fireflied down Sunset Boulevard and braked abruptly in front of the Avenant Building. McGee slid out of the front seat. Two plainclothes officers got out of the back. They were Lieutenant Moses Maglashan, a man over six feet tall, with a rock-hard jaw and the yellow eyes of a lynx, and the bespectacled Christy-French, who looked more like a businessman than a policeman. McGee pushed on the bronze and glass doors. They were locked.
158

He found the porter's bell on a black marble plaque and kept pressing until a voice poured out of the intercom.

"What's going on?" a man's voice muttered angrily through the static.

"Police," McGee announced. "We're coming in."

"I'm coming," the voice said grudgingly.

"Open up."

"Listen, I have orders to..."

"I don't give a damn what your orders are," McGee snapped. "Open up and wait for us on the twelfth floor. Bring the keys to the Andress Agency."

The door hummed and gave way. McGee and his men got in the elevator. They got off and followed the carpeted hallway all the way around the building. The super was already waiting for them with an unhappy look on his face. The keys were unnecessary. McGee took out the lockpick and the door to the offices opened with a smooth push.

"Is something going on?" the porter asked.

"That's what we're here to find out," McGee said.

He groped for the switch and turned on the lights. The metal file cabinet drawers were balancing hazardously on the ends of their tracks. Almost every drawer and paper tray belonging to the eight desks had been emptied out onto the parquet. A porcelain vase lay in two pieces in the middle of a puddle of water. What had once been a bouquet of gladiolas now decorated the epicenter of the indoor earthquake. A pair of legs shod in high heels stuck out from behind the reception desk.

McGee walked around the desk and bent over. When he stood up again he was holding the telephone receiver in his hand.

"Wire's cut," he said laconically. He pointed to the woman with his chin. "I don't think she's dead. See to her." He stepped over the body on his way to the back room. The tremor had also made a mess of the impeccable office that had once been Andress's headquarters. A painting had slipped off the wall and uncovered the safe. McGee looked it over. The assailants hadn't been able to break into it. Nor were there any additional victims. He went back to the front room. The woman lay supine on the desk onto which the policemen had lifted her.

"She's got a lump on her head and she's in a state of shock," Officer Maglashan said. "We should call an ambulance."

"Where's the closest telephone?" McGee asked the doorman.

"You can call from my apartment," he said. He was as pale as a corpse. He looked like he was about to faint.

"You have a master key here?" McGee observed.

The porter nodded.

"So open the suite down the hall."

Then he approached the woman and gave orders to Christy-French to go with the porter and call the hospital.

The two men deserted the office.

"Is it serious?" McGee asked.

"I don't think so," Maglashan said. "She got a good bump on the head. She's semiconscious."

"Go look in the other office and see if there's something strong to drink. If not, bring a glass of water from the bathroom."

Christy-French and the doorman returned almost immediately.

"They'll be here in a few minutes," the officer announced.

Maglashan appeared with a glass half-filled with a honey-colored liquid.

"What's that?" McGee asked.

"Cognac." He sniffed the contents of the glass. "And I think it's the good kind."

"Put it on the chair," McGee indicated. "Try to make her drink a little of whatever it is, but don't get her drunk." He turned to the doorman. "Who is she?" he asked.

"Mrs. Prendergast, the agency receptionist."

"No one else works here?"

"Not these days. After Mr. Andress died Miss Valento let the staff go. Until Monday, I think."

"And that Mrs. Prendergast still comes in?"

"Yes, her and Miss Valento. Just to handle the most urgent business."

"Did anyone unusual visit the agency in the last few days?"

"I don't know what to tell you. During office hours I stay at the main entrance of the building. Most of the people who come to the agency use the Vine Street entrance."

"And there isn't a doorman there?"

"No sir. Only at the Boulevard entrance."

"What is Miss Valento's phone number?"

"She lives in La Jolla. I can check the list in my apartment."

"Go and call. If you find her there, tell her Inspector McGee is about to call her."

The doorman left.

McGee asked Maglashan, "Who was assigned to Valento?"

"Galbraith."

"What time did he start out?"

"Around nine."

"Is there some way of getting in touch with him?"

"He's under orders to call in to the Department every hour. The usual."

"You, Christy," McGee said. "Go downstairs and wait for the ambulance. Otherwise they won't know where to go."

"Okay, boss," Christy-French said.

McGee began to roll a cigarette.

"Is she responding?"

"I managed to make her swallow a little alcohol. She's still in a state of shock, I think, but I'd bet my neck it's more the fright that's knocked her out than that thing she has on her head."

"What the hell could they have been looking for here?" McGee wondered, looking around. He went over the desks and file cabinets and randomly picked up a few of the papers scattered over the floor. Then he dropped them again. "It wasn't money," he affirmed. "And they couldn't open the safe."

"This must have happened in the middle of the afternoon," Maglashan guessed. "Otherwise they wouldn't have found the receptionist here."

"And no one in the neighboring offices noticed anything?" McGee roared, leaving a trail of ashes behind him. "It looks like a hurricane came through here. Things like this only happen in Hollywood. If anyone heard something falling they probably just assumed someone was shooting a movie."

The doorman came back and McGee interrogated him with his eyes.

"Miss Valento's telephone is not answering," he announced in a faltering tone. He looked like he was on his way to the gallows.

"Call Headquarters and find out if there's anything new from Galbraith," McGee said to Maglashan.

The Lieutenant didn't have time to leave. Christy-French came in, accompanied by two orderlies bearing a stretcher. One of them took the woman's pulse and examined the wound on her head.

"We'll have to admit her and see what the doctor says," he

cautioned. "You can never predict the consequences of a blow to the cranium."

They lifted the woman onto the stretcher and bore her to the elevator. McGee stopped Maglashan.

"Forget it," he said. "Let's go back to the precinct. We'll know soon enough if there's anything new." He turned back to the doorman. "You," he added, "lock the door and don't let anyone in without police authorization."

The man nodded. McGee and Maglashan began to move back down the hallway.

"Let's see what the people from Technical can do with this mess," McGee muttered, throwing his chewed cigar butt on the bright fuchsia carpeting.

▶ **11:30 P.M. Los Angeles International Airport** The TWA Clipper alighted on the runway just after the loudspeakers announced its arrival. Jessie Florian was jittery. At the last minute we'd even gone up to the terminal terrace to watch the landing. Since she hadn't seen her son for three months, I preferred not to be present at the reunion. I told her I'd stay in the bar, and that she and Terry could look for me there when they wanted to go back to the hotel. She didn't object.

Meanwhile I thought over my fortuitous discovery of the Plymouth. Of course I had no proof it was the same car that had been following Morton and me, in all probability driven by whoever killed him. I tried to reconstruct the events of the fateful evening: Charles had left the *Times* newsroom around 10:00; his assassin or assassins were waiting for him in the parking lot— they might even have followed him there. They waited for him to get into his car and then shot him without giving him any time to react; the shots could have aroused someone's notice, but it was so late at night, and on Wednesday the weather had been so bad, that the block must have been almost deserted. Next, before anyone could stop them, they got back in the Plymouth and drove straight to the airport. Their mission had been accomplished: first they'd finished off Andress, and then they'd eliminated that unforeseen nuisance who was stirring up the still-warm coals of his death and might eventually raise flames from their ashes. Nevada plates—the thugs could have been recruited somewhere like Reno or Las Vegas, where someone's always available for that sort of work. They'd probably hopped a

162

flight back there. Nulty had identified the two men. Tomorrow, with his help, I could figure out who owned the abandoned car and inspect the passenger list of every flight that had left for Nevada or, if need be, for anywhere in the country after 10:30 P.M. on Wednesday. A bureaucratic, exhausting task, but a necessary one. While I was thinking all this, Jessie Florian and her son showed up in the bar.

Terry was a tall, thin boy, with a gaunt face and a slightly blue pallor (or maybe it just seemed that way under the airport's fluorescent lights). His hair, moustache, and thick beard were a dark chestnut. He was wearing faded jeans and a light-coffee-colored sweater that revealed a flaming red unbuttoned sport shirt. A sheepskin-lined suede jacket hung over his arm, and he was carrying a Samsonite-type bag in his right hand. The look he projected intentionally defied his father's more fastidious image in every possible way. Nevertheless, once he was at my side, I couldn't help but notice the resemblance between some of his features and Andress's: the alert and sharp gaze; the smooth, clear forehead; the thick, sensual lips. I asked myself if the beard was there to hide the same weak chin that had betrayed a secret vulnerability in his father. I could also see Jessie Florian's still beautiful and well-sculpted lines in Terry's face. Something about him reminded me of El Greco's portraits or Titian's *Man with the Gray Eyes,* and Terry was also a painter, or at least had artistic inclinations. The different pictures Jessie Florian and Velma had painted of Terry, and my own, were superimposed on top of each other and merged.

"This is Mr. Marlowe," was all Jessie Florian said by way of introduction.

Terry put down the valise and we shook hands.

"I understand you're investigating my father's death," he offered.

He didn't sound very self-assured.

"In a manner of speaking," I answered. I leaned over and picked up the suitcase. "Shall we go?"

I put his luggage in the trunk and the three of us squeezed into the front seat of the cabriolet.

"I want to know all the details," Terry said. "All I know so far is what I read in the papers. My father's New York representative came to get me at the airport and we talked for about fifteen minutes. I can't say he was exactly steeped in the matter."

I gave him my own version of the events during the trip back to the Roosevelt. I answered the few questions he interrupted my story with without turning to look at him. Jessie Florian's profile was thrust between us. Terry leaned toward the windshield; he'd turned his face to me and was listening intently. Toward midnight, the traffic eased up and I kept a constant pressure on the accelerator; the speedometer needle wavered around fifty miles an hour. A fine drizzle began to fall again— immediately the asphalt became moist and slightly slippery. We had to stop for three lights on Sunset Boulevard before we arrived at the hotel, a little before 12:30. I carried the suitcase to the lobby and tried to make my good-byes right there.

"So, once and for all, are you going to work for us?" Terry asked me suddenly, before I could prepare my exit.

"I already discussed the subject with your mother," I answered. "We still disagree about the focus of the investigation. I don't think we'll be able to come to an understanding. I'm going to go on investigating your father's death. My advice to you is the same advice I gave Miss Florian: get a lawyer as soon as possible and have him defend your interests. Do you plan to stay at the hotel a few days or will you go to the Bel Air house?"

"Listen, Mr. Marlowe. I think we should all talk this over when we have more time. There are various things I know about my father's business that may be useful to you, if you really want to get to the bottom of this. And also, I intend to put the agency back on its feet as soon as possible. My father may have been murdered, but that doesn't mean his politics are going to change. That may mean the threats will start up again when I take his place. This may sound a little shady to you, but I can explain myself if you give me a chance."

"I think I know what you're talking about," I replied.

He observed me carefully, trying to establish how closely our interpretation of the facts coincided.

"If that's so," he said, "you'll probably realize that Velma's involved too. You've hardly mentioned her. What news do you have of her? Where can I find her?"

I noticed the change in Jessie Florian's face, but she refrained from imposing even the slightest resistance.

"I haven't had any news of Miss Valento for about twenty-four hours," I replied. I tactfully omitted the hours we'd spent sharing our grief and her bed. There was no reason for me to wound whatever might be left of Terry's feelings for her, nor did said occurrence really alter the basic truth of what I told him.

"I'm going to get in touch with her right away," Terry resolved.

"Good idea. If you find her, let me know. I wouldn't mind knowing where she is myself—but I don't think Velma or you are at risk right now in Los Angeles."

"Why not?"

"It would be very complicated to explain it to you. Will you be satisfied if I tell you that there is evidence that your father's murderers left the city last night, after they killed Morton?"

"I guess that's something. I'm going to call Velma right now."

Jessie Florian finally intervened, but not in the manner I would have predicted.

"Why don't you come up to your room," she said. "Mr. Marlowe can come with us."

She'd reserved her son a room on the eighth floor, adjoining her own. I lit a cigarette while Terry placed the call. Jessie Florian sank down into one of the chintz-covered chairs. She looked resigned and slightly discouraged. Obviously, she'd decided not to argue with her son about Velma. I asked myself if it was just an interim tactic, or if she was actually terrified by the turn of events and by the conversation we'd had before Terry's arrival. In any event, it was apparent Velma Valento was no longer her main concern, at least not for the moment. At heart she may already have been convinced that any confrontation she initiated with her son over Velma would only make the situation more tense than it already was. For the moment she would establish her alliances and compromise, but I didn't discount my first hypothesis—that it could all be just a tactic to buy time, now that she was faced with this possibly more mature, more self-assured Terry, a more determined young man than the one who had left for Europe six months ago.

He waited on his feet, the telephone receiver in his hand, while the operator tried to place the call.

"Have you got a cigarette?" he said to me.

I held out the package of Camels.

"Thank you," he murmured.

I lit a match out of one of the little hotel matchbooks and extended it to him. He inhaled deeply, and as he took the ciga-

165

rette out of his mouth he stood still and looked it over with an expression I had a feeling I'd seen before.

"I haven't smoked one of these since I left for Europe," he explained.

I remembered Jessie Florian's insinuations that drugs and who knew what else had corrupted her son and her image of him. But as far as I could tell, Terry was an exceptionally intelligent and well-adjusted kid. I even found myself wondering if Velma's fears about Jessie Florian's possible future influence on her son might be unfounded.

"No one's answering," he finally said. He hung up the phone and turned to me. "What do you think? Could something have happened to Velma?"

I tried to hide my own worries.

"It's not even one in the morning," I answered. "She may be out to dinner or attending some evening performance. It's not at all out of the ordinary for someone who moves in the circles she moves in."

I must not have sounded very convincing, because Terry was still looking at me inquisitively.

"Is she still at the La Jolla house?" he asked.

"She was still there last night," I said.

Suddenly I remembered I should call the police department again to find out what had happened at the agency. Discovering the Plymouth in the airport parking lot and my subsequent thoughts had made me forget about everything else. I came to and went to the phone.

"I have to make another call," I explained. "We may know something more in a few minutes."

I asked for an outside line and dialed the number for the Homicide Division at City Hall.

"Inspector Beifus speaking," a voice answered.

"McGee, please."

"He left a while ago. What can I do for you?"

"My name is Marlowe. It's about what happened or didn't happen at the Andress Agency."

"Marlowe? Wait a minute."

I heard him shout someone's name, and in a moment another voice came on the line.

"Christy-French here, Marlowe. We've met, remember?"

"A couple of times at least," I answered.

"You were right. The telephone line had been cut. They

knocked out the receptionist and turned practically the whole agency upside down. Not one piece of paper was where it was supposed to be."

"When did it happen?"

"We think it was between five and six this afternoon. The door hadn't been forced, the receptionist was still there, and the doors to the building are locked at seven."

"Any witnesses?"

"Just that woman, Mrs. Prendergast. I don't think she saw much, though. She's got a pretty impressive bump on her head."

"Where is she?"

"In Hollywood Hospital. But don't get all het up, Marlowe. You won't be able to ask her any questions until tomorrow morning."

"Do you know anything about Velma Valento?"

"We have a man posted in front of her house. No unusual movement. We get updates every hour."

"No one's answering her phone," I explained.

"What are we supposed to do? Do you want to file a complaint?"

"Didn't you consider the possibility that she's been kidnapped?"

"It's too soon to assume she's missing. What are you afraid of?"

"Obviously, that the guys who broke into the agency weren't looking for the receptionist."

"Or anyone else either. Unless they thought she was hidden in a desk drawer."

"Did they get anything important?"

"How would we know? The safe wasn't forced."

I decided to give up.

"Can I talk to Lieutenant Nulty?" I asked.

"He's not going to be in until tomorrow. And if you want to keep up your good relationship with him, I suggest you don't try to wake him up, Marlowe. He takes his sleep very seriously."

"Okay," I said. "What time do you think Mrs. Prendergast will be available?"

"Stop by around ten. I'm not promising you anything; McGee is in charge of all this."

"Thanks anyway," I said, and hung up. Terry and Jessie Florian were looking at me with frightened eyes.

"What happened?" Terry asked.

"Someone broke into the agency. Mrs. Prendergast is in the hospital."

"My God!" exclaimed Jessie Florian.

"Another shooting?" Terry guessed.

"Just a bump on the head. We'll be able to talk to her in a few hours."

"And Velma?"

"No one knows anything about her."

"What are you going to do?" he asked.

"I don't think there is much anyone can do. I'm going to go out there, at least. I'll try to get in the house somehow."

"Do you think..." Terry didn't finish the sentence.

"They may have attacked her at home? It's possible. Ten minutes ago I would have discounted that possibility. Now I don't know what to think."

"I'll go with you," Terry announced.

Jessie Florian and I exchanged a quick look.

"Do you think that's wise?" she said. "You flew twenty hours straight."

"I got a lot of sleep on the plane, Mom," Terry assured her. It was the first time I'd heard him address her this way. It was also my first real glimpse of Jessie Florian's weak spot for her son.

Maybe she was a jealous, authoritarian, and possessive mother, but it was also obvious she'd never learned how to prevent him from doing anything he'd decided he was going to do. Perhaps she'd tried a few times and lost. She didn't want to run any new risks.

"That wouldn't inconvenience you, would it, Mr. Marlowe?" Terry asked.

"It's probably not the smartest thing you could do, but I can understand how it would be even more unbearable for you to sit tight here. Come on, let's go, if your mind's made up."

He turned to his mother.

"There's nothing to be afraid of," he ventured. "Get some sleep and try not to think about it. We'll be back in a few hours."

Jessie Florian sought out my gaze again.

"Now you're working for me," she said in a faltering voice. She'd abandoned her arrogance and the haughty mask she'd worn when we first met. Now she was just a woman bent double by the relentless succession of events. She sensed the trap's doors inexorably closing, and in some way that I still hadn't managed to decipher, she felt as though she herself was being caught in

168

the snare, too. She hadn't foreseen this. "I mean to say, Mr. Marlowe," she added, "that I'm counting on you to bring my son back safe. That's all I ask. Can we come to an understanding, even though it may concern just this one point?"

Her request was almost a plea.

"I'll send you a bill for my expenses," I agreed. "They're going to be hefty."

Terry picked up his suede jacket and we left the room.

"I bet you had a lot of trouble dealing with my mother at first," Terry said.

We'd taken the Coastal Highway, where I could race the engine up to eighty or eighty-five miles an hour without the risk of running into a traffic prowler. The night was falling to a new nadir of rain and gloom. The day had lasted for an eternity. I couldn't tell exactly anymore when yesterday's events had drawn to a close and the subsequent events beginning with my disoriented early evening awakening had begun. Yet again I found myself at the wheel of the Triumph, circling through a route that had become very familiar to me in just a few days. I hardly knew or cared if I was coming or going. Fragments of the day and the night had merged together in my mind until I'd gotten the correct order of events all mixed up. What was I doing here with this kid, who, as far as I was concerned, had until a few hours ago been nothing but a lost name wandering among clouds of opium, the foggy peaks of Tibet or Nepal, the kingdom of the Dalai Lama, and the empty nirvana of the bonzes?

"I have the feeling you weren't listening to me," Terry deduced. "Your mind is somewhere else right now, isn't it?"

I assented with a deliberately vague gesture. I wanted to suggest that I agreed with one half of his statement, but not necessarily the other, without saying which half I agreed with and which I didn't.

"You're thinking about Velma Valento, aren't you?" he insisted.

"That's where we're going, isn't it?" I answered. I held out the package of Camels. After an instant of hesitation he took it from me. Before he removed a cigarette he carefully examined the little cellophane-wrapped box.

"Turkish and American blend," he read. He laughed sarcastically. "I've never understood why they printed the picture of a dromedary there, if they chose the name Camel," he said. He raised the cigarette to his mouth and returned the cigarette package. I took one also and we lit them with the car's electric lighter.

"You've seen a camel, haven't you?" he asked.

"Just in the zoo when I was a kid. I know this one's missing a hump."

"I'd only seen them in the movies. But when I crossed the Greek and Turkish border in a jeep, two hundred kilometers from Istanbul, the first thing I saw was a peasant with an enormous robe and a couple of camels. I didn't see another one in the whole Turkish territory. I bet the tourist bureau put them there."

I smiled.

"How old are you, Mr. Marlowe?"

"Somewhere between thirty-five and forty," I answered. "At some point I lost count."

This time he was the one who smiled.

"I feel uncomfortable calling you 'Mister,'" he said. "Would it bother you if I just called you Marlowe?"

"You could also call me Philip, if you'd rather."

"Okay, Philip or Marlowe, and I'm just plain Terry." He blew out a thick mouthful of smoke. "There isn't anything Turkish-tasting about this blend," he concluded. "Have you ever smoked hashish?"

"No," I answered. "Does it expand your mind?"

"The boundaries of perception, as Huxley says. It's a good thing to try; once you make it a habit, the boundaries begin to contract again. But there is one point when the limits really vanish—the boundary between reality and what isn't quite real, I mean. You perceive reality as something that might be happening inside you or outside you. It's hard to explain if you haven't tried it."

"And what can exist that isn't real? Anything that exists is already real."

"Maybe so. That's why I told you that what it expands is the capacity for perception. You feel things more deeply than before, or you feel other things, other kinds of things. The difference is more qualitative than quantitative."

"A difference that somehow separates you from concrete reality, a reality you can reach out and touch."

"Naturally—that's what hashish is for. Any sort of narcotic, I suppose."

170

"It's a dangerous road; there may not be a way back."

"The Brahmins say that life is an eternal return."

"And the Dakotas, up north, say that the year is a circle around the world, too."

"Really, I never heard that."

"Probably because you never lived with the Dakotas."

"Have you?"

"No. There's no future for a private detective on Indian reservations. There's no crime."

Terry laughed out loud.

"You and I are going to get along just fine," he said.

"That depends on how long you stay in Los Angeles."

"I'm going to settle down here," he announced. "In Los Angeles, San Francisco—I haven't decided yet."

"And manage the agency?"

"In a way. I'll leave most of it to Velma, but there are things I want to do. Things along the lines of what my father was doing."

"You said you had information about the agency that could be useful to me," I recalled.

"Yes, and I want to discuss it with you as soon as possible. Are we far from Velma's house?"

"It's just a few more minutes, so it might be better to talk it over on the way back."

"If there is a way back," Terry pronounced.

It wasn't the Brahmins he had in mind, or the Dakota Indians, or the endless return that opium or hashish create.

Velma's house was visible from the Coastal Highway turnoff. It rose above the highest part of the terrain adjoining the road, so you didn't have to go out of your way to notice it was completely dark; even the glass plaque with the number 6005 that usually shone out over the lawn was dark. I followed the road instead of turning into the driveway.

"Isn't that the house?" Terry asked, turning toward the back window. I nodded. I downshifted and turned left about two hundred yards ahead. I moved the clutch to second, and the car climbed the escarpment leading up the rocks at the edge of the road.

"We're going to take the long way around and try to get in from the back," I explained. "There's a policeman watching the house, and it would be better if he didn't see us."

"Is there a problem?" Terry asked.

"The guys they choose for this kind of job are usually very stubborn. We'd never be able to convince this one we just wanted to go in and check things out."

La Jolla wasn't exactly famous for having been planned on the *Roma Quadrata* model. I turned into a maze of streets and began to trace a wide northeasterly curve, with no idea of where we'd come out. The terrain was as rippling and capricious as a little San Francisco; there were large expanses of lawn and rock between one house and the next and the lighting was poor. The drizzle drew its shiny curtain across the dusty yellow headlight beams. When I came to the first intersection I turned left again.

"I'm going to park right here," I said. "We'll have to remember where."

I turned off the lights and the motor. I leaned forward to open the glove compartment and took out a flashlight and a Walther P-38.

"Are we going to need that?" Terry asked.

"Let's hope not. The flashlight's going to be invaluable."

We got out. Filaments of rain dragged along by the ocean wind stung our skin. "Would you prefer to wait here?" it occurred to me to ask Terry as I took the key out of the car.

"No," he said firmly.

"Okay. Let's walk a little by instinct. The back of Velma's house looks out on a rock promontory. If we're lucky enough to find it we can jump into the garden. The guy is going to be posted near the front door."

Terry had put on his leather jacket. I heard his teeth chattering. It was cold, but for him this was a new experience, quite distinct from the experience of the Orient and hashish. This was the Western world, one of the most civilized regions on the planet. A well-fed society with no major demographic problems: no plagues, indigence, or generalized misery. Los Angeles was a relatively clean city, and its air wasn't very polluted as of yet. La Jolla in particular was a residential area for rich people. All the latest innovations in technology and comfort were at our fingertips. Hygiene and well-being were the essential passwords of our life-style. Whoever was willing to work could get a job, and money ran abundantly—you just had to know where to find it. We had neither castes nor an overly rigid class structure. Upward mobility was fluid; somebody born on the riverbank could reach the highest peaks—it was just a question of audacity, resolution, and a certain lack of scruples. Without doubt we had the highest per capita number of cars, refrigerators, television sets, radios, telephones, appliances, vitamins, antibiotics, hospital beds, methods of entertainment, and houses of prostitution in the whole world. This was the West, this was the United States. The first nuclear power in history. Winners of the Second World War. The country that made the reconstruction of Europe possible. Our marines were on every Pacific, Indian, and Caribbean island, in South Korea and Japan. But Terry's teeth were still chattering, and I was pretty sure such a thing had never happened to him in the tortuous streets of Istanbul, or in Teheran, Kabul, Lahore, or Bangalore. This trembling was particularly Western and specifically North American. I would even have bet money it had something to do with that stretch of Southern California where Los Angeles itself was being seduced by Hollywood's neoned star and footlight paradise.* Tonight Terry was assuming his father's place in an influential, hermetic, and overprotected world where crime and murder were still common coin. A world where power, money, the search for prestige, and the desire for success could determine an individual's life or death from one minute to the next—an individual who in this case had been Terry's father and might eventually become Terry himself. I decided that the best thing I could do was pretend I hadn't noticed anything, and we continued in the direction we thought would lead to Velma's house.

It wasn't hard to find the place. Just as I'd suspected, the street we'd taken led us to a grassy embankment that ended abruptly at a rock ledge. Directly below our feet lay the backyard of Chandler's residence. There wasn't a single street-light in this section, but the stucco walls gleamed softly in the dim, wet moonlight. We made our way down a small staircase carved in the rock. I shone the flashlight beam against one of the back windows, and without thinking twice tapped a pane with the butt of the Walther. The rain-and-fog-impregnated night sucked up the noise like a sponge. I put my hand inside and groped for the bolt; it turned, and the window opened. A trio of bars stuck

*According to Chandler, "Marlowe is like Vergil in Dante's *Divine Comedy*: he says what the reader might say about the world of Los Angeles were he to encounter it himself."

some eight inches out from the wall and curved up at both ends to imbed themselves in the masonry. The space between them was big enough for us to slip through with some effort. I went first; Terry took off his coat, passed it to me through the bars, and then followed himself. We traversed the house, lighting our way with the flashlight. Everything seemed to be in order, but something was floating in the air, a subtle and intangible ambiance; the solitude and absolute silence seemed abnormal, as if they might forebode a flight, a kidnapping, or a desertion. We walked into Velma's bedroom. The bed hadn't been made; the sheets were cold. If Velma had left the house of her own free will, she'd done so quickly and some time before. I didn't know if there was someone who took care of the house. Terry thought he remembered that there was, a woman who came after lunch and left in the middle of the afternoon, but that had been eight months ago and who knew if she still worked for Velma. We looked in the closet, but it contained no clue as to whether anything out of the ordinary might have occurred. I found a large piece of cardboard in the study. After we quickly slipped back out the window I arranged the piece so it would hide the shattered pane. Terry and I hadn't found much to say to each other during our search, but we shared a strange mixture of uncertainty and uneasiness. It was almost three in morning; that prolonged absence and complete lack of news couldn't augur anything good. Suddenly I remembered the note I'd left Velma under the telephone on her night table. I'd looked the spot over; the note was no longer there. It was perfectly plausible for Velma to have destroyed it or taken it with her if she'd left. I didn't mention this to Terry. I suggested we go around the house and question the officer on duty in person.

"If you think we should," Terry hesitated. Sorrow and another deeper sort of dread had replaced the panicky fear he'd probably felt when we'd started off into the night.

At first I was surprised not to see anyone out front. It was Terry who found him. There was a bit of light about twenty yards away, and then, just before the terrain began to rise again, at the side of the driveway, the gigantic form of what might have been a Norwegian maple. The man was leaning against the trunk, but he wasn't exactly standing. He'd found a way to rest against the tree while holding a regulation pistol in one hand. With the other he was trying to stanch the bleeding from a bullet wound between his ribs. He experienced a new wave of terror as he saw us run toward him, but then the hand holding the pistol slackened.

"My name is Galbraith," he gasped. "I need help. Call 50-406, Police Department."

"We can get you to my car," I answered. "I'm a private detective. What happened?"

"Two men tried to get into the house. I tried to stop them, but they fired as soon as they saw me coming toward them. I think I hit one of them. They got into the car and got out of here."

"A gray Plymouth?" I asked, suddenly casting aside all my speculations about the car I'd seen at the airport.

"I don't know what kind of car it was," Galbraith said. "It wasn't a Plymouth."

"And Velma Valento?" I asked one more time.

"She wasn't there. I don't know anything about her."

I couldn't go on interrogating the man while he slowly bled to death. I took out my handkerchief, removed Galbraith's jacket, put the piece of cloth under the shirt, and pressed it to the wound.

"Take his revolver and hold this to him as hard as you can while I get the car," I said to Terry.

I started running back toward the little stairway carved in the rock. It wasn't exactly the ideal moment to think things over, but I couldn't help coming to two airtight conclusions: Velma had disappeared, and Andress and Morton's murderers hadn't left Los Angeles after all.

▶ **8:20 A.M.** **Hollywood Hospital** "You always manage to be where the action is—eh, Marlowe?" McGee said.

Nevertheless his tone wasn't provocative. He'd shot Marlowe his mocking look, soured by the years and by his occupation. After all, Marlowe had saved the life of a policeman, one of his men. Today or tomorrow the same thing or something like it could happen to him.

Marlowe passed his hand over his face; the tips of his fingers felt the taut skin of his left cheek while his thumb pressed a smooth dent on the other side. He had a twenty-four-hour beard. Those hard and bristly thorns growing out of his flesh could be as much a sign of life, flourishing despite bodily fatigue and lack of sleep, as they could a sign of vital weakness, carelessness, or negligence. Marlowe thought that as so often happened, the extremes resembled each other: the life force creating cells, tissues, and adrenal secretions, and the nervous centers resisting growth, the mind asking itself what all the fervent activity was for, what purpose could possibly be behind that blind preservation of existence mandated by instinct and nature.

"How is Galbraith?" he asked.

"He'll survive," McGee said. He was toying with a half-rolled cigarette, wavering between his desire to smoke it and the fat red *X* clearly superimposed over the outline of a smoking cigarette on a sign on the wall. McGee respected the language of codes. His was a black-and-white world of prohibitions, limits, and impediments. As far as he was concerned reality consisted of two vast, clear territories: the law on one side and the immense territory exceeding the boundaries set by the law on the other. Signs had been invented to make sure no one stepped over the line. And no prohibition conveyed its message as persuasively as a sign on the wall. A sign spoke to your eyes; it had a vigorously inhibitive power. He suppressed the desire to lift his cigarette to his mouth. "The bullet fractured a rib and buried itself in his lung," he added. "A delicate operation, but he'll survive. Probably they'll have to operate again later; for now he's out of danger."

"Did he say anything else about the men who attacked him?"

"What else could he have said? It's a very badly lit area, it was raining, and the guys shot him from twenty yards. Anyway, we know who they were: the same ones who did the job on the offices in the Avenant and who probably killed your friend Morton."

"Aren't you forgetting Andress?" Marlowe said.

McGee didn't answer.

"Are you going to let me talk to Mrs. Prendergast or not?"

"The doctor doesn't want any questions," McGee answered. "The woman's nerves are shot. Anyway, what do you want to know? They didn't make an appointment first, she barely had time to stand up. One of those characters grabbed the flower vase and broke it over her head. After that she was in limbo."

"And Velma Valento wasn't in the office."

"Miss Valento didn't set a delicate foot inside the agency all day. We already searched her house; she also seems to have flown out of there in a hurry. By the way," McGee spat, suddenly remembering something. "By any chance it wasn't you who broke the glass in the back window, was it?"

"I told Velma she had to fix that window," Marlowe said.

McGee looked at him for a minute.

"I could arrest you for breaking and entering, for something like that," he said.

"Frankly, I hate the smell of hospitals," Marlowe confessed, standing up. "And you can't smoke in the halls. Since you won't let me see Mrs. Prendergast the best thing I can do is leave."

"And who was the kid?" McGee asked. "Andress's son?"

"Correct."

"Do you know what his plans are? Is he going to take over his father's business?"

"I think so."

"Where is he now? Did he move into the Bel Air mansion?"

"He's at the Roosevelt, with his mother."

"Well, Marlowe. Now you see what's going on: two dead, two wounded, one a policeman. The boss is ready to go through the roof. If those two butchers wreak any more havoc the whole city is going to blow up like a keg of gunpowder."

"Thad Brown?"

McGee nodded.

"You can't say I'm not collaborating with you gentlemen in every respect," Marlowe said.

"Your collaboration would be more widely appreciated if you stayed in one place."

"What do you want me to do? Lock myself in my room until it's all over? It's not a very safe place, either. And someone has to find Velma Valento, since that problem apparently isn't part of your plan."

"The alleged Miss Valento must be in safekeeping," McGee sputtered. "Use your brains a little, Marlowe. Those two guys wouldn't have tried to break into her house if they'd already let her have it. That Miss Valento is the only one who's behaving with a little intelligence, at the moment. She knew she was in danger and vanished into thin air without saying anything to anybody about where she was going; it was the best thing she could have done. Do you know if she has family or trusted friends somewhere? I understand she used to be married to a certain Mr. Grayle."

Marlowe didn't bother to mention he had reason to believe Velma wouldn't have left town without letting him know where she was going first. But he wasn't too convinced of that, either.

"Didn't it occur to you that maybe those men didn't go to La Jolla looking for Miss Valento, McGee?" he asked.

"Then why did they go there?" McGee snarled.

Marlowe shrugged. "To look for whatever it was they couldn't find at the agency," he answered.

"You seem to know a lot more than I do about this mess. Why don't you just tell me everything you know, Marlowe? You call this collaborating?"

"It's pure conjecture," Marlowe said. "Obviously, these people are on the trail of something that interests them a great deal. Something that can be kept in a desk drawer, a filing cabinet, a breakfront, or a safe. They don't have any problem killing or hitting anything that crosses their path, but what they're looking for now isn't a person. It's not money either, to judge by what happened at the Avenant. What more can I tell you? Draw your own conclusions, McGee."

"Who are you protecting now? Who are you working for? Andress's partner, I suppose. Who the hell else could have told you that?"

"Believe me," Marlowe said, raking one hand through his hair. "For the first time in a long time I don't know who I'm working for, or even if I'm really working for anyone. I have potential clients coming out of my ears and various offers up in the air. All too abstract. The only one I had a firm deal with was Morton."

"I don't know why I should believe you," McGee muttered. "You don't play completely straight; you pretend to collaborate up to a point. You come to us when you need our help, but you always keep one or two cards up your sleeve. I don't like your kind of gambler, Marlowe. You already have a couple of wild mastiffs on your tail; if you want to break the law to boot I wouldn't give a nickel for your life. Suit yourself."

"What do you want me to do?" Marlowe asked.

"First, tell us everything you know. And then get out of the way and let us do our job."

"You forget I need to earn a living too."

"Somebody told me that Andress's ex-wife wanted you to protect her and her son. Is it true? Well, accept her offer. Go set yourself up at the Roosevelt. Don't let them leave the place until we get our hands on those two guys, and don't you leave either. That's a form of collaboration. That would give us three fewer problems to worry about."

"I'll think it over," Marlowe answered.

"And if you have anything else to say, say it now."

"I'm an open book," Marlowe said. "Your problem is that you overestimate me. I assure you, McGee, it's just instinct. If from time to time I give the impression of getting to the scene of a crime right before you do or of knowing a little more than you know, it's just a question of professional training. I grope around in the dark, and once in a while I bump into something and grab it. Think about it. You have to wait for something to happen to go into action; people call me when they're afraid something's about to happen, or when whatever has happened is too petty to bother the police with. That's my only advantage; the rest is just an illusion. And now, if you'll excuse me, I'm going to go to sleep for a while. In my apartment, not at the Roosevelt. On Shetland Lane. You know where I live if you want to follow in my footsteps."

"Go to hell," McGee exploded, unable to contain his rage.

Marlowe followed the long third-floor hallway, turned around to look at a nurse who smiled as she went by, and stopped to wait for the elevator. The main door of the hospital was on Alta Brea Crescent, West Hollywood. It had stopped raining, but the cold wind blowing in from the ocean hadn't cleared the air yet. Marlowe stopped at the foot of the little flight of steps outside and lit his first Camel of the last three or four hours. He filled his lungs with smoke. Fleetingly he recalled the final day of the summer that had been left behind—a summer when the sun shone with enough strength and the air was warm enough for the chorus of sylphids who met at the pool next door to splay their legs across the tiled terrace in their tiny, tight bikinis. That was the day Morton had called him up and they'd lunched together next to the ocean, in the shade of the squalid palm trees at Lonely Sands. Then came autumn's brusque irruption—a storm that had already lasted four days and had settled in over the hills, the beaches, and the drawn-out urban disintegration of Southern California like some sort of demonic calamity, a gloomy backdrop for those days' dramatic events: Charles's death and now Velma's disappearance. What new catastrophe might he have to look forward to in the next few hours?

A dark blue Ford traversed the hospital's driveway and stopped. Marlowe thought he recognized the car, and immediately saw Nulty's elevated shoulders emerge on the other side of the hood. He stayed where he was and waited for him.

"You're up early this morning, Marlowe," Nulty said by way of a greeting.

"Yeah. Last night about nine."

"Go home and get into bed as soon as you can. Around this hospital here someone might mistake you for a corpse."

"That was my plan, but I'm glad I found you."

"Did you talk to the Andress employee?"

"No."

"Who's upstairs? McGee?"

"None other."

"Then you're out of luck. Try again around lunch, or maybe this afternoon."

"I don't think it would do any good." Marlowe scratched his cheek. "Tell me something, Nulty. You know who killed Morton, don't you? Full description?"

"What do you want to know? Their names? That won't help you, Marlowe. The police in five states are already looking for them, and the FBI is looking for them all over the country. Anyway, I'm going to give you a present." Nulty put his hand in his inside jacket pocket and took out a bulky yellow envelope. He held out a couple of photographs. "Keep them," he added. "This is what the boys look like. One is my height. The facts are on the back. And be careful. They kill without warning."

"Skalla and Soukesian," he murmured. "So that's who we're fishing for."

"You've seen them before?"

"Skalla, maybe once. I've heard talk of Soukesian." He glanced at the photos again. Then he put them in his pocket. "Nulty, do you remember me mentioning a four-door Plymouth following me and then Morton?"

"We're assuming that's how they're getting around. We're following up on that tip of yours now."

"Well, there are a couple of things I've been meaning to tell you about that Plymouth. Last night Jessie Florian called me to ask if I'd come with her to pick up her son at Los Angeles International. While I was there, the Traffic Department truck towed a car that had gone past the twenty-four-hour deadline. It was a lead-gray Plymouth sedan—Nevada plates, number 6330. It could be a coincidence, but it was parked there around 10:30 Wednesday night. Half an hour after Morton died."

"Nevada 6330?" Nulty repeated. "We'll look into that right away."

"It seemed logical to assume the murderers left town after they killed Charles," Marlowe said. "Then those other two events occurred: the break-in at the agency and the attempted break-in at Velma Valento's house. So I rejected that hypothesis."

Nulty scratched behind his ear.

"And then?" he asked.

"When I rescued Galbraith I asked him if he'd been able to identify the car of the men who shot him. He wasn't sure what it was, but he was sure it wasn't a Plymouth."

"Could they have switched cars?" Nulty guessed.

"It's plausible."

"You're right. To be extra careful, after they got rid of Morton."

"What do you do in a case like this?" Marlowe inquired.

"Start over again, I guess. But I'm going to check out that Nevada Plymouth. It must still be in the Traffic pound."

"Can I call you later to find out what happened?"

"Where are you going now, Marlowe?"

"I wasn't lying, I'm landing in bed."

"Are you a hard sleeper?"

"Not lately."

"Then I'll give you a call in a couple of hours."

"I appreciate it, Lieutenant."

It took Marlowe twenty minutes to get to his Shetland Lane apartment. He took a scalding shower and made a couple of fried eggs, some toast, and two cups of coffee. He finished his second cigarette of the morning and went to bed. The shave could wait until later.

▶ **9:13 A.M.** **Hollywood Hospital** Nulty quickly flashed his police shield at the front entrance and went straight to room 332. McGee was still impatiently pacing back and forth like a caged tiger, with an unlit cigarette in his hand.

"Do you have the pictures?" he asked, without saying hello.

Nulty nodded and they went into the small hospital room. The blinds overlooking the lawn on Alta Brea Crescent had been partially drawn, and the leaden, damp, still, dawnlike light had sucked all the color out of the room. Mrs. Prendergast's eyes were closed but she wasn't asleep.

"What did the doctor say?" Nulty asked.

"Nervous shock. They'll discharge her in a day or two."

Nulty lit the lamp on the night table.

"Mrs. Prendergast," he said. He waited while the woman turned her head on the pillow and wearily opened her eyes. "We're not going to bother you much longer," the Lieutenant added. He pulled over a metal chair and sat down next to the bed. "Just one small effort and we'll let you rest until you're completely recovered. I want you to look at these photographs." He put them under the cone of light cast by the lamp. "Do you recognize either of these faces, Mrs. Prendergast? They're alleged to be the men who broke into the agency."

With all the energy she had left in her, the woman cast her eyes over the photographs. She didn't seem to care very much about finding whoever was responsible for the outrage. More likely, she wanted to forget everything that had happened as soon as possible—to erase those dizzying seconds in which some stranger had added an inexplicable dash of tragedy to the tranquil flow of her daily routine. It couldn't really have happened; it must have been a bad dream, and even these minutes of semi-consciousness—when she found herself in a room that was not her own, a room without flowers, its walls painted in pale hospital colors—were part of the nightmare.

182

"I can't remember anything," she said. "It happened too quickly. They were wearing hats and dark raincoats and they were very tall. That's all I can tell you."

"Look carefully," Nulty insisted. He tilted the shade so that the edge of the light fell directly across the photographic paper's shine. He placed two fingers on the upper edge of the mug shots, blocking the men's foreheads and hiding the domes of their craniums as well. "Do you recognize them now?"

Mrs. Prendergast barely managed to raise her head.

"It was that one," she said, focusing surely on one of the photos. "I stood up; he came up to me without a word, picked up the vase, threw the gladiolas on the floor without so much as looking at them, and hit me over the head."

"Thank you, Mrs. Prendergast. Rest now, and don't worry. We won't bother you again."

Nulty stood up and turned off the lamp.

"Skalla," McGee murmured.

The two men left the room.

"Well, now we have something definite to go on," Nulty said.

"About time," grumbled McGee. "I didn't know what was going to happen to that cigarette if I had to spend ten more minutes in that place. I probably would have swallowed it. Let's go to the Department."

They walked through the lobby and stopped on the short staircase that led down to the lawn. McGee raised the tobacco to his mouth, struck a match, and inhaled deeply. Nulty followed suit. He smoked Dutch cigars; it was one of the few luxuries he allowed himself and one that cut deep into the personal-expense column in the family budget.

"I have something to do," he explained. "I'm going to check out a tip Marlowe gave me this morning."

"Marlowe?" McGee rumbled. "So you had the good fortune to run into him, too? You know something, Nulty? That guy drives me crazy. I can't stand his arrogance and the way he has of subtly bragging about his teeny feats—as if he weren't doing everything possible to rub your nose in them. I'm going to recommend they revoke his license once and for all."

Nulty looked at the thick peg of ash forming at the end of his cigar. The sight gave him a deep sensation of well-being, as satisfying as the taste of the tobacco and the aroma that usually frightened people off when he exhaled his mouthfuls of smoke.

"Come on, are you going to let me in on this tip or what?" McGee sputtered.

"I'll tell you in an hour at Headquarters. First I have to make sure."

"Don't look at me with that satisfied baboon face," McGee said. "And don't breathe in my kisser while you're sucking on one of your disgusting cigars. Not only do I have to put up with Marlowe's insolence, I also have to watch while he gets guys like you to waste your time when you should be doing something useful. If it was up to me, I'd put him out of service right now."

"It's a shame it isn't up to you," Nulty said good-humoredly. "You could put in for a transfer to the 77th Street Precinct any time. There are always opportunities for action there. Anyway, I think I'm going to see the Chief in an hour. And I'm on duty, even though you may not think I am. See you later, McGee. I'll bring you new developments soon."

Nulty left Inspector McGee stone-cold halfway down the staircase and squeezed himself into his car. Just getting his legs into the Ford's front seat was no small feat.

He took the smooth curve of Alta Brea Crescent, continued his descent through Greenwood Place, crossed Griffith Park, and within a few seconds had buried himself in the flow of cars coming off the Boulevard. As he drove he couldn't stop watching his large, yellowed hands, or the wrinkled shirt-cuffs sticking out below the brown jacket. Twenty years on the force, first-lieutenant rank, a wife and three kids to support, a salary that barely got him through the month with a half a tank of gas to spare and obligated him to lower his precious cigar ration to two or three a day maximum—but in spite of everything he liked his job. It gave him the kind of freedom and independence Nulty held very precious. He wasn't a guy who could sit behind a desk or do any other kind of bureaucratic work. He had too much adrenaline coursing through his two hundred thirty pounds to sit still for more than an hour at a time. Maybe he could have been a boxer, as someone had told him when he was a kid, or even a truck driver. But a person didn't finish high school at great personal sacrifice merely to install himself on the seat of a heavy-truck cab going back and forth over the endless highways of the United States at a piddling forty miles an hour. Instinctively,

Nulty turned his gaze eastward and contemplated the mountain-tops emerging above the tattered rainclouds. Incredibly, he'd never been past those hills in all his forty-three years. He'd never even left California. Nobody had wanted to see all the states as much as he had, to explore the immense country from west to east, north to south. To be sure, he loved California with all the patriotism he could muster, and he doubted there was another state in the country that could compare with it. California had everything a man could want or need. When he looked at the big picture Nulty couldn't help feeling real satisfaction; his only true occupational hazard was that he hardly ever had the time to step back and contemplate that big picture, to appreciate the true significance of the freedom that was his once he was sealed tightly inside the capsule of his automobile. Too often his work made him lose sight of what was important, mired him down in the minutiae of his daily routine and swaddled him in the sordid reality of the gutter. And of course now and then he had to sweep the hard seats of the Department clean with his butt for a few hours. However, the final sum was clearly positive; now and then Nulty was able to satisfy his vital urges by rough-ing up some deserving type who was asking for it, and to exercise his mind when circumstances required him to. There were mo-ments when he envied Marlowe's unrestricted freedom to do more or less what he himself did without having to answer to anyone. And there were moments when he hated people like In-spector McGee whose brains were the size of mosquito heads and who made up for their sad lack of imagination by making life miserable for everyone else. The job that for Nulty had become a way of life lay halfway between those extremes of envy and dis-gust.

Nulty left Sunset Boulevard on Doheny Drive, at the foot of the slope of the Strip, and took the road for the Los Angeles Police Traffic Department's pound. He stopped at the wide gate on South Highland Avenue. This was where they piled up months' worth of stolen, abandoned, and unclaimed vehicles. The officer on duty at the entrance recognized him, letting him by with a smiling salute. Nulty drove in and parked the Ford next to the office of the Sergeant in charge. His name was Art Huck.

"Hi, Art," he said, opening the door to the office. "How's business?"

The man took his legs off the tabletop.

"What brings you here, Lieutenant?" They shook hands. "A used car? You already know how that goes: the supply is always greater than the demand."

"I'm looking for a piece of junk they towed out of the airport parking lot last night—a Plymouth sedan, Nevada plates, 6330."

"Ah, yes. No one came for it. Want to see it?"

"Is it locked?"

"Yes, but that's easy to fix."

The Sergeant picked up a screwdriver and a coathanger-shaped piece of wire.

"Right this way, Lieutenant."

They walked through the enormous asphalt compound. Cars of all brands, types, and colors were piled up along the wire fences. They found the Plymouth at the back of the strip. Lead gray, as Marlowe had said. Nulty leaned over the window and looked inside.

"Just a minute, Lieutenant."

The Sergeant put the screwdriver against the upper edge of the glass, pushed down, and when he'd managed to push the glass down a few inches, slipped the wire in until it was hooked around the doorhandle. He jerked it up and the door opened.

"It's that easy, huh?" Nulty said. "And then people complain someone stole their car."

They hadn't left anything on the seats or the dashboard. Nulty was careful not to touch the steering wheel. He pressed the button that opened the glove compartment. The top jumped out; in the hollow were a rag and an empty cigarette box. He picked the box up with a handkerchief and put it in his pocket. As he went to close the compartment he saw a label pasted to the back of the door. *George W. Hicks—Used Cars—Carson City, Tel 13-572,* the black letters on the orangy background read. He wrote down the name and the number in his notebook.

"Let's call Carson City," said the Lieutenant. "I want to know who this Hicks sold this car to, and when. And I'm going to get a man from Technical to take fingerprints."

He slammed the Plymouth's door shut.

"What's this about?" Art Huck asked.

"Couple of birds who've been giving us a lot to do in the past few days. They abandoned this buggy at the airport, but they must have had a reason. They probably wanted us to think
186

they'd skipped out. They're still here, and they must be getting around in something. Do me a favor, Art." Nulty stopped at the door to the Sergeant's office. "Call that guy and ask him for the name or at least a complete description of the guy who bought the Plymouth from him, also the date of sale. When you have that information, give me a call at the Homicide Division. I'm heading over there now."

"Okay, Lieutenant. What should I do if someone comes to claim the car?"

"Have him show you the papers, and keep him here. Get help, because these guys are armed and dangerous. But I don't think that's going to happen. If we're wrong and the Plymouth belongs to someone else... well, I'll come beg your forgiveness in person."

The Sergeant smiled. Nulty brandished his cigar stub in the air in farewell and squeezed himself into the front seat of the Ford.

▶ **11:07 A.M.** **Los Angeles Police Department** Captain Thad Brown and Inspector McGee were in their office. They looked up as Nulty walked in without knocking and sat down in his usual chair in front of the Chief's desk.

"Huck called five minutes ago from the pound," Thad Brown said. "One certain George W. Hicks of Carson City doesn't know the names of the guys who bought the Plymouth from him. There were two of them. The description he gave us matches Skalla and Soukesian. They also bought an Oldsmobile 98, California plates, number 3-416. It was Monday, the twenty-third of September, at nine in the morning."

"Aha!" Nulty said. "The day Andress was killed."

Thad Brown didn't comment.

"I don't think those two guys were swimming in dough," he interjected. "They must have collected on some other job first. You don't just buy two cars the same day, and abandon one of them two nights later. The Plymouth cost $600. They must have been well paid."

"Oldsmobile 98, plate 3-416," Nulty noted. "What color did you say?"

"I didn't. Light green. That one cost $859."

"Monday the twenty-third, nine in the morning. How long a drive is it from Carson City to Los Angeles?"

"Via San Francisco, with luck, anywhere from thirteen to fifteen hours."

"Which means they could have easily been here by eleven that night. They killed Andress an hour or two later. Good guess," he suggested, "or not?"

"Let other people draw the conclusions," Brown said drily. "Stick to your own job. Take a look at this."

He held out a gray piece of mimeograph paper. Nulty knew those stamps by heart. He read:

CIRCULAR NO. 237. 2709/56. 0800 HOURS.
FROM: LOS ANGELES POLICE HEADQUARTERS
TO: HEADS OF DEPARTMENTS AND SPECIAL SECTIONS. CONFIDENTIAL.
RE: VERIFICATION OF IDENTITY AND VARIOUS ITEMS OF EVIDENCE AGAINST STEVE SKALLA A.K.A. LOU LID, AND ARIZMIAN SOUKESIAN A.K.A. MOOSE MAGOON. (SEE ATTACHED PHOTOGRAPHS AND IDENTIFYING DESCRIPTIONS.)
PRESUMED ASSASSINS OF REPORTER CHARLES MORTON PERPETRATORS OF AVENANT BUILDING ASSAULT AND MURDER ATTEMPT AGAINST OFC. JOHN GALBRAITH. DUE TO PRIORS AND EXTREME DANGEROUSNESS OF ABOVE, ALL PERSONNEL DETAILED TO SEARCH HEREBY ORDERED AND AUTHORIZED TO SHOOT ON SIGHT ONCE POS ID CONFIRMED WITHOUT PERMITTING DELAYING TACTICS ON PART OF SAME. DEPARTMENT HEADS, SUPERVISORS OF SPECIAL SECTIONS, AND OPERATIONAL COMMANDING OFFICERS TO CONVEY APPROPRIATE ORDERS TO SUBORDINATES.

"That's what this is all about?" Nulty commented, dropping the memorandum on the glass desktop. "It's more or less what you already told me, isn't it, Thad? Who are we protecting now?"

"The system," Thad Brown answered. If his voice betrayed a trace of cynicism, Nulty was too used to that certain way the Chief had of talking and dealing with things to notice any change in tone. "We're looking for a couple of murderers while we also do everything we can to keep the structure on its feet. That's more or less the job we have cut out for us."

"Understood. Then my job is the Oldsmobile, and yours is to make sure the system's cement blocks don't come tumbling down," Nulty stressed. "I suppose last night's hunting party didn't come back with a trophy."

188

"No. Those boys are very careful. They probably didn't stay at the Sheraton or a Holiday Inn, but someone must have put them up someplace comfortable and very secure."

"And the Los Angeles boys' choir?" Nulty asked. "No soloist interested in earning extra credit with an operatic aria?"

Thad Brown had begun to fill his pipe with calm and meticulous movements. Out of habit, Nulty's gaze wandered toward McGee. The Inspector was smoking his tobacco impassively. Although it was the twenty-seventh of the month and he was down to the last of his twenty-five-cent Dutch cigars, Nulty decided he would join them. He took a Van der Graff out of his breast pocket and bit off a piece that must have been worth at least five cents.

"And what's the story on Velma Valento?" he asked.

"She's my problem now," Thad Brown said. He made a smooth flame jump out of his Ronson and dextrously rolled his pipe bowl back and forth until he'd managed to keep it lit. "And I was under the impression yours was Marlowe," he added. "But according to McGee here, Marlowe has been running all over town without anyone giving so much as a folderol about what he does or where he sticks his nose."

"I put Nogard on him. With Fulwider relieving him every three hours and with orders to report all his movements to me immediately. But when I gave the order, Marlowe wasn't in his apartment, and no one managed to find him until he appeared at the hospital with Galbraith wounded. You already know he's a slippery character. Right now I've got him sleeping at his apartment in Brentwood Heights."

"You assigned Nogard and Fulwider. I was under the impression that I had put you on Marlowe personally. If I didn't make myself clear before, let's try to avoid any future misunderstandings. Find him immediately and don't let him out of your sight for a minute. Listen to me carefully, Nulty," he added, resting his elbows on the desk. "I'm under enough pressure; you just read the circular: shoot first, ask questions later. Straight from the top. There are at least two people dead and a third in critical condition. I myself subscribe to the brass's point of view: until Miss Valento turns up, Marlowe is the most likely bait. I'm holding you personally responsible for his continued good health."

"Understood. Then I'm going to put the bait on the hook."

"Leave the bait to its own devices. Just follow him and wait for the fish to nibble. Light green Oldsmobile 98. Hold on to the rod with both hands, and when they bite, reel them in tight.

189

Once this particular problem is solved we'll have plenty of time to consider the more general issues."

"Yes," Nulty said, standing up. "Like seeing how and where we begin to rebuild the system."

▶ **2:53 P.M.** **Brentwood Heights** *Rinngg, rinngg, riiinngg* sounded the telephone in the living room. I woke up convinced I'd just closed my eyes; my watch, however, tried to make me believe I'd been asleep for about four hours. I couldn't remember anything. *Riiing, riing* . . . the phone went on calling bossily.

"I'm coming!" I yelled.

It wouldn't shut up. I'd lost four precious hours of my life submerged in some deep well—no light, nothing to see, no ill-omened shadows, and no memory. Freud was just a two-penny bungler, and sleep was just a labyrinth spiraling down to something similar to death; it wasn't filled with symbols or images, it was as empty as the hold of a shipwrecked boat run aground against some deserted shore.

Riiing, riiing, riiing.

"Who's there?" I muttered.

A far-off and vaguely familiar-sounding voice surged from the other end of the line.

"Marlowe? I'm glad I found you alive."

"Who's there?" I repeated.

"Chandler," the voice said.

"Who?"

"Raymond Chandler. I believe we've met."

"I'll be damned. Christ almighty. It sounds like you're on the other side of the world. Are you calling from England?"

"Not yet. I'm taking a rest while I write a novel: my last."

"I promise I'll read it. I bet it won't be the last."

"Listen, Marlowe. I've got someone here, someone you'll be interested in talking to. Wait a minute, I'm handing over the phone."

"Hi, Philip."

"Velma?"

"What a surprise, huh?"

"What happened to you? Are you all right? Damn it, we'd imagined the worst. Where are you?"

"In a very beautiful place, in the mountains near San Bernardino. The town is called Big Bear; there is a little lake and

190

the air you breathe is very pure. At least that's what they tell me—it's barely stopped raining since I got here."

"Christ. How did you end up there?"

"Have you always sworn this much? I'm getting the impression you've been corrupted in the past twenty-four hours."

"It's only been twenty-four hours? We've been looking for you everywhere. They broke into the agency; Mrs. Prendergast, or whatever she calls herself, was beaten up, and she's in a state of nervous shock. Someone tried to get into your house."

"My God," Velma gasped.

"Now do you want to tell me a little something about how you got there? And your plans for the future?"

"It's a long story. Chandler convinced me he had to hide me somewhere. At first I resisted; now I see he was right."

"Well, that was sensible after all. What does Chandler know about all this?"

"He can explain it to you better than I can. Can you come see me?"

"Not only can I—it's what I want to do immediately. Listen, there's someone else who wants very much to see you."

"You mean the police?"

"No, not for the moment, at least. Terry."

"Who?"

"Terry Andress."

"Terry's here?"

"He got in last night. He flew from London to New York and arrived in Los Angeles about eleven-thirty. He's decided to take over his father's business, and I've formed a very favorable impression of him. Jessie Florian's attitude has changed as well."

Velma didn't respond.

"Would you mind if I brought Terry with me? He'd never forgive me if I didn't."

"Of course not, but I'd rather his mother have nothing to do with this."

"Don't worry, there's no reason she has to know. Now tell me how to get there."

"Chandler will tell you. I'm getting off. Kisses."

Her lips emitted a soft crackle from six thousand feet above sea level in some lost, distant corner of the Sierra Nevada.

"Listen, Marlowe," came Chandler's alcoholic rasp. "You're familiar with the San Bernardino mountains, aren't you? There's a big lake nearby, a tourist spot with cabins and bungalows scattered around it: Arrowhead. You won't have any trouble finding it. The town of Big Bear is about fifteen miles from Arrowhead. When you get in, ask in the Totem Pole Art Shop or the Teddy Bear Café for Chandler's cabin; everyone knows me around here. The best route to San Bernardino is Wilshire Boulevard, Canyon Drive, Lost Canyon Road, etcetera. Get a good map of the area."

"Okay, Raymond. See you soon."

Without wasting a minute I called the Roosevelt. Apparently Terry had been waiting right next to the phone. I briefed him on my conversation and promised to pick him up in an hour. I asked myself if it might not be a good idea to tell someone else. Nulty had said he would call me, but he hadn't—the Plymouth business had probably been nothing but a perverse coincidence. Nevertheless, the threads of the plot were becoming capriciously tangled. Skalla and Soukesian were still on the loose. A few hours ago I would have sworn the police were in no hurry to catch up with them. Now things were different. They'd wounded a policeman: they weren't playing by the rules. Poor Galbraith, a bullet lodged in his lung, had turned out to be a convenient sacrificial lamb. McGee's fury in the aftermath of Morton's death had been nothing but a reflex, the necessary daily excretion of bad temper. As far as McGee was concerned, Morton and I belonged to a category of life forms that also included parasites, vultures, and other creatures who fed off garbage and carcasses. For a minute I tried to look at things from his point of view and in so doing almost let myself be swayed by an improbable wave of sympathy. The effort almost did me in. After all, what the hell did I care what McGee might think or want to do about this whole business? The question had as much to do with my own doubts, disillusion, and fatigue as it did with Inspector McGee. I wondered if a mysterious parallel might exist between Chandler's decision to write his last novel and the deadly apathy that had been sneaking up on me gradually over the endless, sterile months and years. Maybe Chandler had decided to stop writing just as I had arrived at the no-less-compulsive decision to stop giving a damn. I was hungry, and a hot shower wasn't a bad idea. I needed a shave. I glanced out the window. The sky was still gray. What the hell was going on in California? First summer had evaporated in the wink of an eye into some equinoctial emulsion, and then one of the murkiest and coldest autumns in my memory had rushed in from the curly ocean crests to take its place. I decided the shower had top priority and might boost my morale; I could stop for something to eat on the way. *Come on, Marlowe, let's get going.* My God, would I ever finish this absurd race against time, fight off the panic of my own or someone else's fears, stop wasting all my energy fleeing death? Deep down I began to suspect Freud was right after all: Eros and Thanatos, their mortal battle was the crucial one; the choice was simple—act or die. I thought of Faust in his alchemist's laboratory. In the beginning there was action—it was the act, not the word, that had created the world.

Terry was keeping a lookout through the glassed-in entrance of the Roosevelt. I opened the door of the Triumph and he jumped inside. He looked uneasy and nervous, no doubt at the prospect of seeing Velma. Was he still in love with her? In any case, I'd decided not to consider him a potential rival, nor did he see me as such. He'd put on his suede jacket and was wearing exactly the same clothes he'd been wearing the night before. Immediately I started the car, bore north on Fifth Avenue, turned west on Flores, and went straight toward Glendale on Glendale Boulevard. I knew that shortcut would put me out on Lost Canyon Road, via Laverne Terrace, to begin the ascent to the hills, avoiding the traffic and the lights on Wilshire Boulevard and Canyon Drive. I didn't need a map to get to San Bernardino; the road signs would be good enough. Once there, it would be easy to get directions to Arrowhead Lake and then Big Bear.

It was almost five in the afternoon. The wind got colder as we climbed higher, and the setting sun sent slanting rays through the wispy clouds. Somehow, amid all that gray, the autumn had begun to glaze with a rich gold the birch and maple branches flowing by us and the immense oak trees on the other side of the highway. There was still an hour to go to San Bernardino and I was hungry. The gas gauge read half a tank. I stopped at the first service area. The luminous billboards crackled with the light of the setting sun, advertising a motel and a snack bar and a coffee shop.

An attendant wrapped in white overalls approached us.

"Fill 'er up and leave it over there," I said. "Hold on to the keys for me—we'll be in the snack bar."

"Okay, boss," the man said, sweeping the keys out of the air. He had fast reflexes.

We sat next to a window. I ordered a double burger, French fries, and a beer. Terry didn't want anything but a cup of coffee. I decided it would be a good idea to drink something hot afterwards and told the waitress to bring enough for two.

"We still haven't discussed what you were going to tell me about your father's business," I reminded him.

"That's right," he answered. "But since we'll be seeing Velma soon, what do you think of discussing it when she's present?"

"Let me see," I said. "Would it have something to do with arrangements between your father and a few of the writers who weren't on the official list of agency clients?"

Terry observed me thoughtfully. He was probably trying to guess or simply calculate how much I knew about the business.

"Then you know all about it?" he asked.

In a few sentences I summarized what Chandler had led me to believe about Andress's political inclinations, and then told him about the coded list Velma had found among his personal papers.

"I knew my father kept that list," Terry said. "There's more than that—there were documents more incriminating than a mere list. That's what the men went to find at the Avenant offices. And also the reason they killed him."

"What sort of documents?"

"Contracts. Secret contracts, but completely in order. It was my father's way of protecting himself against any form of extortion or threat."

"That remains to be seen. Go on."

"Well, you must have an idea of the identity of the writers my father was trying to protect. I met two or three of them while I was staying at his house. They were people who didn't want to show their faces too much around Hollywood. At the time I didn't know very much about the blacklists. I found out about McCarthyism while I was at the university and we did a certain amount of organizing against it; it wasn't anything but a form of student revolt—you've got a pretty good idea of what that meant. We protested against global politics and defended very abstract ideals. We knew people were being interrogated, obligated to retract their political beliefs, threatened with losing their jobs and even with going to prison. We knew people were informing on their friends and relatives. All of that made us indignant. We saw Nazism settling down in our very own country; the hatchet of terror and persecution was being brandished, and those responsible weren't a few stray fanatics, it was our

194

own government. But whatever we might have been able to do had nothing but a symbolic meaning. No one knew an effective way of fighting it. So later I came to find out my father had known—he was fighting McCarthyism in an organized and brave manner."

I may have had a few reservations on the subject, but I nodded anyway.

"First he worked to organize the Hollywood literary agents into an association. Before then the agent was a solitary mediator between the writer and the big producers. He couldn't exert any sort of pressure. The studios went over his head and left him on the sidelines whenever they could, and they didn't like the percentage they had to cede to the agent for his contracts. There was also a lot of controversy about whether or not the agents' association should be legal. Well, maybe I'm a little far off the mark, but to the best of my knowledge the law benefited the authors as well as the agents. It's easy for a movie studio to push one little writer around. A person can make a lot of money on a truly exceptional screenplay, but you could count those on one hand. The Association pioneered the requirement of going through an agent. And the agents taught the writers how to handle the studios. They established norms, tariffs, percentages, and minimums. It was an organized and rational form of making contact. Although some parties still may protest against it, the general consensus is highly favorable."

"Tell me a little more about the writers you met at your father's house," I said.

"As I explained, two or three of them couldn't be seen in Hollywood, men who had been in jail and were on the studio blacklists. No one would buy what they had to offer, or if they did they only paid a few cents. My father said he would negotiate those scripts. He couldn't do it publicly, but he didn't want to do it illegally, either. He set up fully executed contracts in the authors' legal names, although the studios used pseudonyms for these authors in their film credits. My father's name appeared and was compromised on those contracts, but the studios also had to sign on the bottom line. Like I said, it was the only way he had of protecting his operation and himself. It didn't do him much good," Terry reflected bitterly.

"And you think those contracts still exist somewhere?"

"They have to—there's no other way to explain the break-in at the agency. Otherwise they wouldn't have tried to get into
195

Velma's house either. They probably didn't find them at the Avenant and thought Velma had put them in a safer place."

"That's plausible. Why didn't they look for them at your father's house?"

"I don't know. I suppose they must have gone there to look for them. My father refused to hand them over, so they killed him. They couldn't mess the place up too much, because if they had no one ever would have believed the suicide story."

"You'd make a good detective," I admitted. "But I still don't think your father would have come out alive even if he'd handed over the papers. When you use people like Skalla and Soukesian the intent is very clear. Those men are guns for hire. Whoever's responsible for your father's death probably thought that getting rid of him would close the case whether the contracts appeared or not. Things got sticky when Morton's column brought certain things to light that indicated your father had been murdered. From that moment on, those responsible were afraid that if Morton stirred things up too much, those contracts would finger them as the brains behind your father's death. Only then did the documents become so important; I don't think the attack on the agency and the attempted assault on Velma's house would have occurred if everything had happened the way it was originally planned."

"I think you're right," Terry agreed.

I consulted my watch. We'd spent more than twenty minutes in the snack bar. The darkness had deepened and a blinking oval Esso sign threw red and then blue flashes across the pavement outside. Shadows were quickly settling into the creases of the distant hills. I drank the last sip of my coffee, lit a Camel, and picked up the check to pay at the register. The white-overalled employee came to meet us.

"That's four twenty-five," he said. "Here are the keys."

I held out a five-dollar bill and told him to keep the change.

"Thanks, chief," he answered.

"How long from here to San Bernardino?" I asked.

"If you know how to drive the mountain roads, about forty-five minutes," he replied.

As we got in the cabriolet an immense green Oldsmobile pulled up in front of the gas pump.

All the neon lights were lit on the main street of San Bernardino. There was something about the bustling of the city in the icy mountain air that would have fit right into the revelry within the walls of a remote Carolingian free town. Miraculously, the storm had been bogged down a few thousand feet below us in the crags and the barrier of gigantic oaks that grew in the lap of the hills. We passed a honky-tonk that was making the whole street tremble; six feet above its entrance an enormous multicolored headdress hung over the prognathous profile of an Indian chief; its feathers moved in and out and lit up and turned off in time with a sign blinking *Indian-Head Dancing Club.* A little farther we came across the Olympia Hotel and an enormous drugstore that announced it was open twenty-four hours, while dozens of humming fluorescent tubes did their utmost to keep that promise. I slowed down as I passed the bowling alley, and stuck my head out the window.

"Which way to Arrowhead Lake?" I asked a couple about to enter the alley, bags of rented shoes twirling cheerfully in their hands.

"Straight ahead," the young man answered. "About thirty miles up."

We waved to each other, and I put the car back in gear. As soon as we left the main road behind we plunged back into thick clouds; the moon was trying to punch through wisps of cumulus and stratus. The road zigzagged upwards. It was fairly good for a dirt road, with wide shoulders that ended abruptly against a pine forest. After the third or fourth curve we caught sight of San Bernardino through the trees, just a neon cluster and a few scattered points of yellow light. I decided we'd climbed about six hundred feet; the air was getting drier but it was filled with the odor of wild resin, a penetrating aroma of pine and eucalyptus. The car stirred up the dust whirling down from the top of the canyon. I drove on for a long half-hour. Terry had succumbed to the vice of the Camels, which he didn't seem to regret, as I'd once thought. Suddenly the spaces on either side of us grew larger and the night cleared into the almost spectral reflection of the lake. This was Arrowhead. We went around the far south edge. By day the view must have been spectacular. The silhouettes of the bungalows and the piers with their empty launches cut across the shore looking out over the shining, dancing water. The road traced a semicircle for about fifteen minutes until we found a two-story, terraced brick building overlooking the lake, called the North Shore Tavern. I got out to ask directions to Big Bear, and it seemed like a good bottle of bourbon wouldn't be a bad idea for either Terry or me. I chose the cherished and almost

197

forgotten Old Forester. Back on the road the pavement turned abruptly to gravel. On one side was the immense granite mass that made up the western wall of the mountain and along the other ran a dried-out boulder-filled gully. We tossed back a couple of shots of bourbon each; so far everything was going fine. It was past eight, so we'd probably spend the night in Big Bear provided Chandler had enough room in his cabin. If he didn't, the North Shore Tavern wasn't a bad spot. Terry recalled a few things about his travels through the Orient, and suddenly he asked me if I'd read a Jack Kerouac novel called *The Dharma Bums*. I told him I didn't know who Jack Kerouac was.

"He's one of this generation's writers, that is to say, mine," Terry said. "A kind of prophet for many of us."

"Is that so? What sort of prophet?"

"Well, it's complicated. The Dharma Bums are something of a symbol—they're the type of people who refuse to be consumers, and therefore they refuse to work for the privilege of consuming everything North American society offers: freezers, televisions, cars, hair cream, deodorants, all that stuff that's going to end up in the garbage in a week anyway. This society is trapped in an endless cycle of labor, production, consumption, more labor, more production, more consumption..."

"And so?"

"Kerouac envisions a great revolution of backpacks, of thousands of millions of North Americans traveling the world with their knapsacks on their backs, escaping the system and living like that, in complete freedom, liberated from the slavery of consumption."

"And also the slavery of work," I said.

"Right. Not all the bugs are worked out yet."

"And so you grabbed your knapsack and went to travel through Europe."

"Sort of. But in my case there was always a check from my father waiting at an American Express agency. I don't think Kerouac would have approved of that."

"Your friend Kerouac probably lives off the checks his editor sends him," I said to make him feel better.

He was thoughtful for a moment.

"What made you think of that now?" I asked.

"I don't know. Something about all this reminded me of *The Dharma Bums*."

"What do you mean 'all this'? You mean the situation?"

"No, more like the landscape. Somewhere in the novel Kerouac says something like this—I don't remember the exact words—Dirt roads are like that: you feel like you're floating in a Shakespearean paradise and that any minute you're going to see nymphs and flute players, when suddenly you're struggling forward under a burning sun in a hell of dust, thorns, and nettles— just like real life.... I'd forgotten dirt roads like this still existed in the United States."

It was true. The road narrowed as we climbed until it was nothing but a path just wide enough for two vehicles to pass through at the same time. As we climbed, the gully dropped away and the massive peaks in the distance, still flooded with the recent rains, began to give off magical gleams of light. The escarpment wound down between ravines carpeted thickly with bushes, thickets, and pines. It wasn't great for night driving; the path we drove hugged the rock wall, and the curves were frequent and blind. I took the precaution of signaling with my brights every time we approached a bend in the road. We continued for some fifteen miles without passing a single other vehicle. If Chandler had come all the way up there in search of solitude, he'd undoubtedly found all he'd ever need. We reached the peak and came out on another lush, rolling plateau. Before us lay Big Bear Lake, smaller, less impressive, and probably less attractive than Arrowhead, but also wilder and with the appreciable advantage of being an almost unapproachable refuge. I recalled Chandler's instructions and drove directly toward the concentration of light in the village. I found the Totem Pole Art Shop right off the bat, but its doors were already locked. The Teddy Bear Café, on the other hand, was still open. I got out of the car and this time Terry came with me. I was wiped out.

"Another cup of coffee?" I suggested to Terry.

He nodded and we sat down at the bar.

"What can I get you?" asked a freckle-faced blonde with a complacent smile. Strangers probably didn't abound at that time of year, much less at that iffy time of the day.

"Do you know where Mr. Chandler's cabin is?" I asked.

"The writer?" she responded jovially. "Of course, everyone in Big Bear knows where he lives. Is that where you want to go?"

"You got it right on the nose, beautiful," I answered. "Is it hard to find?"

"Five minutes, if you've got a car."

"Actually, we've toiled all the way from Pacific Point."

She chortled. "I never would have thought of that. Why don't you give him a call?"

"What a brilliant idea. Do you have his number?"

"It's 2306. They just put the phone in. You can get him from the booth."

I left Terry in front of the coffee cups and made the call.

"Where are you, Marlowe?" Chandler asked. "Velma and I were beginning to worry."

"According to the fair damsel of the Teddy Bear we're five minutes from your shack. It's not easy to find this place in the dark. We're pretty tired. Is there somewhere around here to spend the night?"

"The best I have to offer is my house," Chandler said. "I can make up a couple of sofas next to the fire. You won't get cold."

"That sounds magnificent," I answered. "My consultant and I are on our way."

"You can't get lost. Just follow the shoreline. It's a relatively large cabin, redwood walls and stone trim. The roof is slate and the shutters are painted green."

He neglected to mention the insides were paneled with pine. Terry and I found that out for ourselves ten minutes later.

▶ **8:13 P.M.** **San Bernardino** "Hello, Chief? Nulty here."

"Where are you?" Thad Brown asked.

"San Bernardino. I'm calling from the sheriff's substation."

"What the hell are you doing way up there?"

"We're trailing the Olds."

"They're up there?"

"We haven't caught up with them yet, but there's no way they can give us the slip. We left a car blocking the exit from the village, so no one can go back to L.A. without answering to us first. There isn't any other road."

"And Marlowe?"

"We're assuming he's leading the caravan. He seems to be heading for a place about thirty miles from here. Arrowhead Lake. At least, a man who answers to his description asked how to get there."

"Where did that happen?"

"Here in San Bernardino. A couple gave us the information."

"We're assuming, he seems... it's all very vague, Nulty."

"The trail is fresh. I need help."

"What kind of help?"

"Send us a prowl car. The sheriff here has a car available, but we need it too."

"You don't want me to send you an armed division?"

"We've got to block all possible exits. Marlowe had a twenty-minute lead and the Olds must be on his tail. We don't know exactly where he's going."

"Okay, I'll send you a prowl car. Find Skalla and Soukesian immediately. Stop worrying about Marlowe."

"Is this a joke? We have to know exactly where Marlowe is heading to catch up with that Olds."

"What's that place you mentioned, Arrowhead Lake?"

"A vacation spot. I don't know what the hell he could possibly want to do up there. Unless he's taking the kid for a joyride."

"Kid? What kid?"

"Terry Andress."

"The son of...was in Marlowe's car? And what did the man we have at the Roosevelt do to stop him?"

"Nothing. He's still watching the widow. Those were his orders."

"Son of a bitch. Heads are going to roll when all this is over."

"What do you want me to do? We're following your instructions to the letter."

"Is that so? And you don't even know where Marlowe is?"

"Marlowe left his apartment around four. He went to the Roosevelt and picked up Terry Andress. The Oldsmobile still hadn't showed up so we stayed about a hundred yards behind him. All of a sudden he turned up Glendale Boulevard and started speeding like a crazy man. He's got a very fast car—one of those little English sports cars, a Triumph. We lost him and had no idea what direction he was heading in. We kept on going to Glendale, but there was no sign of him anywhere. We backtracked toward Lost Canyon Road and found out he'd filled up on gas halfway to San Bernardino. That was where the Olds showed up."

"Come again?"

"The service station attendant remembered that right after the Triumph left he filled up a green Oldsmobile 98 with two guys inside."

"Allow me to explain what probably happened," Thad

Brown said, his voice hoarse with anger. "You stayed a hundred yards behind Marlowe's car; they stayed two hundred yards behind. In effect, Skalla and Soukesian just got on line; when you lost Marlowe, they stayed on his trail without deviating an inch."

"If that's what happened, they must have followed his scent. Marlowe isn't the type of guy who leaves little arrows along his trail like the Boy Scouts."

"I don't give a damn how they did it. The fact is you lost him and they didn't."

"Like I said, we think they're heading toward Arrowhead Lake. I left a car at the entrance to San Bernardino, and the Sheriff is going to watch the mountain pass. According to him, there is only one decent road there; they had no choice but to go that way. When you send me a prowl car, I want it to go directly to the lake."

"Fine, but it'll take over an hour to get to San Bernardino, even with all the stops pulled out. You should get going right away yourself. You don't have the slightest idea what they could be looking for there?"

"The sheriff says there's an inn on the lake, a place called the North Shore Tavern. We're going to ask there."

"Do it fast. Don't let these guys get a leg up on you."

"That's what I'm trying to do," Nulty said.

He hung up the phone and spit out at least eight cents' worth of Dutch tobacco.

▶ **11:05 P.M. Big Bear Lake** "So that's the story, more or less," Chandler concluded. He savored a mouthful of whiskey. He took out his tobacco pouch, and with his thumb, index finger, and forefinger initiated the delicate operation of pouring fibers of aromatic Amphora tobacco into the bowl of his pipe. "When Wade came out from Hollywood just to see me, and burst forth with all that concern for Velma Valento, I started to get suspicious about what might be behind it. At first I thought it might simply be a question of personal and somewhat juvenile concern; then, coming from an individual like Wade, I was forced to decide something more had to be going on. The puzzle pieces fit together too neatly. It had almost all the elements required for a story. Fifteen years ago I wouldn't have given it a second's thought; I would have rolled up my sleeves and sold it to the *Black Mask* or *Dime Detective Magazine* for a nice piece of change."

The four of them had settled around the fireplace in the main room of the cabin. It was a warm and comfortable spot. The walls were lined with light, fragrant wood; the fireplace was made of stone; and there were built-in bookcases and cabinets. Against one of the windows Chandler had put an old oak desk and an ilex-wood chair with a couple of pillows. The typewriter, a transistor radio, and a tall stack of typewritten pages secured by a paperweight rested on top of the desk. The living room's center was occupied by an enormous jute or hemp rug covered with Indian designs and colors. Books and examples of totem art were scattered here and there. Between the sofas and the quilted leather armchair Chandler had claimed for himself was a low, full-sized table. Clustered on top were a bottle of Talisker, a half-empty bottle of Old Forester, ice, glasses, and an abundance of ashtrays and cigarettes.

"So you believe Wade is directly involved in all this?" Marlowe asked.

Chandler sucked meditatively on his pipe.

"Wade, perhaps not personally," he said. "The problem in a case like this is that nothing is personal. Wade is part of a system now. More than ten years ago, when I met him, he was also part of a system, but in a different way. Now he's an integral part of a production process. A film company is infinitely more complex than a watch movement; each piece fulfills its function and knows little or nothing about the rest or what they do. Therefore, each piece never obtains a picture of how the whole mechanism works. There's just one thing every piece is aware of: if just one falters, the entire mechanism is paralyzed. Such a disaster must be prevented at any cost—it doesn't matter how. That goes for individual studios and also for Hollywood as a whole, conceived as one immense and unique piece of machinery. Am I making myself clear?" Chandler seemed to throw his question out to the air, without expecting a response. He sucked luxuriously on his pipe and went on. "Well then, Wade must have had a pretty good idea of what would happen if the Andress case were to be thoroughly investigated: the scandal would contaminate all of Hollywood; it would become necessary to impede the infection to prevent the scandal. Up until Wednesday night there wasn't anything to be afraid of, but then he came across you two at

203

Lucey's." The pipe stem inexorably pointed first at Velma and then at Marlowe. "The line of reasoning he subsequently embarked on was about as sophisticated as figuring out two plus two equals four. Up until then, Velma represented a single, loose link; you, Marlowe, if he had taken you into account, were another. The two of you together were no longer isolated links; you were the beginning of a chain, is that clear? So he comes to ask me the friendly favor of finding out if you two were old friends or if it was a question of a recent acquaintanceship. The connection to the Andress murder was too obvious. That was when I began to suspect that Miss Valento might be in danger—I still don't know what sort, but the events that followed give us a pretty good idea: the appearance of those two hired guns, the agency break-in, the secret contracts Terry mentioned. In order to seal the Andress case shut once and for all, it had become necessary to eliminate the loose ends: Morton was one; you're next, Marlowe; eventually it might be Velma's turn; and yours might come too, Terry, if they find out you want to get to the bottom of your father's death. I admit I was primarily worried about Velma, perhaps because we used to be neighbors and I've always been one of her secret admirers. And so I went to her house and managed to convince her to come with me to Big Bear until the entire matter had been wrapped up. You gentlemen brought the rest of the story with you. Nothing I could add can shed any further light on things."

"We're acting on the basis of that theory," Marlowe agreed. "Now we have to decide what we want to do about it. We're confronted with a machine, as you said—an anonymous, faceless, impersonal, powerful organization with influence, resources, and two visible instruments named Skalla and Soukesian. The police are on their trail. If they dig their heels in around here much longer the police'll hunt them down in no time. I don't think Skalla and Soukesian are our primary threat at the moment. The greatest danger is the organization behind them. And I only see one way of exposing it: the police have to capture Andress and Morton's murderers and make them confess, and Velma and Terry must supply them with the evidence that will bring the rest to light."

"Then what do you suggest, Marlowe? Do you think Velma should go back to Los Angeles?"

"I think so. And go straight to the D.A.'s office. Velma?"

"I guess so. The police will have to protect me until those two individuals are put in jail."

"And you, Terry?"

"Frankly, yes. It's the best thing we can do. It's not in the least soothing to think that those two murderers are still loose out there somewhere, but if things are the way Marlowe says they are, there is an entire police operation on their trail. I don't think we have anything to be afraid of."

"Then it's unanimous," Chandler announced.

"In that case, let's start back tomorrow morning," Marlowe said. "And you, Raymond? Will you be able to stand it here for long without Velma to keep you company?"

"I'll manage," Chandler promised. "After all, I'd already decided to come and finish that lucky novel. La Jolla is an absolutely sterilizing place. I went mute there, thinking I had escaped Los Angeles and the Hollywood scene, but even there someone was always making the telephone ring or pushing my doorbell at the most unexpected hours. The place is also rife with temptation. I can't stand to be alone, but when I seriously get down to writing, I have to do it alone and in silence, without anyone looking over my shoulder or telling me what to do."

"You couldn't do that in La Jolla?"

"In La Jolla I was the perfect hypocrite. I was pretending to seek out solitude, but at the bottom I was really avoiding it any way I could. Here, in Big Bear, I can't do anything but accept it. I embrace this fortunate solitude as I embrace a bottle of whiskey, and sooner or later it will make me sit down at the typewriter."

"I've found this to be an exceptional opportunity to watch you work," Velma admitted. "I know very well how it's done in Hollywood. The studio gives its writers a three-, four-, five-week deadline, a couple of months at the outside, and they have to shut themselves up in the office and fill up pages with very little or no inspiration. But you no longer write exclusively for Hollywood, and I'm sure you're not disappointed."

"No, thank God," said Chandler. "I already went through that stage and I know it very well. I'm completely fed up with stories that have been fired off sitting on the edge of a chair. Now nothing satisfies me but to create leaning back in a comfortable sofa, with a pipe in my mouth. Add a double scotch, and the rest comes on its own or not at all."

"But in your case it always comes," Terry observed.

"I wish it did. But it doesn't. I've been working on this novel for three years, and I'm always a long way from finishing. I'm tired, and so is my novel's hero. Neither he nor I know how to get out of the mess we're mixed up in. Sometimes I think the best thing would be to give up and resign myself to entering the brief history of the American mystery novel as the author of *The Long Goodbye* and four or five minor works, plus a dozen truly accomplished stories. But I don't know what obsession is compelling me to write this last one; it's like the need to finish a cycle. A novel made with snippets and remnants of the work I kept leaving behind—sewing it all together the way Indians sew their blankets, a sort of patchwork."

"Patchwork?" Velma said. "Stupendous—why not? If that technique can work for quilts and collages, I don't see why it can't create a good novel, too."

"I even considered naming it that at one point," Chandler replied. "But then I decided on another title: *Playback*. You know, that technical trick one sees so often at the movies: the actor appears in front of the public, moves his lips and makes singing gestures, but the voice is really coming from a scratched record or a magnetic tape behind him. Usually, the voice belongs to someone who stopped singing long ago, someone who is already dead or has been silenced forever. That's sort of how I feel. I really don't know whose voice is playing behind the curtain, unless it's the voice of my own ghost; but what I do when I sit down there"—with a melancholy glance he gestured toward the desk where the Underwood portable mutely gathered dust— "what I do is a sort of parody. A series of empty gestures that aren't even very well coordinated with the sounds coming from behind me, from the past. I was never a good actor, and so perforce this can't be a good playback performance."

"That statement could be either pathetic or moving," Velma said with almost maternal fastidiousness, "but it's neither, because it's essentially false. *Playback* is a stupendous idea. Brilliant and original. And while we're on the subject of whether or not you'll be remembered for *The Long Goodbye* and other minor novels—as I've heard you say dozens of times in the last twenty-four hours, Raymond—it sounds like false modesty to me. I have a list in my head that includes at least four or five titles that have nothing minor about them. And when someone has already written half a dozen novels which have sold by the hundreds of thousands in this country and abroad, is also the person responsible for many of the best suspense stories—some of the few good screenplays Hollywood has produced in the last few years—and has written articles and essays not always praised by members of my profession but published in some of the most exclusive magazines in the country, he can't consider himself a minor writer. That style doesn't suit you, Chandler; it makes you seem old and soft. That's the most sensible thing I can tell you."

"You think so?" Chandler thought it over, probably asking himself if this stimulating reproach didn't remind him too much of some of the arguments he'd had with Cissy, or, more recently, with Natasha Spender, Helga Green, or any of the other few women who had truly filled his life. "My private tragedy—just among ourselves and without any false modesty—is that I began to write too late, and never felt as though I was a very important writer. In each generation there are incomplete writers, people who seem incapable of reflecting enough of themselves onto paper, men whose work always adds up to something incidental. Often, as in my case, they've begun late, and have an overdeveloped critical sense. At times they lack the necessary selfishness and think that the lives of others are as important as their own, others' happiness as essential as the expression of their own personalities, if they have any. I imagine I'm one of them. I've had enough material success to understand that phenomenon and I lack that particular sense of destiny I'd need to believe that what I do matters very much."

"In this instance, your own judgment is perhaps the item of least interest," Velma interrupted. "Others' opinion of your work is much more important. Perhaps you think of yourself as just another mystery writer—and we already know a very deep prejudice exists against the mystery novel, as if it were a minor genre intended for distraction or entertainment, simply because many are published and everyone likes them. But yours is a very special case: you've managed to write mystery novels that contain something more than the simple intrigue of crime; you've created characters, you've described a city and certain ambiances such as Hollywood and Los Angeles society in a way that no one has ever described them before. That puts you up there with the great North American writers. That's not the opinion of a literary agent, Raymond, it's just the opinion of a close reader of your work. And of a usually rather demanding reader, I should add."

"Hell, who would have told me I'd ever have to listen to all that about myself," Chandler smiled. "You could easily convince me, Velma; you're too pretty and you seem completely sincere, and I'm a sucker for both those things. I'm going to confess something to you anyhow: if I'm truly jealous of anyone it's of those people who consider art and literature to be worth whatever sacrifices have to be made to achieve them, but I'm not one of them. I like money and success too much—perhaps the fact that they came late has made me like them even more. My salute to posterity is my thumb on the end of my nose and my fingers in the air. Editors and agents read too many reviews, because their business requires them to, naturally. But who are the critics, after all? Most of them are little people whose dignity and credibility depend on perpetuating a handful of false values thought up by other critics, who are also little people. I can admit that although I don't consider myself a great writer, my standards are too high to allow me to be a great admirer of successful mediocre writers, and too unorthodox to make me care what the wise men say.

"In conclusion," he added after a pause, "none of this is worth a hill of beans; but a writer, to be happy, should be required to be a nice average guy, not a starving genius like Laforgue, or a lonely man like Heine, or a lunatic like Dostoyevsky. And above all he shouldn't have to be a mystery writer with a certain magic touch and fear of plots, which describes me to a T."

"Dostoyevsky was also essentially a good mystery writer," Terry said. "A tremendous mystery writer, in fact. Works like *Crime and Punishment, The Brothers Karamazov, The Possessed,* and even *The Idiot* are essentially suspense novels; they offer crime, mystery, and a search for the guilty. And the reader is presented with an enigma from the very beginning, too. Isn't that more or less the definition of a mystery novel?"

"That discussion is one that would have to go on all night, through tomorrow, and for a few more weeks after that," Chandler replied. "But the fact is that you have to leave tomorrow, and it would be best to do so early. So we can broach this topic again next time. In my opinion, the difference isn't to be found in the genre of novel one writes; the only valid distinction is the one that separates the good writers from the bad. And a good writer is the writer who is capable of giving up everything else to wholly dedicate himself to his writing, even if it means risking dying of hunger. Not necessarily because of the bravery such an act implies, but rather because it's the only proof that for him literature, or better said the necessity of being a writer, is far more important than anything else. I once knew some Hollywood writers who told me they wrote because they had to, or because it was a comfortable way of earning a living and traveling the great wide world, but that when it came right down to it they hated to write. But a writer who hates the actual writing, who gets no joy out of the creation of magic by words, to me is simply not a writer at all. The actual writing is what you live for. The rest is something you have to get through in order to arrive at the point. How can you hate the actual writing? What is there to hate about it? You might as well say that a man likes to chop wood or clean house and hates the sunshine or the night breeze or the nodding of flowers or the dew on the grass or the songs of birds. How can you hate the magic which makes a paragraph or a sentence or a line of dialogue or a description something in the nature of a new creation?"

The question lingered in the dense, smoky air. Marlowe bent toward the table, sipped his whiskey, and lit a lone Camel that had been mashed between the folds of the package.

"My God, this has been more of a tobacco and alcohol orgy than a literary discussion," Velma said, apparently with the intention of breaking that crystallized silence.

"As far as I'm concerned, this is the last one of the evening," Marlowe said.

"Camus once said there are two cigarettes that cannot be given up," Terry recalled. "The last one at night and the first one in the morning."

"Who was that, son?" Chandler asked.

"Albert Camus. Didn't you read *The Stranger*? In its own way, it's a mystery novel, too."

"Has it been translated? I read French very badly, or better put, I completely gave up reading French at all."

"In any event, he was right," Marlowe admitted, getting to his feet. "The first fresh cigarette in the morning is the one that obliterates the bitter taste of the last one the night before."

He had the vague sensation he was quoting someone, but it was probably just the result of the white-night inspiration of his long day's journey.

▶ **9:45 A.M.** **Big Bear Lake** After a hearty mountain break-fast we said good-bye to Chandler. The rough weather had at last conclusively crossed over the barricade of mountain peaks; the sky looked as limpid as a mirror and beneath the slanting autumnal sun little Big Bear Lake was a sheet of lapis lazuli. The dry, cold air penetrated deep into my lungs. I sat at the Triumph's steering wheel and let the motor warm up. Velma lingered, tearing herself from Chandler's melancholy and somewhat drunken embrace; he was probably already a little in love with her. Terry watched them, absorbed in his youthful seriousness. In the raw morning light, his beard and pale skin made him look like a Hindu ascetic or one of El Greco's lanky martyrs. I asked myself what he could be thinking, and what his present feelings for Velma might be. I incinerated the first cigarette of the day, the one that had to wipe out the bitterness of the tar and nicotine of my last Camel the night before. For the first time, I noticed the dramatic panorama that spread out from where we stood. The lake extended eastward until it was lost behind a pine-covered peninsula, and the gray walls of the stately Sierra Nevadas on the southern bank twisted west through the small village and fell off into the canyon. Along the wall the road stretched out, that fifteen-mile track of gravel snaking toward the edge of an abyss like a narrow, dangerous serpent. Far away in the distance the ocean vanished into the unattainable horizon like a pale, diffuse, foggy shoreline. We weren't in any hurry, but I glanced nervously at my watch. Velma placed herself at my side. Terry slipped in on the far end of the seat, slammed the door shut, and opened the window to wave at the solitary Chandler, standing erect in the cabin door. His pipe hung out of one side of his mouth, his jowls hung slack, and his hands were buried in his pockets. It was a good-bye, but not necessarily a long one, or the last one, either. I pulled away from the curb.

We stopped at the Teddy Bear Café to replenish our supply of Old Forester and cigarettes. Velma and I stayed in the car.

"What is this?" Velma asked. "The beginning of something or the end of something?"

I bent over her and kissed her.

"I'd say it's more like the middle of the road."

Terry returned with a bottle and a couple of cartons of Camels. It was as if we were going on a weekend outing. It was Saturday and the morning's intoxicating splendor encouraged such thoughts. I turned on the radio. From a live LP, Nappy Lamare's Levee Loungers assaulted High Society's "Evergreen Ramble" with old fury, and Matty Matlock's clarinet wailed out his solo like some inspired, virtuous dare. We covered the miles winding around the west bank of Big Bear Lake and the car entered the gorge. Then I happened to look into the rearview mirror. That was the first time I noticed the green Oldsmobile, about a hundred yards behind us. There was nothing sinister about the car's outward appearance, but immediately I realized it was gaining on us too quickly. I stepped on the accelerator and began to increase the distance between us.

It would have been crazy to try to drive down that narrow strip of loose gravel at more than forty or fifty miles an hour. The Olds didn't seem to see things that way. I practically steered the car into the abyss, and took the first curve blindly without taking my foot off the gas pedal. If a car had been coming toward us on the far side of the curve it would have been disastrous, but I had to take the risk.

"What's going on?" Velma asked with frightened eyes. "You're driving like a madman."

"We're being followed," I answered. "We have to get out of the canyon as soon as we possibly can or they're going to corner us."

Simultaneously, Terry and Velma turned their heads toward the back window. The Olds was now about twenty yards away. It was a solid, heavy car and it held up well on the gravel; it could allow itself luxuries I no longer could with the lightweight, spindly Triumph.

"It's them," I said, now without the slightest trace of doubt, "Skalla and Soukesian." I even managed to make out Skalla's bloated bulk in the small rearview mirror. "Let's pray we get out of here before they do."

"How far out?" Terry breathed.

"At least as far as Arrowhead Lake. Once we're on asphalt they won't be able to touch us."

We started down a long straightaway. Conditions were ideal for the Olds to cut into our lead, and I confirmed that it was gaining on us at the speed of at least eighty miles an hour. I pumped the gas pedal. I felt the Triumph skid and its front tires hailed pebbles in one direction and then the other. The Olds rushed forward and managed to hit our back bumper. We jumped forward, but I kept on going.

"My God!" Velma gasped. "There's no way out."

I sped up and steered back toward the granite wall again. If Skalla was planning on pushing me over the cliff, I wasn't going to give him the chance. I wasn't happy about the prospect of being smashed against the mountain, either. I eyed the rearview mirror; I saw Soukesian stick his arm out the window with a .45 in his hand. Now they were ten yards behind me. The next curve was about fifty yards away; I opened out to repeat my last maneuver. They launched their second attack; I managed to speed up in enough time to diminish its impact. Velma and Terry got jostled around and thrown against the windshield.

"Hit the seat!" I yelled.

I took the curve and managed to put myself some fifteen or twenty yards in front of the Oldsmobile again. A shot rang out, whistling as it grazed the Triumph and unleashed a chain of echoes up and down the entire length of the canyon. There were two hairpin curves in front of me, and for a minute the Oldsmobile disappeared from my rearview mirror.

"Don't put your heads above the seat," I told Velma and Terry. "We're under fire."

"But how..." I heard Velma's faltering voice begin to ask itself, "how could they have followed us here?"

It wasn't exactly the most convenient moment to list all the possibilities. I left the second bend of the hairpin and came out on a long, six-hundred-yard straightaway down a very gradual hill. I took the speedometer needle to seventy and the other car appeared in the rearview mirror again. I thought I could get enough of a lead on them, but Skalla was also an expert driver. The Oldsmobile's green muzzle began to loom closer in the mirror and I realized they'd catch up to me before the next curve. The race had to last another four hundred yards. I accelerated to the outer limit of prudence and looked up. In that instant, I saw Skalla's next attack and the next blind curve approach. I twisted the wheel to the left, putting distance between myself and the edge of the abyss just as the Oldsmobile came in for the kill. Soukesian's long arm squeezed the .45's trigger a couple of times and Skalla tried to change his aim, but I didn't give him the time. Just as they caught up to us I spun back toward the edge of the gravel and rammed the Triumph's spur into the Oldsmobile's front mudguard. I had to turn the force of their own attack against them. Skalla spun the wheel like a crazy man, and I saw Soukesian finger the gun again. He was going to try to shoot us point-blank. In that split second I attacked. There was a violent crunch of frames and chassis, and we heard the strident screech of the Oldsmobile's brakes. It was the worst possible thing Skalla could have done. Soukesian was impelled forward by inertia. The gunfire was buried in the general din; the projectile whizzed past us, grazing the Triumph's windshield and tearing splinters of rock out of the mountainside. Skalla couldn't avoid the curve that rushed up hungrily toward him; the Oldsmobile essed across the gravel, raised a dust cloud that darkened the pure morning light, and plunged over the cliff. I felt the Triumph skid dangerously over the gravel, but the impact with the other automobile had diminished its momentum. I stepped on the brakes and managed to bring it to a stop just as the tires began to take a detour into the void. I jumped out of the car and ran toward the deep tire skids that marked Skalla's desperate attempt to brake as he came upon the curve by surprise; farther on a tumult of dust and pebbles indicated exactly where the Olds had gone over the edge. Within seconds Terry and Velma joined me.

It wasn't a cheerful sight but it wasn't a total catastrophe either. The heavy vehicle had spun surely through the rocks and bushes and had finally flipped over as it crashed through the barrier of pine trees. Slowly, the door facing up into the air began to open toward the sky, and Soukesian laboriously began to get out of the vehicle like some apparition from beyond the grave. Skalla emerged behind him. The two men were completely dazed, bloody, and their clothing was in tatters, but they were still alive. I ran to the Triumph; the poor old thing looked like hell. I took the P-38 out of the glove compartment. Skalla and Soukesian weren't about to offer any resistance. They scratched at the rocks and stretched their arms toward the bushes in a desperate attempt to get back to the road.

And suddenly, as if they'd been awaiting that precise end-of-act curtain to make their appearance, Nulty's blue Ford and a prowl car irrupted onto the scene from opposite directions. The two cars braked brusquely as they reached the curve. I turned my head and watched Nulty approach, hurling his more than two hundred pounds of weight toward us. He had his regulation Colt in his hand, and behind him two more policemen came running. Four uniformed officers got out of the prowl car; two of them were carrying Thompson machine guns.

"How did you do it?" Nulty squawked, looking into the gorge. "We saw the Oldsmobile come out of the grove and throw itself behind you just as you went into the canyon. I thought I drove fast, but hell, we lost sight of you after the first curve." Skalla and Soukesian continued their painful climb through the boulders. Suddenly, in the midst of their daze, they seemed to notice the police deployment awaiting them at the edge of the road. They both froze in their tracks, then straightened up and slowly raised their hands in the air.

"Fire," Nulty said to the policemen aiming the Thompsons.

I looked at him incredulously.

"Don't do it!" I managed to scream. I hurled myself crazily onto the two policemen just as the deafening rattle of machine-gun fire burst forth. Skalla and Soukesian's bodies twisted convulsively; for a moment it appeared as though they were going to be dispatched into outer space, but finally they crashed down heavily onto the parched earth. I turned toward Nulty with all the fury and rancor I could muster.

"Why did you do that!" I screamed into his face. "Why did you have to kill them? They weren't armed and they weren't going to be alive much longer anyway."

"They were a couple of murderers," Nulty said. His face was still impassive. If he had something to hide, or if the slightest emotion was running through his guts, he wasn't allowing any of it to show.

"It was the only way to get to the bottom of this," I said in a tone of combined ire and desperation, as if it were something that could be fixed. "Now we'll never be able to do it."

"To the bottom of what?" Nulty said in the same inflexible tone of voice, from behind his immobile stone features. "There are the guys who killed your friend Morton. Bullets or electric chair, what difference does it make? We just saved them the nuisance of a few hours of beatings and repentance."

I just stood there looking at him incredulously.

"They weren't Andress and Morton's real murderers," I muttered between my teeth. "The real murderers were behind them. You arranged things so we'd never find out who they really are."

Nulty had lit a thick cigar, and for the first time he looked at me with something more than the hardened mask of a veteran policeman.

"Come on, Marlowe, don't take it that way," he said. "You did good work and you should feel more than satisfied. Your friend has been avenged, and neither you, Miss Valento, or the Andress kid has anything to be afraid of anymore. What was it you wanted to find out? Who was behind Skalla and Soukesian?" He blew a large mouthful of smoke against the radiant morning

214

sky and stood and watched as the cloud vanished swiftly into the air. The policemen had climbed down to where Skalla and Soukesian's riddled bodies lay and were beginning to identify them. "No one was behind Skalla and Soukesian," Nulty added. "Or, if you want to hear it another way, the system was behind them. Get my drift? The system, Marlowe. Not you, or I, or all the policemen in the whole state can mount an armed attack against the entire system."

For a few seconds we looked at each other in silence. I shut the P-38's safety catch and dropped the gun at his feet. A little cloudlet of dust rose as it crashed against the gravel with a dry sound.

"Keep it as a souvenir," I said to Nulty. "I'm retiring from the profession."

I turned to Velma and Terry, who were a few steps behind me. The three of us walked to the Triumph in silence.

This novel has attempted, perhaps to a fault, to pay tribute to Raymond Chandler and by extension to all the "Chandlerians" who have at one time or another been taken over by his work. With very few exceptions not worth the trouble of listing, the characters, addresses, locations, locales, license-plate and telephone numbers, whiskey and cigarette brands, general toponymy, and both cited and uncited references have been taken either from Chandler's fiction or from his life; in the latter case I have relied almost exclusively on the invaluable support of Frank MacShane's work. The following quiz has a number of different uses: it can be used as a sort of supplementary diversion for Chandler fans, as a reference point for the curious reader who may not be overly familiar with Chandler's work, or simply as a guide for following the itinerary that I myself used as I selected the nomenclature for this novel. Obviously, a fourth choice would be simply to read it (or not read it) and forget it altogether.

I GIVE YOURSELF TEN POINTS:

1 For determining the meaning of the body of Yensid Andress.

2 For requesting the services of any of the following policemen:

- [a] Captain Thad Brown
- [b] Commissioner Fulwider
- [c] Assistant Inspector Beifus
- [d] Agent Nogard

3 For determining the true identities of:

- [a] Fuentes
- [b] Vincent Starret
- [c] Howard Melton

4 For discovering the precise location of:

- [a] Room 332
- [b] Chateau Bercy
- [c] Restaurant La Plaza

216

d	Romanoff's
e	Lucey's

5 For finding any of the following streets:

a	Alta Brea Crescent
b	Altair Street
c	Drexel Avenue
d	Idaho Street
e	Laverne Terrace
f	Spring Street
g	West 54th Place

6 For coming across these license-plate numbers:

a	12–216
b	13–572
c	6330
d	3–416

7 For managing to get an answer from any of these telephone numbers:

a	Haaldale 9–5033
b	50–416
c	2306

8 For smoking a Van de Graaf cigar.

II GIVE YOURSELF FIVE POINTS:

1 For unmasking these hired guns:

a	Steve Skalla
b	Arizmian Soukesian

And their respective aliases:

a	"Lou Lid"
b	"Moose Magoon"

2 For determining the true identity of the victims:

a	Charles Morton
b	Mrs. Prendergast
c	Galbraith

3 For entering a nightclub and discovering a blonde dressed in green in front of a mirror that is not oval but perfectly round.

4 For finding a vaguely Egyptian-looking ornament.

5 For knowing exactly where the voice of the pianist whispering "My Little Buckeroo" and later improvising on the theme of "We Can Still Dream, Can't We?" is coming from.

6 For discovering:

a a dark gray Plymouth sedan

b an Oldsmobile 98

c a Lincoln Continental

7 For sharing Marlowe's admiration for the woman whose "hip-swinging strut wasn't something you learned in commerce school."

III GIVE YOURSELF THREE POINTS:

1 For being interrogated by either of the following policemen:

a Moses Maglashan

b Christy-French

2 For managing to gain entrance to any of the following places:

a Doreme Inc.

b Indian-Head

c Hotel Olympia

d Shamey's

3 For finding the exact location of:

a a cabin "with redwood walls, a slate roof, and lined in pine"

b 6005 Coastal Highway

c The Avenant Building

d Hotel Roosevelt

4 For driving a car down any of these streets:

a Doheny Drive, at the end of the Strip

b Wilshire Boulevard

c Franklyn Avenue

d Sixth Avenue

5 For finding the source of these citations:

a "On the right the great solid Pacific, trudging into shore like a scrubwoman going home. No moon, no fuss, hardly a sound of the surf. No smell. None of the harsh wild of the sea. A California ocean."

b "I smelled Los Angeles before I got to it. It smelled stale and old like a living room that had been closed too long. But the colored lights fooled you. The lights were wonderful. There ought to be a monument to the man who invented neon lights. Fifteen stories high, solid marble. There's a boy who really made something out of nothing."

218

6 For managing to get a tire patched in Art Huck's garage.

7 For correctly naming the hair color of one George W. Hicks.

IV GIVE YOURSELF TWO POINTS:

1 For obtaining the services of:

a Lieutenant Nulty

b Inspector McGee (and one more point for discovering why they call him Violets)

2 For locating these Los Angeles suburbs:

a Brentwood Heights

b Arcadia

c Bunker Hill

d and, incidentally, Shetland Lane

3 For getting a room or losing a few hours in:

a The North Shore Tavern

b The Teddy Bear Café

4 For attending a meeting of "The Fictioneers" and obtaining autographs from each one of its members.

5 For running into the starlet who would "very soon...fly off toward a prestigious, futile, luxurious, artificial, and asexual world" and would "never again...be a creature made from flesh and blood. Just a voice on a sound wave, a face on a screen."

6 For petting Taki the cat without getting scratched.

V GIVE YOURSELF ONE POINT:

1 For finding Marlowe at 428 Bristol Apartments.

2 For getting a table at the Café Nikobob.

3 For receiving Steven's personal attention.

4 For meeting, on two separate occasions and in two different stories, a certain person named Terry, drunk in a car, late at night.

5 For correctly naming the novel that wraps up with this paragraph:

"What did it matter where you lay once you were dead? In a dirty sump or in a marble

219

tower on top of a high hill? You were dead, you were sleeping the big sleep, you were not bothered by things like that. Oil and water were the same as wind and air to you. You just slept the big sleep, not caring about the nastiness of how you died or where you fell."

6 For knocking back an Old Forester in the company of Marlowe and McGee.

7 For crossing the corner of Western Avenue and 9th Street.

8 For smoking a Camel on any of the multiple occasions in which Marlowe lights one up.

The scoring criteria are as follows:

VERY DIFFICULT:	10 points
DIFFICULT:	5 points
RELATIVELY DIFFICULT:	3 points
RELATIVELY EASY:	2 points
EASY:	1 point

Grading Curve:

EXCELLENT:	300 points and up
VERY GOOD:	Between 200 and 300
GOOD:	Between 100 and 200
SATISFAC-TORY:	Between 50 and 100

I urge you to read the works of Raymond Chandler.

Hiber Conteris, a noted Uruguayan writer and intellectual, was a political prisoner in Uruguay from 1976 to 1985. While he was in prison Mr. Conteris wrote four novels, a book of short stories, and three plays. He was released from prison after the change of government and came to the United States, where he is currently Visiting Professor of Hispano-American Literature at the University of Wisconsin in Madison. After his arrival, the Governor of Wisconsin proclaimed May 14, 1985, to be Hiber Conteris Day.

Mr. Conteris is an honorary member of P.E.N. and recipient of the Letras de Oro Prize, among numerous other awards.